Allison's Gambit

M000312859

Allison's Gambit

C. A. PRICE

CIRCUIT BREAKER BOOKS

Circuit Breaker Books LLC
Portland, OR
www.circuitbreakerbooks.com

Author photo by Diana Jahns

Book design by Vinnie Kinsella

ISBN: 978-1-953639-10-3
eISBN: 978-1-953639-11-0
LCCN: 2021909892

I dedicate this book to my patients, who have enriched and taught me so much. I can't tell you what a privilege it has been to listen to the stories of thousands of patients through the years. I would especially like to mention LT, who was the one who started me on the philosophical journey that became the book, Allison's Gambit. *It was she who said one day with startling conviction, "I will never stop smoking, I want to die young. I don't want someone to have to care for me like I had to care for my mom."*

Oh yeah, life goes on...
Long after the thrill of living is gone.

—JOHN MELLENCAMP

PART 1

1

July 2012

THE DEATH OF MY FATHER CAME SLOWLY, WITH INCREDIBLE SPEED.
Bright lights humming loudly drowned out by the scene below.
An all-too-common hospital code, ending an all-too-common way.

Forty-six years he had smoked, ever since his tour in Vietnam.
He quit as many times as he started. The last time, a full year before
his passing.

After the small army of doctors, nurses, anesthesiologists, medical students, and scribes left the scene, the smell of utter defeat
remained. Blood, a pale chest, brown patches of betadine glaring
back along with lackluster eyes.

Twelve years before he died, he had retired from his job as a
construction foreman. This was a major part of his life, along with
a family he adored.

No one was allowed in until the janitors sanitized the mess
to avoid the impression of chaos and failure. The breaking of ribs
went unheard. The imperceptible flinches from the eighteen-gauge
needles went unseen. Remaining were the blaring lights, the respectful white, warm blanket draped over his body, and a family
slowly realizing their sudden loss.

Eighteen months before the final code, his wife had called 911.

The emergency was sudden shortness of breath. Or maybe his
collapse could be blamed on his heart. It had only been a mile walk,
fifteen minutes past the familiar mailbox. His doctors diagnosed

him with chronic obstructive pulmonary disease, which seemed implausible as he had already been smoking less due to difficulty breathing. With his diagnosis, multiple inhalers adorned his bedside table offering minimal relief. Contentment came with his now-diminished circle of friends and distance.

In 2012, he found himself encircled by drawn light-blue curtains three times. Each ER visit provided hours of tests and fear along with new treatments that would improve his quality of life. When his heart and kidneys began to worsen later that year, his drug regimen grew exponentially. Each month there were three to five visits to doctors, who provided hopeful expressions, more complicated treatments, and pills added to or subtracted from his days-of-the-week container. Testing helped fill many of the other days in the month. Lab tests, chest X-rays, CT scans, a lung biopsy, visits to the physical therapist and respiratory therapist. Like a child with more and more toys, he started to accumulate devices: a CPAP machine, a cane, a front-wheel walker, an oxygen tank, a wheelchair—and a hospital bed that kept him from sleeping with his wife for the first time in their marriage.

Three months remained, though no one knew, with the exception of everyone involved.

They placed a pacemaker, the type that helped his worsening heart failure, fluid overload, and gasping for breath. And to help justify the $100,000 cost, it also would kick him in the chest with a bolt of electricity each time his heart dared to stop. Unwilling to take this recurring grenade explosion in his chest, he began to beg. First to the doctors and then to his family.

None could comprehend why he would want to remove the implantable defibrillator he had agreed to just months before to save his life.

"Do you want to die?"

2

April 2019

CONSIDERING I HAD A FRONT-ROW SEAT FOR MY FATHER'S LAST days, it might seem ironic that I took up smoking. The fact is, my habit has nothing to do with him and everything to do with my mom, Nancy MacPherson. Now they have both passed away, and I smile when I think of my father. The emotions I go through when I think of my mother are complicated. On a good day, I manage a slight smile, but on most days, I just feel relief that she finally died.

Now it is so clear that, despite knowing what my father went through, if I had to choose a death, I would choose his in an instant. He died; my mom suffered. Actually, that's not exactly true—everybody else around her suffered.

It must come across as callous to those who don't know what happened, but my mom's dementia caused a suffering like no other. It made me realize that there are different ways to die. I won't say I became fixated on death; I just became aware it was going to happen, which I know sounds stupid. We all know we are going to die. It's just...we don't think about it. We push it into the recesses of our minds. But somehow I know I'm destined to die like my mom. And I have consciously decided to try and alter that reality. Why die of Alzheimer's when you can die of something else—anything else?

I have generally learned not to express my uncommon beliefs, so they won't attract disdain. No one enjoys opening themselves up for criticism and feeling like an emotional punching bag. Reticence seems the wiser option. But I have decided to change that and tell my story despite realizing that many will look at me like I am a pariah. If this diary were a YouTube video, I would likely have far many more thumbs-down than thumbs-up. How do I know this? Because this is not my first foray into asking the world to pass judgment on my feelings.

Though you have probably already learned this lesson, don't say anything political or controversial on social media. Random people you don't even know will actually threaten you because you provided tips on how to save water. Water! I wish I were making this up, but I speak from experience.

I'm sure the same surprise hits people after they post their first video on a public site, maybe of their six-year-old daughter at a ballet recital. The social-media affirmation complex doesn't make up for the rather surprising number of thumbs-down they receive. It's enough to make you question yourself. "Maybe she isn't such a good dancer? Perhaps I should have made her practice more."

Now that it has been a while since my mom passed away, emerging from my cocoon seems imperative somehow, and there doesn't seem to be a minute more to lose. I need to reach out to all of those other caregivers who are like me. I realize now that I have not only been grieving; I have been avoiding the well-wishers who often leave me more depressed. But mostly I have been avoiding telling my family and friends about my philosophy.

It is time to tell my story and convince at least my friends that I have something to offer from my experience. I am stronger now emotionally. I'm ready to take on the world, even the strangers who will pleasantly yell at me, "Just shut up and die already."

3

April 2019

CIGARETTES BECAME THE SYMBOL OF MY REBELLION. MY CAUSE? To choose happiness in death, not misery. I guess that is my philosophy in a nutshell. How can that be so controversial? I don't want to live forever. And news flash, you won't either, no matter how many Pilates classes you attend or kale salads you consume. It's just that longevity isn't all that it's cracked up to be. In fact, I want no part of it. As Patrick Henry famously said, "Give me happiness; then give me death." OK, I'm not so good at history or remembering quotes, but my version does have a pretty nice ring.

I may have restarted my smoking habit from anxiety alone. But the more I thought about it, the more perfectly it seemed to symbolize my newfound life goals. The nicotine provides both instant and long-term gratification. The instant is obvious—oh, they make you feel good. As for the long-term, that is all part of my idea.

As is the case with any revolutionary idea, I didn't expect instant acceptance, no matter how brilliant or obvious it seemed to me. Thus, my best friend Janine's reaction was not a surprise that winter day when I revealed I had started smoking.

"Allison. That's perhaps the most ridiculous thing I've heard of in my entire life. Certainly from you."

I was baring my soul. Sympathy, understanding, compassion—were those too much to expect?

"Janine, I assure you I've thought about this a great deal, and no, I'm not just trying to justify something that I know is wrong."

"There...you said it. You know it's wrong. Even you know stupid when you hear it. Is there something you're not telling me? You're one of the brightest women I know. So, for God's sake, just put down the cigarette and no one gets hurt." Janine laughed, mirthlessly, a little at her attempt at levity.

I knew she wasn't joking. Like your average, trying-to-be-healthy fifty-year-old, she didn't require a leap of faith to find cigarettes horrible in every way. They stink, they make your clothes smell, they make you and those around you miserable, and—we can't forget—they kill you. Minor detail. And yet here she was having a discussion—actually, maybe a fight—with her closest friend.

I was not only intent, I was defiant. And maybe a little hurt. "You just don't remember. Not like I do. You don't share my fear. But I'm not crazy, Janine. In fact, I think I'm the only one who really gets it."

"Gets what? Seriously, can you talk me through this? I just can't wrap my head around what you are saying."

"Maybe you're just afraid to see." I sighed. "I didn't just wake up one day and decide I wanted to be a smoker. I have decided that I don't want to live until I'm old. I'm making a conscious decision to hasten my body toward death. Because dying of cancer or a heart attack or anything else seems like a better alternative than no longer knowing you are alive."

There, I had said it. The first time out loud, and it felt...cathartic.

I suppose that I had been saying tiny versions of this before to similar, slightly less dramatic reactions. I'm probably not the only one who does this. You come up with an idea, and you wonder how others might react. So, you give a little hint as to what you are thinking. If your friend starts looking at you as if you have a third eye, you back off and quickly retract what you have said. You soften it by saying that's not what you really meant. Peace between you is reestablished. I wasn't going to do that this time.

"You've got to be out of your freakin' mind!" Janine paused. She was breathing heavily. Angrily. It was the reasoning behind my decision that so exasperated her. I think she would have preferred hearing I was struggling with a bad habit I just couldn't break, try as I might. Then she would throw her full weight into saving me from myself. But I no longer wanted to hide my feelings. I was ready to share them with the world. Or at least my best friend. Plus, some things are easier to masquerade than others. Even a pregnancy you can hide for a few months. But concealing a one-half-to-one-pack-a-day cigarette habit is nearly impossible. The smell betrays you to everyone but those with chronic sinusitis. Your clothes, hair, and car announce your bad habit to the world.

"Janine, just hear me out. We've all got to die of something, right? And chances are you have your own phobias or biases, things that you will do your best to avoid. You know, like being eaten alive by a crocodile."

Since we had sat down for our coffee, this was the first time I saw Janine smile. She really is radiant, the most naturally beautiful of all my good friends. If she diets, you would never know it, because she always seems to eat whatever she wants and still maintains an adorable figure. If it weren't for push-up bras and Spanx, I wouldn't be able to wear half of my clothes. Janine, at coffee sporting an auburn dye job and short cut, can still rock her little black dress from college.

The smile was short-lived, and I guess I knew we would have to revisit this topic a lot before she understood. And maybe she never would.

I persevered. "So, if I had a choice between getting eaten by an alligator, being taken out by an axe murderer, or dying suddenly

by heart attack, it would be a no-brainer. Sign me up for the MI."
I felt this was a rather rousing end to my speech.

"This is about Nancy, isn't it?" queried my best friend.

"Hell yes, it's about my mom!" Now it was me who was getting a little hot and bothered. "I never want to live like that. Ever. I don't want you, my husband, my kids—anyone—having to..." And before the tears came, I had to leave. "I'm done explaining. I've got to run anyway. Thanks, Janine. I mean it, thanks. We'll talk soon."

Though the café was kind of noisy, all I heard was the chair scraping harshly against the floor. Then the sound of my heels against the tile echoed in my ears, and I suddenly thought I was going to pass out. *Come on, Allison, get it together. Just make it to the car.* Yet while I was fumbling for the keys, the tears came. Not many, but more than I wanted to show in public. I had to get away from my friend. I didn't want anyone to see. I had started to bare my wound publicly. A wound that had been more private than I realized. And a sense of shame. Because what I was saying was that I resented what I had had to do for my mother. I resent my mom for so much, and she never knew.

4

October 1988

IT'S A WONDER I HAVEN'T SPENT MORE TIME IN THERAPY. I THINK it's because I have known so many therapists. It's funny that when you grow up with someone, it's hard to take them seriously, even if they later turn out to be an orthopedic surgeon or defense attorney—or therapist. They still are just Martha or Bill to you.

I was a sociology major. Half of us became teachers, half became therapists, and the other half never found well-enough-paying jobs to pay off student loans. And clearly, none of us were good at math. But at the time, we knew everything.

Even as freshmen, we started to feel we were more emotionally intelligent than pretty much everyone walking the planet. After learning something fascinating in class, I felt compelled to analyze random people I came across, and 429 Hart Hall became my favorite destination. It was home to the class I looked forward to and absorbed more than studied.

Professor Stevens, always wearing tweed jackets with elbow patches, might have looked boring in a photograph, but his eyes danced with excitement. And I myself would dance out of each class, heading straight to the library or to huddle in our makeshift sociology club.

The subject one day was caregiving, and Professor Stevens got us to think right back to the beginning.

My first experience with caregiving was absolutely wonderful, or so I was told. How could it not have been? I was the one being cared for. Like everyone else who has no memories of their first few years, I learned from the stories of others.

A typical day would have probably started with undeniable hunger, but it didn't matter because screaming seemed to be the only volume setting with which I had been programmed. The story was that I was rather indiscriminate with my vocalizations. Other babies cried; I yelled. One volume, any reason would do. One of my grandmother's favorite sayings was that if she shined a light into my mouth, she would see right down to my toes. "You would get your mouth so wide."

When I look back at my early photos, I say I was adorable from the outset. Who would not love that smiling, albeit scrawny, infant in that black-and-red dress? I even had a cute hat with matching shoes that I'm sure never touched any pavement. What parent could have resisted the charms of my smile and bright-green eyes? Despite these obvious gifts that made me the cutest baby in the whole wide world, stories of my temper still circulate to this day. "Someone's having an Allison tantrum" became a saying in our household, one that even I later used.

Professor Stevens moved on the following day to one of the debates of the time—the impact of nature versus nurture. In the eighties, with skyrocketing divorce rates, it seemed this discussion morphed into quantity versus quality time. *Time* being the critical word in all of this. Babies, though pretty darn cute, are an amazing, soul-sucking usage of time. Who would have known? Oh yeah, every single mother on earth. But despite being a know-it-all, I was only nineteen, and babies still seemed a long way off.

Stevens could paint a picture, though, and only halfway through the week, we all began to wonder if having kids might not be the best idea after all. "That infant you just had demands every single moment of every single day, seemingly forever. Which may be what led to what I am convinced is the cruelest experiment in all of history."

My interest was piqued.

Professor Stevens continued, "When you're king, I guess you can do whatever you want. And back in the thirteenth century, King Frederick perhaps had had enough of his many illegitimate children. The story goes that he wanted to prove that German was the first language a baby spoke, that it was somehow innate. So, he snatched a bunch of babies from their mothers and had them raised by women who were instructed only to feed and change them. They weren't allowed to speak or do any other touching."

When I got out of class that day, I didn't know where to go next. I knew I had to tell every last person about this experiment, but I also needed to learn more. Maybe I just needed to fact-check my own professor. Could he really have been telling the truth?

"And so what happened?" asked my college roommate. I had just come back from the library to research the question because I didn't really believe anyone would actually have done this experiment. Even if they were a king.

"They never spoke a word." I replied.

"Until what age?" came the obvious follow-up question.

And what I learned that day still stuns me. "No one knows—all of the babies died." The conclusion was from lack of touch, from not being loved.

Now, this was an experiment you would think would never be attempted again. But sadly, this is not the case. Not only have there been countless somewhat similar studies, there have also been cases of orphanages with institutionalized neglect, their infant mortality reaching as high as 30–40 percent.

If this doesn't make you want to send your mom a Mother's Day card, then I don't know what more you need. And yes, you might as well send one for Father's Day too.

I don't think I needed to have learned about these experiments in college. Nor do I believe I had to have children of my own to love my mother unconditionally. For as long as I can remember, I had a love and admiration for my mom that knew no boundaries. She, the vivacious, caring freedom fighter—it is this version of my mother that I want to remember. Strong and loving. Nancy was always fighting something. A true rebel, always had a cause. She seemingly joined every Earth-type of group you could imagine. First it was Greenpeace and saving the whales. Then it was Beyond War, education in Latin America, overpopulation. Every few years, there was a change.

What didn't change, however, was that whichever group she joined, Nancy wanted to comfort the downtrodden. Like the babies who died from a lack of love, I think my mom would have lost her purpose if she were no longer able to provide that love for others.

5

October 1984

YOU MIGHT ASSUME THAT MY MOM, A PACIFIST TO THE CORE, never got mad. And you would be right, notwithstanding her anger at my brother and me. She said I made her turn gray fifteen years early. This was unfair, but also it didn't make a difference in my mind, as she colored her hair anyway. I wasn't trying to hasten her march toward old age; it's just something that daughters are naturally good at. In other words, I wasn't trying to do anything other than survive my teenage years and live my own life. I had no plan. Certainly, I wasn't trying to end my life prematurely—that's not why I *first* took up smoking. That's another story altogether. And to really tell the story, I must go back to that time because time becomes most impactful when you fall in love.

I was fourteen the first time. Sometimes I wonder about those who question whether or not they are in love. For me it was simple: I knew I wanted to be with Nate every minute of every day. Which in the ninth grade simply meant the classes we had together, math, PE, and US history. In that order. Oh, I so wished PE were last. There was little worse than going to history class feeling all gross and yet hoping he would notice me all the same. Though if it weren't for Elizabeth, I don't know if I would have ever uttered a word to him. We were best friends then, Beth and I.

But I could have killed her when she crumpled up a piece of paper with *Allison ♥ Nathaniel* on it and threw it at him one day.

He noticed me then, all right. From that day forward he didn't look in my direction. Or if he did, he would look away as fast as he possibly could.

It's funny about time—when you are fourteen, it can move so slowly. You hear adults say how it speeds up as you age, and maybe they are right. But when you're in ninth grade, waiting for the second hand to slowly move around the clock until class lets out, this seems a very far-off concept. It was a full two weeks before Nathaniel "accidentally" knocked the books out of my hand. Two weeks that felt like two years.

Meanwhile, my emotions had been manifesting as crying, tantrums, boredom, and acceptance. This amusement ride of sentiment probably drove my family and friends crazy. I would like to say that my doldrums started to abate as I had all but forgotten about him. But that would be a lie. It's hard to forget someone completely when you spend eight hours a day arguing about whether he looked better with long or short hair. For weeks he had been completely ignoring me. So, I spent another ten hours a day on the phone with Beth to never let her forget how she had ruined my life.

That is, until one day I found myself screaming somewhat hysterically. I don't know why, really. It's not like he had hurt me. Nor had he ruined some project. He had touched me—intentionally pushed me, actually. The sudden silence was unnerving. When I looked up, gathering *Algebra 1* and George Orwell's *1984*, I felt a sudden wave of embarrassment. At everything. My scream, everyone looking at me, my one sock that had fallen down around my ankle, and...Nathaniel staring at me!

"What'd you do that for?" I screamed. And then, he just ran. Turned and ran. Soon the whole crowd parted, and the day just went on like any other.

Was the second hand even moving at that point? Truly it was a day that would never end. It's strange looking back at your life and remembering how intense your feelings were at that age. Life went from spectacular to not worth living in the space of a few hours. And since time marched with the speed of a glacier before global warming, when things were bad, they were going to stay bad forever.

My brother didn't seem to have this problem. He just didn't care very much—about anything. He never wanted to go to a dance, never wanted to go out with a boy...well, I guess, a girl, in his case. He just seemed happy going through life, doing his homework and going to school. It was disgusting! Why couldn't he ever get in trouble? But we did get along, I guess. He could often get me out of a bad mood. So, he was good for something. In fact, maybe he gave me the idea to try out for the soccer team. I forgot to say, he did love soccer. And perhaps, rather than hating it like I pretended to do when I was forced to go to his games, I liked it more than I thought.

Gibson High School, home of the Eagles. I hated school. Not that I was particularly bad at it, but I didn't stand out like the unicorns either. You know, the ones who never seemed to try yet had perfect hair, who never had to wear braces, and who were allowed to use makeup. I wanted to think they were as rare as unicorns, but they seemed to be everywhere. You know how it is, when you are feeling down about yourself but all you notice are those who have got it all together.

As I've matured—such a funny word—I have started to compare myself to those beneath me. It's a lot easier to feel good about yourself when you contrast your life to that of a hooker or a drug addict. I think this is why *Married with Children* and *The Simpsons* did so well. We all felt that we were better than those characters, and it boosted our self-image. When I was fourteen, we didn't have shows with such irredeemable characters. But we did have Sandra Jenkins.

Everybody seemed to make fun of Sandra Jenkins. She missed probably half the school year. And when she did come, we were awful to her. I guess, in retrospect, I'm not particularly proud of myself for that. But there was little to like. She had no friends, she dressed like a goth transvestite, and she was mean. Not that I ever talked to her, but she exuded an anticharm.

But that comparison could only make me feel confident for a while. It was not long until my mind would wander away from someone else's train wreck back to reality. Back to the unicorns who didn't even seem to sweat in gym class. Not me—I could sweat like a guy. Not the super-smelly, "wish I were wearing men's deodorant" sweat. But still the kind that would leave a stripe down your back all the way to your butt.

One day in PE, though, I scored a goal in soccer. It was really more luck than skill. But it went in, and I felt great. I'd never really been that into sports before. All I had ever done in that stupid school prior was try to get an A in PE. It just made your whole report card look a little better. That goal probably changed me in more ways than I could have ever imagined. I didn't exactly have much skill. Remember, I had never played other than in PE. I guess you could count kickball and practicing with my brother, but it's likely that wasn't what got me on the soccer team. I really think it was that goal. The PE coach just happened to be the girls' soccer coach. And so, when tryouts rolled around in October, I think he remembered.

The funny thing also about that team: a couple unicorns played for the Gibson Eagles. And they were really good. Seriously, what weren't they good at? But even more strangely, we kind of became friends. They started to look out for me at school. It's not like they would hang out with me and Beth, but they did recognize my existence. Which was odd because, like most ninth-grade girls, I wasn't exactly much to look at. "My nose." That was my answer when people asked about my best feature. I think I said that because it was the first thing I could think of that wasn't totally offensive. Plus, the answer caught people off guard.

Beth would look in the mirror from one side to the other as if she were having a serious debate about which was the better side to look at. I thought her best feature was her eyelashes. She didn't even have to try. When we started wearing makeup, she didn't really have to do anything with her lashes. But when she did, boys noticed. Everyone noticed. Which was good because we were inseparable back then, and so people couldn't help but notice me a little too. It certainly wasn't my nose that helped us be in the "not totally losers" crowd. Remember that movie *The Breakfast Club*, where everyone was a certain type of person? That's truly what being in school is like. You become pigeonholed into some stereotype, and you can't escape it. And since your only goal as a teen is to fit in, you don't want to escape it.

It was my second year of high school when I saw Nate, no longer Nathaniel, smoking with his friends. It was in the parking lot, and I didn't think he saw me. But I was everything all at once. Disgusted, hurt, turned on, fearful, and envious. It was not as if we were dating or anything. But we did talk to each other now and then. My braces were finally off, and so perhaps I wasn't quite as repulsive as I had been the year before.

What was he thinking? Was he not the boy I thought he was? Where did he get the cigarettes? What if his parents found out?

But I was saved again by soccer. Who would have thought a sport I had only played for a couple years would have had such a profound effect on me? It certainly gave me confidence. It provided me with several really good friends. And it made me realize cigarettes are not for me.

Of course I tried them, though. How could I not? The guy I so wanted to date was smoking, and that was my in. What other girl would be daring enough to ask him for a smoke? Everything about my plan worked. With the exception that smoking was awful. I still remember the brand: Lucky. Prophetic. I coughed my way through the cigarette but instantly became the cool chick among his friends. The euphoria was tremendous. Maybe the nicotine, maybe what was happening to me. I was surrounded by five of the cutest guys in high school, we were laughing, and Nate actually put his arm around me for the first time during a prolonged coughing fit. No wonder people smoked—it was great. Well, great for a while. In this case, not longer than forty-five minutes. I had to run to soccer practice, and that was when things changed.

That was my last cigarette for a very long time. I couldn't run. Worse, after I had tried to catch Carly, who wasn't particularly fast, I had to stop. I went straight to the bathroom and vomited the tuna on rye, the pickle, the twenty-four raisins and apple juice and maybe even some of my breakfast. It was the first time I had ever done that, and it didn't take a genius to correlate it with my cigarette "habit." My habit truly was a one-and-done. Well, almost done. I would sometimes take a drag just to be cool and hang out with the guys. But I conveniently lied to them about getting into serious trouble with my folks, and they didn't force me to do more. Probably because I was a girl, but maybe because Nate kind of liked me by then.

My fifteenth birthday came with some fanfare. My parents were really pretty good sometimes. A day where everything was suddenly my choice. I could choose whom to invite, what we were going to eat, the flavor of the cake, and everything else.

Maybe some people just know, but was chocolate really that much better than lemon? And what if Clarissa, a unicorn from my soccer team, didn't like chocolate? Clearly, the pressure of so many decisions wasn't good for my skin. The week leading up to March 13 brought an army of zits and a corresponding full-on meltdown in the bathroom one morning. I never complained much about going to school because of the work. But shame. Shame is a powerful motivator, and I was feeling very motivated that morning not to go to school. Years later, when I spoke of that day with my mom, she remembered—one of the few things she did seem to remember. I guess it was more of a tantrum than I wanted to believe. Maybe it was because she also recalled what it was like feeling so ugly that you had no self-worth. But, whatever the reason, that was the day Mom allowed me to wear makeup. I probably still looked like crap because my eyes were pretty bloodshot. Neither Mary nor Kay has figured out a way to fix that. But my skin was smooth. I couldn't believe how much better I looked. Even the volcano just left of center on my forehead looked more like a gopher's mound.

I started to cry again when I hugged my mom, resulting in a needed touch-up. But I went to school, and no one noticed. So, it was a good day. Despite the fact that we all want to excel in something and want to do something extraordinary, as teenagers, goal number one by far is to avoid notice for being different.

6

October 1988

GOING AWAY TO COLLEGE WAS A THRILLING TIME FOR ME. Months before taking the unpleasant middle seat that would carry me far away from home for the first time, I threw my mortarboard in the air like so many of my friends. We were high school graduates, and that seemed to be a sufficient achievement to warrant a celebration that lasted for much of that summer.

For years family and friends had asked me, "What do you want to be when you grow up?"

I soon realized that "How should I know? I'm only twelve!" wasn't the answer that they were looking for. And though sometimes I couldn't keep from being a smartass and saying something like "A school janitor," I realized you got people to gush when you said something that reached even higher than their dreams. "I want to be a doctor! In fact, I want to be a surgeon so I can cut out cancer and keep people alive."

"Oh my gosh, Allison, that's amazing, truly amazing. And I bet you could do it too," my uncle might say as he pinched my cheeks.

The fact was, though, I really had no idea what I wanted to be. I'm sure I made up my fair share of answers during that time, pilot, astronaut, lawyer, and physicist among them. The truth was I didn't even feel confident about choosing a major. I was eighteen, tall and wiry, with long hair and a flat chest, stylish but not Barbielike, with far less experience than I had imagined. Not just sexual experiences (there had been only two of those). It's just that until I went to college, I had no idea how much I hadn't been doing. I really had taken my parents for granted. Suddenly I had to navigate a million things—and fail often. I had never signed a lease before and was embarrassed I still needed my parents to cosign. I had a savings account but not a checking account. I couldn't figure out how to sign up for all my classes. My car insurance got canceled because I forgot to make my payments. I missed the English entrance exam because I thought it was on Wednesday and not Tuesday. All in all, I quickly realized my "dream" of becoming that surgeon was pretty unlikely to come true. I wasn't exactly med-school material. In fact, I didn't know if I was sociology material. Though it was my favorite class, I still killed myself to get an A-.

What I did become good at was making friends. And friends, the kind that you make in college who stick around for a lifetime, are the ones who saved me. Without women like Khatia and Lindsay, I don't know if I would have even graduated. I can't count the number of times I was saved by a random comment like "If I didn't get the notes for statistics from the student center, I'd have had no chance on that midterm."

I learned to weasel myself into the conversation and say, "What notes are we talking about?" And suddenly, I would have a chance of getting a good grade instead of barely passing.

And I met my best friend from college while trying to pledge a sorority that I wasn't cut out for. Janine was smart too, and she helped me have a social life. She was the kind of girl who seemed to party, drink a fair bit, always have a boyfriend, and yet still manage good grades. I wanted to be her. She made everything seem easy. She was my friend magnet. Once I latched onto her, so many others became my de facto friends.

One day Janine showed up at my door. "Do you like to ride? Bicycles, I mean, not men," she amended quickly, perhaps because she saw the look on my face. "It's just that you seem athletic, and I hate doing anything alone."

I didn't know Janine that well at the time, despite having been at a few parties together. Yet somehow, this flyer she saw advertising the Ride of the Century—a pun on the word for a hundred-mile bike ride—changed our friendship from close to lifelong. We started training together during our freshman year, riding on Sunday mornings for one to two hours at first. We would finish and treat ourselves to breakfast at this greasy diner called Pancake Circus. Say what you want about the Circus, it couldn't be beat for both the prices and the portions that we justified after pedaling our little butts off. And exercise can be as intoxicating as alcohol. At least, at the end. The ride itself could be dull for long stretches, despite the scenery.

To get through those boring times, we started to play this game called Ask Any Question. We figured, why shouldn't we be able to tell at least one person in this world all of our deepest secrets? This even blossomed into a short fling after being asked, is there something that a man can do that will get you to orgasm every time? It was probably a good thing for our friendship that we mutually enjoyed—but not enough—this foray into bisexuality. This is also something I've never told my husband about. He never thought to ask.

"So, Allison, what do you want to be when you grow up?" Janine asked one day after a four-hour ride.

A laugh with a bit of pancake came out as I had just stuffed my face with a rather large bite.

"And I don't want the stupid answer of some random profession. I want to know what kind of person you want to be. Are you going to stay Little Miss Perfect and become a proper housewife? Will you marry your career instead? Will you be one of those discontented housewives with three kids who feels they gave away their whole life to a man they no longer love or admire? Or—"

"Just stop already!" I managed before I took another large bite. I chewed for a while, then said, "I get it, I get it, but how am I going to keep all of those options straight if you keep on asking questions?" I didn't go on.

"Well?" she asked while I continued to stall by drinking my coffee.

"Seriously, Janine, how am I supposed to know? You're asking me to predict the future."

"Oh no. Not at all. That would be just a random guess. I'm asking what kind of future you want. That's quite different. You may say you want to be a well-respected dentist but end up a bartender with two kids from two different men and a rather nasty meth habit. I'm not asking you to guess what will happen; I want to know what you hope will happen. Which Allison would you want me to see twenty years from now when I run into you at the grocery store?"

Luckily the century bike ride took a lot of practice; it took that entire summer to come up with what seemed like a good answer at the time. I wanted Happiness with a capital *H*. And what I had learned so far in my nineteen years on the planet was that the circumstances don't really make as much difference as you imagine. Otherwise, why does it seem all those silver-spoon Hollywood kids with great careers and all the money in the world end up crazy, on drugs, or even dead?

While we pedaled, I gave Janine my response.

"Is that your final, stupid answer?" she cajoled. She had a way of smiling while tilting her head that made her biting remarks less painful.

More timidly than I had hoped came my yes reply. I added, "I don't think it makes much difference if I get married once or twice, have one kid or three, or go to Princeton or Cal State. I just have to decide to be a happy person."

"Come on, don't you think you'd be a little happier with a job that provided you enough so you didn't have to worry about student loans or your mortgage?"

"Happier than what?"

"Than living in a rundown two-bedroom on the wrong side of the tracks, with condoms and needles frequently found on your streets," insisted Janine.

It seemed the rest of the summer Janine tried to get me to fundamentally change my answer. Maybe it was because I never truly believed I would end up a homeless drug addict, but I just couldn't see that struggling a bit financially would make me sad. Maybe it was just because my life experience to that point was pretty limited. Looking back now, though, I realize my answer has evolved with time. I'm starting to believe that there is one thing that can consistently derail happiness, and it's not lack of money—it's poor health.

What was great about Ask Any Question was that when you got deep into someone's soul, they could turn around and ask an even deeper question in return. This time it was me asking Janine about suicide. My question evolved to "How much pain and suffering do you think you could endure before you asked to be put out of your misery?" A query long before the likes of Dr. Kevorkian made it a national conversation, and a question that I knew would tug a little at her more religious background.

"Really, Allison? That's your question? A bit general, don't you think?" stalled Janine. "Are we talking an injury where you know your death is imminent?"

"I'm not sure that makes any difference," I retorted. "If your guts are hanging out and you shoot yourself in the head, how is that different than learning you're going to die of brain cancer and doing yourself in before the craziness and the pain begin?"

"It makes all the difference in the world! If I knew I was just about to die and I was in agony, then I'd want to die right then. Seriously, Allison, I would be begging you to shoot me if I had only minutes left to live."

"What if it's two hours?" I pushed.

"Same answer."

"Eight days?" I pushed harder. "In fact, wouldn't that make it more important? If you are only going to suffer for fifteen minutes, that's bad. But eight days of anguish—that's misery, don't you think? Wouldn't that make you even more inclined to kill yourself?"

"You realize I hate you, Allison," she said, not only smiling but tossing a clump of grass at my face. It was a beautiful day, with cumulus clouds close but still distant enough we didn't have to worry about rain. "I hate you because I'm going to be thinking about something that should have waited until I was about sixty years older. Next you're going to wonder why I don't just kill my-self right now!"

"Are you saying this question is so awful, you'd rather just end it all now than go another fifteen minutes, despite having the most charming, vivacious, beautiful woman at your side?"

"Since you put it that way, *yes*!" And we laughed. We couldn't stop. A few bicyclists rode by us and probably wondered if we had been eviscerated, holding our sides and rolling around in the grass.

We never did come up with a clear answer that day, nor did we in the next few weeks before our Ride of the Century. However, I think there are some moments that live on in our subconscious. Having truly contemplated something, you may find that it can recur with renewed interest. So, my answer evolved with each news story or personal tale that became a variation on the topic. But I never really gave thought to when would I consider ending my life if I knew I was losing my mind. Until, of course, I had to confront the idea head-on when my mom began to lose hers.

7

May 1953

At five feet eleven inches, my mother was a force to be reckoned with from a young age. She reached her full height at just fifteen, when she was in the tenth grade. Growing up in rural Ohio, she would have dominated sports if she had had any interest. But though she was athletic, competition was not her thing. Mom preferred hiking and the outdoors. She loved nature and could spend hours studying outside. What set her apart and made her an outsider in that area of the country was her love for every living creature. If it had been accepted in this part of the country, she would have definitely been Buddhist. All of God's creatures were perfect, commanding respect.

Grandad had been an avid hunter. Weekends, he would alternate between pheasant, duck, deer, and whatever else was in season. But she must have worn him down. Not by crying—that wasn't her style. Mom would either debate or give you a doe-eyed look of disappointment to get you to change your ways. With her moral compass stuck on compassion, she couldn't fathom how anyone could approach life in a different way. So, by the time I came along, I never knew he had done much hunting until I saw old photo albums providing evidence of his prior passion.

Not to abuse the analogy, but my mom was truly a fish out of water in Clarksburg, Ohio. It was not that she didn't have friends; she didn't have allies. Stating all that she was thinking would have been social suicide at Lincoln High School. In the 1950s, they thought that Elvis Presley was a bad influence. Certainly no one was ready for the Village People, and thus no one was ready for my mom. Not that my mom necessarily hung out with groups of flamboyant, homosexual men, but she would see nothing wrong with them and would have staunchly defended their rights to do and dress as they pleased.

The soup kitchen run from a neighboring church in Clarksburg was staffed entirely of volunteers. Probably no one would have used the term *ghetto*, but the Methodist church that served the poor was definitely on the other side of the tracks. Mom would ride her bike every Sunday and often on Tuesday nights to do what other kids did as a punishment. She felt it her duty. It was something that defined her.

Apparently, Grandma Louise was not very happy about it. The main reason was that this was the wrong crowd. No one believed color had much to do with it, though there were definitely more Black people at that church. Certainly, no single race had a monopoly of needing clothes, food, or shelter. What Grandma seemed most worried about were the "bad elements": the teenage mothers, the alcoholics, the potential for violence. Louise saw these dangers in other people, but my mom never did. My mom seemed to have a filter; she only saw the positives in people and the world in general.

I recall one time coming back to my parents' house as an adult to find ants everywhere. I sarcastically said to my dad, "Have you not heard of Raid?"

He rolled his eyes. "You have no idea what I have to live with. Your mother has decided we can't kill the ants; we can only persuade them to go somewhere else."

"Please tell me she's not trying to talk to the ants?" I laughed and pleaded at the same time.

"She doesn't think she's Dr. Doolittle, if that what you're imply-
ing. She's using lemon juice to break up their communication trails."
After I shared a good commiserating laugh with my dad, we agreed
that all the lemons in the world weren't going to solve this problem.

I was the one who bought the Raid in the end. I didn't even tell
Dad, lest he be thrown on the witness stand as a coconspirator in
the great ant genocide that I laid down one night while they were
out. To the end, I think Mom always believed it was her lemons. I
bought the lemon scent, after all.

When you get to the age that you start to learn more about who
your parents were when they were young, you find several surprises.
What was not a surprise to anyone was that Mom wanted to be a
veterinarian. She loved everything and everyone, but she was not
immune to hurt. People can be cruel. People can fight against you
and dissuade you from your dreams. Animals will return you love
in kind. Unconditionally.

I don't know how many pets she had had when growing up.
It just seemed to Grandma and Grandpa that they couldn't
say no often enough. Other children might get into trouble
for sneaking off at night, returning home drunk. Not my mom.
She would be caught with a new dog or cat in her room that
she had to save. She might go weeks caring for an abandoned
kitten until she found someone to permanently take it home.
Or she got into trouble—whichever came first. Maybe that
was her secret to weight loss. She gave all her food to the pets
she tried to hide.

And while she was working at a veterinarian's office, she met
my dad. It was a story that got retold at many Thanksgivings and
always brought laughter.

When I was in my twenties, I started telling the story to some
friends at my parents' house. I'm not sure why she let me go on
and on. She was probably just being kind. "Allison can definitely

tell a story. She's so passionate," my mom would say. But then eventually, she came and sat with us and took over. The story was lyrical, funny, detailed, and absolutely wrong.

She told us, "There was a dance for those in the military after they finished boot camp. Larry was a trim, handsome cadet who likely could have had numerous women line up to join him for the end-of-the-year ceremony. He chose Kathy. I don't really know anything about Kathy, but I must thank her for being awful to your dad that week.

"He had gone through a lot of trouble to please her. He had rented a tuxedo for the event, which came with some classic, slick, black wingtips. He and his friends had been able to borrow a car to bring a total of six of them to and from the dance. And what he would always say was the primary reason he didn't back out was that he had bought a five-dollar corsage. 'Do you know how much money that was?' he would always exclaim when he told the story. 'Oh, it's not much money now, but in 1953, that was a *lot* of money. And that's when she told me.'

"You see, it was after he had bought the corsage, he got the phone call from Kathy that she would not be able to come with him to the dance that weekend. Larry was brokenhearted. He didn't like to emphasize how much he cared for Kathy, but he didn't need to give details. It seemed that she was the only thing that got him through some of those awful days where he would be running, or climbing, or carrying more than he felt was possible. She was the last thing he thought of before he collapsed with exhaustion. That stupid, cruel girl—she gave no reason, which broke his heart all the more.

"It was two days before the dance, and his buddies couldn't console him. And so the only thing that led him to me was the five dollars. The tuxedo place would have allowed him to return it for a full refund, but the corsage was his. Unwilling to give up on this five bucks, he agreed to just come to the dance to have fun; they all deserved fun after all those weeks of boot camp misery.

"It was about an hour's drive from the military base to the dance hall. Along the way, he got some good ribbing, especially after the two other girls had gotten into the car. And that's when my life changed. Larry was not going to have his happiness spoiled by Kathy any longer—he was going to do something about it.

"They were stopped outside an apartment complex where three women were standing outside talking. 'You know what I'm going to do?' he calmly informed the others. 'I'm going to take this stupid corsage, walk up to those three women, and persuade one of them to come dance with me.'

"What I didn't know until after is that they circled the block three times. I'm not sure if this was for Larry to work up the courage or for the other five to work up the dare. No one could believe he was actually going to do it. But the next thing I knew was this drop-dead gorgeous man had gotten out of a car and was walking toward us. You could tell he was military just by the way he carried himself. He had short hair, and those shoes. The whole outfit just gleamed, and he didn't break stride for a second.

"Though there were three of us and we were all staring as if a movie star had just walked up to us, I felt the whole time he was talking just to me. Not that I can really remember a word he said; I just knew my answer was yes before the question even came.

"Maybe he chose me simply because it was where I lived and I promised him I could be out, ready to go, in less than ten minutes. I was only nineteen, and I knew no other place than Ohio at the time, but before that night was out, I knew I would follow this man to the end of the earth if I could just be with him. I just knew."

8

September 2013

I WAS IN MY MIDFORTIES WHEN THE DOCTOR TOLD ME THAT MY mom, Nancy MacPherson, had dementia. It was a crisp September day, and it began like so many others. Yet there, in the offices of Drs. Jones, Stemple, and Metcalf, my life was changing.

We had left the 1990s-styled waiting room with dated magazines to wait some more in room two. A room which, once Dr. Metcalf delivered the news, suddenly became different. Smothering. Blue-and-white tile, fourteen by twelve feet at best, a small sink. A faint smell of something covered up.

My senses began to open while my mind began to close. I think I was listening, but my focus was elsewhere. Because Dr. Metcalf had said the word.

Staring at Dr. Metcalf's pen, I became hypnotized, not allowing grief to invade. The dialogue became so quiet I no longer heard anything. My mind was shutting off. An IED had exploded in my brain, leaving me with ringing ears and sudden nausea.

Stealing a glance at my mom, I would catch the rare word spoken by the doctor in a quiet monotone. The only word that sank in, however, was *Alzheimer's*. The disease with no cure. A disease so awful I had never allowed my mind to wonder about its effects.

"One thing a colleague said to me to comfort the needlessly worried" came the solemn voice of our white-coated expert "is this: 'if a patient is afraid that they are losing their mind, they are not. Everyone gets distracted. But if a family member brings someone and has concerns, then you had better do a careful evaluation.' So, unfortunately, you're not one of the needlessly worried; I was concerned about Nancy from the moment you both walked through my door."

"Needlessly worried"—that was what I thought I had been. "Allison, you're overreacting," my husband loved to say. A phrase he repeated even after my mom's primary doctor gave us a neurology referral. Which had brought Nancy and me to this fucking sterile office at 1820 Twenty-Fourth Street with crappy parking and this smug Tom Selleck–wannabe doctor in his annoying white coat. This fantastically serene, monotonic, purported expert trying to tell me about being a little high-strung, pointing out in contrast how calm Mom seemed to be even though she was the one with the disease.

"There is no specific test," he continued, "that will definitively make the diagnosis. But in some ways, it doesn't matter. The signs from the history are typically all one needs. But let's test her anyway."

My blood on boil and my ears growing as red as my nails that had been done just yesterday, I calmly—at least I want to believe I was calm—raised my hand like a schoolgirl. "I thought you just said there was no test, and now you want to give her a test. I'm sorry, but I guess now I'm confused."

"The time-honored test is the Mini-Mental Status Examination. It won't take long. Let's do it today, shall we?"

I didn't really believe this was a question, more of a statement from the doctor, but what did I care. He already knew! I thought he was doing the test to appease me. But I didn't need the test. I knew too. I just had never acknowledged it until that moment. I think I had known for years.

That's not to say that I had never really given it thought, but I preferred to see the changes as part of growing old. Of becoming lonely. It may have begun with her taking five minutes to find her keys, but I knew it had been worsening.

After my father died, being alone really did a number on her. She started to call me a lot. And at first it was nice that we began to converse when I got home. By the time the day of reckoning at the doctor's came, however, it was not unusual to talk four or five times per day. I had stopped answering her messages. Really, there was little point, as she would be calling again soon enough anyway.

The test started off somewhat innocuously. "Nancy, can you tell me what day it is today?" She looked up, and he continued, "Actually, tell me everything about today. What day of the week, the date, the month, the year?"

Dr. Metcalf listened politely to the rambling response. Had it been a dinner party, this would have been an unremarkable conversation. "I think it's a Tuesday. Yes, it must be Tuesday," Nancy added a little more emphatically. "I know this because Allison always comes by on Tuesday, and we get coffee. Don't you, dear? You know my favorite place isn't Starbucks. Not that there's anything wrong with Starbucks; they're just so busy, and they talk too fast. I like Mr. Bean—such a funny name. It's just a few blocks farther, and they are much friendlier. Kind of like you, Doctor. I think you would prefer Mr. Bean too. Have you ever gone there?"

I detected a small pause as Dr. Metcalf was not only taking notes on his computer, he was also judging her intently. Her shoes, the Velcro type that suggested that ease and comfort were the only things that mattered any longer. The brightly colored blouse she wore even during these cooler months. The ill-fitting polyester pants with what was probably a permanent stain. And I wondered if he noticed her blush, the poorly applied mascara, the somewhat bold and uneven lipstick. I'm pretty sure I had done her nails last, and that was two weeks ago.

Now I was looking at her with a similar critical eye, and that was it. I had to walk out of the room. I just had to go. I don't really even know what excuse I gave; I just ran out. When I got to the bathroom, I shed a few tears. I think I was too hurt to cry. *He* was judging my mom. Negatively. What did he know about my mom? This was not who she was. Not who she had always been. Until then. That moment. When she suddenly became fragile and confused...to me.

I returned only a little more composed. I was angry, I think. At the doctor? At the world? I should have stayed in the bathroom.

"Can you draw the face of a clock for me, Nancy?" This seemed somewhat innocuous. As the seconds ticked by, I was struck by how long it was taking just to write in twelve numbers. I couldn't really see because she was left-handed. But when she finally announced she was done, it looked more like the work of Salvador Dalí than Rolex. The clock literally seemed to melt and transform along the page. How could this be a product of her mind? How could she not see this wasn't even close to a circle?

So, when it came time for him to ask the dreaded Serial Sevens, I couldn't control myself—I tried to help her. I started muttering, "Ninety-three," under my breath, but who was I kidding. Who would be more likely to hear me? This doctor, who looked barely older than Doogie Howser, or my mom, who could fail to hear the TV when it was on so loud the neighbors would complain? I received a disapproving look from Doogie and felt even worse when I heard, "I was never good at math anyway."

No, no, no, no, no, no, no. Mom, that's just not true! Dad was hopeless. Once we passed algebra 1, he became as helpful as our cat, but Mom helped us clear through high school when we got stuck, even with calculus. These and future interjections remained in my mind. I had been shooshed once by Dr. Metcalf, and I wasn't going to continue embarrassing myself.

And what made it even more sad: Mom didn't seem to care at all. She wasn't embarrassed. She wasn't even bothered. She seemed to love this man while he continued to be judge, jury, and executioner. "Allison, doesn't he have nice hair!?" winked my mom. *She winked! What the hell was that?*

This thirty-minute test felt like eternity. The mental judgment day exam mercifully came to an end. Out of thirty points, Mom scored fourteen. He may have even rounded up. Anything less than twenty-six is considered abnormal.

Maybe I tuned everything out at that point, or maybe he had spent enough time with us and left quickly, but the next thing I knew, we were in the elevator, headed to the car.

They say a sudden diagnosis often brings shock and waves of different emotions. Well, whoever "they" are, they are right. I was shocked. Mom, not so much. She was blissfully unaware and showed absolutely no concern at all. I couldn't decide if this was a blessing or not. Was she better off not knowing she had a disease that would eat away at her mind?

All I knew was that I had my marching orders—papers to get blood work and a head CT scan to ensure nothing else treatable was going on. Then, three months later, we were to return to relate progress, a statement that was a laughable oxymoron.

9

September 2013
Nancy

"COME ON, MOM, THEY'RE CALLING US."

"Allison, can we listen to the end of this song? I've always liked this song." Nancy couldn't remember the song's title or the singer's name, but that didn't seem to matter. She knew it better than she knew anything in that moment. "You know, I cried a lot during that time. I think most people think this was about their husband or lover. For me, it was about the two of you."

The slightly bothered tone of the medical assistant broke through. "Just through here, Mrs. MacPherson. After taking off your shoes, can you stand on the scale for me?"

"OK, 174.3. You and your—"

"Daughter," Allison interjected.

"—can come into this room. The doctor will be with you in just a moment."

"Allison, why are we here again? I don't really like going to the doctor's—you know that. And I feel totally fine. I keep on telling you that."

"Mom, this isn't exactly easy for me. In fact, I was supposed to be at Sloane's basketball practice now."

"Sloane? She has a basketball game today?"

"But that's not the point, sorry. Ever since Dad died last year, you've lived in the house all by yourself. Brother and I have begun to worry about you being there all alone."

That song began playing in Nancy's head again. How she loved that song.

"We've, I guess, started to notice that your house is not like it always used to be. Recently I must have done ten days' worth of dishes. Do you remember at Christmas we bought you several new outfits that Sloane and I picked out together? Mom. Are you listening? When I went through your closet, they were all there, still sitting with their tags on. You used to love wearing new clothes. Even when I was a girl and picked out something probably a little crazy, you still wore it with pride."

Nonplussed, Nancy tilted her head, "I still love whatever you do. You know that. You're the most wonderful daughter in the world. Do you remember that song 'You Light Up My Life'? It's going through my head right now. I don't know what got me thinking about it, but I've always loved that song."

The doctor entered. *Oh, he's pretty good-looking. Maybe this doctor's visit won't be so bad after all. But no manners at all. He just burst into the room. I was having such a nice time with Allison.*

"Mrs. MacPherson, hello. I'm Dr. Metcalf." He extended his hand and did give me a warm smile. Your doctor has asked me to see you. Is that OK with you?"

"Of course. It's not like I had any pressing engagements this morning. How can I help you?"

"Well, I'm not sure if you are going to like the idea of doing a test. Who likes a pop quiz? But this one is really kind of fun. Nancy, can you tell me what day it is today?"

Nancy looked at him.

He continued soothingly, "Actually, tell me everything about the day. What day of the week, the date, the month, the year?"

"I think it's a Tuesday. Yes, it must be Tuesday. Or maybe Wednesday. You see, I'm retired, and it really doesn't make any difference to me."

He asked some more questions.

"The president? That handsome Black man. I can't remember his name just now, but I do like him."

"Can you draw the face of a clock for me, Nancy?" the doctor serenely continued, handing me a pen and paper.

As pen went to paper, the clock began to take shape.

Why can't I draw a circle? It looks kind of oval. It reminds me of when you are dizzy and you are trying to walk a straight line but you just can't. Allison and this lovely man look so intent upon my progress. It seems I am disappointing them. Well, at least Allison — she looks sad.

"Can you put in the numbers?" Nancy heard vaguely.

This seemed just as easy, or rather, hard. Nancy got to nine and realized she was already at the top. *This is a strange test. Maybe I should just put ten, eleven, and twelve on the outside.* Nancy sensed pity. *I'm not sure what is so disappointing. It's not as if I need to draw a clock to get my Social Security check.*

"Mrs. MacPherson, if you started with the number one hundred and you subtracted seven, what number would you get?" the doctor inquired.

"Are we still doing the test? I rather hoped it was over by now. I thought you said it would be enjoyable," Nancy replied.

"Yes, we are just about done. Are you able to subtract seven from one hundred?" he asked again.

Why is he asking me this? Nancy shook her head. "I was never good at math anyway. Are you married, doctor? Do you have big family?"

Did he even respond? I'm not sure he did. Now, he seemed to be talking intently to Allison. *I wonder what they are talking about.* They both seemed animated, but they were talking softly, so Nancy didn't hear much.

She frowned at the paper in her hands. *That test really wasn't all that fun. I've not been asked those kinds of questions before. I was never good at drawing.*

She looked at the doctor again. *I really wonder if he is married. Maybe I should ask him again, though I think he ignored me the first time.*

What a nice day it is today. Maybe Allison and I can go for a walk along the river. It should be beautiful this time of year. Oh yeah, that was one of the questions he asked: what is the season? It's spring, obviously. I wonder why he bothered asking me when he surely should have known himself.

I just love that song, I'll have to play it when I get home.

"He just left. Mom, I guess it's time we go."

"OK, Allison, that sounds like a great idea. Do you have time to go for a walk?"

10

September 2013

Traffic was probably bad. I didn't notice. I changed the radio's all-Disney channel to the easy-listening station I had programmed just for Mom. Looking at her gazing absently out the window made me want to cry. What was different about her?

The half-hour drive to Park West vanished along with the sounds of Gordon Lightfoot and our polite conversation. After shifting the Volvo into park, instinctively I rushed to help Mom out of the car, but she was already shutting the door. The diagnosis had created a feeling of frailty, yet she didn't need physical assistance. She had already begun to shuffle toward the front door in her beige Velcro shoes.

I didn't go in. I couldn't. As if I had learned a secret about someone, I felt this diagnosis had changed us. It changed me. From that day forward, I would look at her through a different lens. I would begin second-guessing every decision, every conversation. I began to doubt if she would remember things I said or the memories we shared. When might she even forget carrying me through this very door when I broke my ankle? I couldn't go in now; I just wasn't ready.

My husband, Carl, asked me to keep it in perspective. "It's not like she's dying of cancer. Tomorrow will be just like today. She's happy, she's living well on her own, she's got friends and family. And she's not in any pain. Really, hon, I think you're—"

"*Stop!* If you say that word, I'm going to scream. I'm serious, Carl. Nothing is ever a problem in your mind. But the fact is, my father's dead, and today I learned that my mom's officially losing her mind. At some point, I will have no one left. Can't you even acknowledge my sadness?"

And then he did something I'll never forget. Carl hugged me. At just over six feet tall, he is much stronger than I am. But this hug wasn't about power. It was an embrace. With him whispering in my ear words of love, enveloping me with his arms, I lost it. I lost my fear and every last tear I could possibly shed. After thirteen years of marriage, we had had our ups and downs, but in moments like that, there was no doubt how much he loved me. How much I needed him.

Carl reluctantly, gingerly, brought up what would happen next. He probably thought he was still entering a minefield. I gave him a rundown of the appointment, her fourteen out of thirty score, her Salvador Dalí clock.

"So, what is the point of the blood tests, head CT scan, and follow-up appointment?" Carl queried—and I don't think just to pretend he was listening. He truly wanted to know. Always healthy and muscular, he tended to believe most things in medicine were just a scam to make more money. "I thought you said he already knew the diagnosis."

Neither of us had any answers. And I was already a little touchy, making Carl as careful as a lawyer with his words. What saved us, as it often did, was the girls. As difficult as life could be, there was a constant, pleasant, distracting chaos known as Meredith and Sloane. Two years apart in age, they were so different in temperament that it was hard to believe they came from the same genetic material.

Meredith, our first, was amazingly independent. She asked for little affection and gave less. She was intensely competitive—to a fault, Carl would add. Sloane was more like a cat. She just wanted to curl up in your lap and purr. She was not competitive at all. She was the one who would chase a butterfly instead of an onrushing soccer player.

With children, no matter what the day brings, you still have to feed them, bathe them, and keep them from killing each other. This day was like any other in that respect.

Carl had picked them up from child care on his way home from work. Soccer practice for Meredith came right after, and so they hadn't been home long before I walked through the door. And it wasn't a surprise when Meredith came into the kitchen and said, "Lasagna. We had lasagna yesterday. Can I just have a peanut butter and jelly sandwich?"

I realized I sounded a little like my mom when I heard myself say, "Hon, I've had a hard day, so just be happy you're getting anything at all."

Even Sloane kind of groaned at this response. I guess I was not surprised. When I was their age, I hated leftovers. As an adult, I love yesterday's casserole. Not because it tastes so wonderful a day or two later; it's because prep time drops to about ten minutes—warm up the casserole while making a quick salad, butter a little french bread, and voilà! Dinner is served. Almost as good is that cleanup time is similarly improved. In five minutes, plates and cups are in the dishwasher, the casserole is put away, and we move on.

On to the next chore of the evening—homework. Even though Meredith was in the sixth grade, homework seemed like too much had arrived too early. Tonight, though, I didn't mind. I began to think less and less of Mom's diagnosis. The appointment with Dr. Metcalf and all its implications began to recede further as Sloane, curled up beside me, began to draw while I instructed Meredith on division. This was a typical, gloriously dull and happy evening for us. The type of evening that I would become nostalgic for.

11

September 2013

I CALLED MY BROTHER, JEREMY, THE NIGHT AFTER GETTING THE confirming diagnosis. We both cried a little. Well, I did a lot. It had been a rough day for me. What's strange is how things hit you suddenly even when you already know about them on the inside.

Maybe I became this way because of my mom. I remember her almost sobbing when I was awarded the top prize in my school for the debate team. It was at the end-of-the-year ceremony, and we all knew it was coming. Which was good, as I had to prepare a speech. I imagined it was like the Academy Awards, where you go up there and pretend you just put something profound together, all the while continuing to act like you are so surprised you won. Hence, when I saw Mom crying, it seemed so incongruous. "I just got overwhelmed. I'm so happy for you. You worked so hard." It's funny how I can actually hear her voice now when I think about it. And when we got her diagnosis, I was doing the same thing.

Who was I kidding that I had just suddenly found out she had dementia? She was driving us all crazy at times. She had become somewhat paranoid. She would make sure the door to the garage was locked at least ten times a day. Ants became a problem, as she fed her cat so often that food would just sit there. And I can't tell you how often you could say the same thing. Even if it was just a repeated comment to which you felt compelled to respond: "You're right, the weather is pretty bad right now."

So why were we crying? We had already known.

Jeremy finally commented, "You've been in denial for quite a while, you know."

Did my brother really just say that? "Oh, and what were you doing about it, Mr. Know-It-All?" I retorted.

As one might guess, that conversation didn't go well. In fact, I was getting really pissed off. Seriously, what had he been doing with our mom the last five years? He stayed in touch, true, but he never gave my dad a break, went shopping for them, ensured she made it to her appointments. None of that. That was all me. And now he had the nerve to say I was in denial.

Maybe it was good that I hung up on him. I couldn't take it any longer. Really, if he knew things weren't right, if he were the omniscient one, why didn't he insist she get on some kind of medicine three years ago when he already *knew*? Jesus, he pissed me off.

But was I too late? Were we all too late? It wasn't as if my dad had insisted something must be done earlier. Was this like cancer, where the doctor kind of shakes her head, thinking, *Had she only come to see me sooner, I could have saved her.*

So, I did what any self-respecting, college-educated person would do at that moment. I consulted Google. When it feels like your life is on the line, you do some serious research. I first learned that there are many types of dementia, and that there are some that can be treated at least a little. Like Parkinson's dementia, sometimes known as Lewy body dementia. The problem with this was that you needed to have Parkinson's disease. Mom didn't. Perhaps she was a little bit of a klutz and could drop things every once in a while, but that wasn't enough to diagnose her with Parkinson's. Her handwriting was enough to give it away. She could never have been a physician—even in her late seventies her cursive was beautiful. Also common was multi-infarct dementia—basically numerous small strokes that affected how well your mind worked. Definitely associated with heart disease, cholesterol, and all of that. Again, sadly, Mom really didn't fit that picture. Ditto for alcohol-type dementia. In fact, everything I looked up seemed like a long shot at best. And they were long shots you really couldn't treat much anyway. Which got us back to Alzheimer's.

You may be asking, who was this Alzheimer anyway? Well, I'll tell you.

His full name was actually Aloysius Alzheimer, and he was born in Germany in 1864. The overachiever was both a psychiatrist and a neuropathologist. Luck seems to play a part in everyone's career somewhere along the line, and Aloysius's luck was named Auguste Deter. She was fifty-one when she ended up at the insane asylum where he worked. She had no short-term memory and was extremely confused. She couldn't function well on her own, and her husband could no longer care for her. The problem was that they didn't have enough money to keep her at the asylum — I guess this isn't just a twenty-first-century problem. So, Auguste's husband made a deal with young Dr. Alzheimer. Alzheimer would keep her at the asylum if the family allowed him to dissect her brain after she died. This feels somewhat wrong. Dr. Frankenstein–like. Some might say it was a deal with the devil. But I guess, what choice did the husband have? He could no longer take care of her, and agreeing to the dissection seemed the only way he could get his wife care.

Dr. Alzheimer's luck didn't even end there. Surprisingly, despite being so young, it took only five years for Auguste to die. That was when, upon dissecting her brain, he discovered the neurofibrillary tangles and amyloid plaques that are the signature of this awful disease. Think of a vine that starts growing in the brain. As it grows, it begins to wind its way all throughout the brain. Further, it seems to leak out a waxy substance that hardens with time, creating plaques that prevent good communication from one brain cell to the next.

And it won't stop growing. That was what Dr. Alzheimer saw. No wonder she couldn't think normally.

It was not lost on me that he made his deal with Herr Deter when Deter's wife was only fifty-one years of age. Though this seems incredibly young, Dr. Alzheimer also died at age fifty-one, presumably long before he could have shown any signs of dementia. I'm sure it didn't help that he was an avid cigar smoker. In the end, he died at such a young age from heart failure. Maybe he really had made a deal with the devil.

Treatment for Alzheimer's could be summed up as "better than nothing." There was very little from Dr. Google that suggested any therapies were going to be game-changers. It seemed that most patients continued to decline in any case, and the only debate was whether there was some slowing. I yearned for more. More knowledge, more hope. I was afraid that when we returned for her follow-up appointment, I wouldn't know the questions to ask, that we would get shuffled off quickly with a prescription and a good-luck handshake. The fact was, the more I read about the disease, the more I found life stories and the more scared I became.

In retrospect, I really knew nothing at that point, not unlike the expectant mother who reads books about bringing up her newborn. You can read for nine months straight, but when the day comes and your baby is screaming with a fever, you freak out and realize that you are woefully unprepared.

It may seem odd to compare a patient with dementia with a newborn baby, but as time went on, I started to feel they were remarkably similar. There are differences, of course. For thirty or more years, your parent was your caregiver, your teacher, your confidant, a source of unconditional love. At the end, they are similarly helpless, confused, angry, incontinent, beautiful, fearful, and demanding. They demand all of your attention, every minute of every day. You get no sick days, no days off, no time to stop worrying and assume they will do well. You break down as a caregiver. Not only because the job is that much more daunting. A two-year-old with a tantrum is difficult; an eighty-year-old has strength and spits and kicks. It's not too hard to change an infant's diaper. Blowouts from an adult can require a two-hour cleanup. You break down in the end because you know it won't improve. Your parent won't grow out of this stage and start taking care of themselves. It will only get worse... until you leave, you pack them off so someone else can care for them, or they finally pass away.

12

June 1986

THE JOKE IS THAT ONLY YOUR SIBLINGS KNOW HOW CRAZY YOUR parents really are. Everyone else just sees the polished version. And at no time is this more acute than when you are a teenager. It's the time when everything they do seems to embarrass you. What child actually wants to be seen with their parents in high school?

But one of mine always came. Pretty much to every soccer game. Mom would even show up for some of my debates when she could. I could feel her cheering me on, telepathically emphasizing points we had ironed out together. Before the debate, when I was nervous, she would distract me. I'd see other parents going over the debate questions, but Mom would start babbling about our last vacation. She somehow knew that my mind had to wander and not fixate. And suddenly, time was up, the debate was on, and I wasn't really nervous anymore.

She knew me better than I seemed to know myself. I couldn't keep a secret even if I tried. Remember when I had thought they never found out about me smoking? This wasn't entirely true. She knew. I don't know how she knew, but I heard her talking to my dad one night. "Larry, don't worry, she's not... How do I know? I just do, that's all; she's not smoking anymore." And I supposed I could try to prove her wrong by occasionally taking a drag, but that wasn't really smoking.

I think it's because she had so many sources. Not that my mom was a big gossip, but she was always involved in local activities, and somehow she just got to know a little about everybody in the neighborhood. And now that I'm looking back, I can see her as more than just Mom. She was somewhat sexy when she would dress up for work. She wasn't over-the-top in any way. Just a classic, clean look: matching perfectly, cute earrings, the couple bangles, and always the right shoes. She must have had eighty pairs—or 140, according to my dad. But he didn't complain much. She made her own money and was similarly successful. Not that they didn't argue—they did. But not so much about money. Maybe if they hadn't had kids, they wouldn't have fought at all.

I remember once when Jeremy stole money from Dad's wallet. I think he did it more than once, but...after he got caught when he was twelve, that was the last time. I had never seen Dad get that mad. I am pretty sure Dad would have hit him if Mom hadn't saved him. Then she took the brunt of Dad's anger for the next three hours or more after we went to bed.

After the United Nations brain trust went into action, the sentence came down the next morning. Jeremy was under house arrest for two weeks. No more friends over, no basketball practice or games. It seemed that every homework assignment was grilled and repeated just because Dad "said so." And they gave him every chore they could think of.

OK, I'll admit, this was kind of fun at first. I didn't have to do the dishes, vacuum, or dust for two whole weeks. And I did tease him mercilessly at the beginning. When Saturday came, though, and he couldn't play basketball with his team or even go to the game, it felt like someone had died. Our house just stayed silent. I would start making excuses to go out just to enjoy something.

Jeremy was not the only casualty as we went through high school. Out of the two of us, I was the one who got into more trouble at school. But my mom's punishments were really quite different. In fact, they weren't punishments at all. They were far worse. She became sad, distant. It could last for days. Some might call it the silent treatment. It felt more as if she had learned a horrible truth about you and she couldn't deal with the disappointment of raising such a child.

Once my friend Doris and I just decided to go to the movies instead of our afternoon classes. We made ourselves up and snuck into an R-rated movie. It was exhilarating, and we felt so grown-up. But when we were caught, Mom fell apart. It was the polar opposite feeling of winning a debate and seeing her beam with pride. And it felt as if I had just broken a piece off her heart. I know she told my dad, but he didn't add to my punishment. There wasn't even a written decree. It seemed like I did dishes for a month straight. I could iron, make sandwiches for everyone—and nothing. It was almost as if I didn't exist for a while.

I'd like to say that I never disappointed my mom again, but that's the kind of lie that would just get me into more trouble. There was the time I took her shoes without asking, the time I missed my curfew by about one hour and forty-seven minutes, the time I snuck some rather nasty-tasting vodka, and I'm sure more that I don't care to remember.

Sometimes as adults, Jeremy and I would reminisce about our foils. One time we did totally get away with something. I was sixteen and hadn't been driving very long. We had an old 1969 Buick Skylark. My dad, for some reason unclear to everyone else on the planet, decided to paint over the nice sky-blue color. What did we get in the end? A yellow-and-black bumblebee. It was so not cool. But it was a car, and thus, we were grateful to have it.

One morning while driving us to school, I reached into the backseat to grab the tape player. This was distracted driving at its best. Suddenly, Jeremy was screaming, and I turned to see that I was about to crash into a car pulling out of the driveway right in front of me. I think I hit the brakes, but it didn't seem to make any difference. I crashed directly into the right rear end of that car.

My brother is usually pretty cool, but he was as hysterical as I was. What were we going to say? This old lady then got out of her car and ran up to us. "Are you hurt? I'm so sorry. I just pulled out and wasn't paying any attention. I never saw you. Are you OK?"

Jeremy and I weren't exactly lawyers, but we weren't stupid either. This lady thought it was *her* fault. Needless to say, we didn't exactly go out of our way to tell her that my torso was in the back-seat when I should have been steering the car. We didn't even lie to our parents. We just omitted that rather important aspect of the truth.

At our parents' twenty-fifth wedding anniversary, somehow we all ended up joking about the crazy things Jeremy and I did that caused them to become prematurely gray. When this one came up, we all had a good laugh because that was the first time they had heard that part of the story. It's the only time that I can remember getting away with anything substantial. And it's a good thing too. I don't even want to guess what they would have done to me had they found out. Maybe I never thanked my brother enough for lying. As brothers go, he really wasn't that bad.

13

December 2013

NEXT ON THE AGENDA WAS OUR RETURN VISIT TO THE NEUROL-
ogist. I had eagerly awaited this appointment. I hoped it would
provide me some ray of hope. I was beginning to feel emotionally
worn down. So much so that one day I arrived at the office with
different-colored shoes. In my defense, it was still dark when I
left the house—I had wanted to get to work early so I didn't feel
guilty about taking an extended lunch break. But my mind was
clearly elsewhere, and within two hours I had to be across town
for Mom's appointment. Little did I know at that point that there
is no point rushing to a medical visit. They are always running at
least a half hour behind.

"Dr. Metcalf will see you now. Follow me," said the pleasant
but curt medical assistant. I grumpily thought, *I really don't know
why we need to weigh Mom at every visit.* She had been pretty much
the same for the last twenty-five years, give or take ten pounds. I
watched her teeter. *One day she'll just fall off the scale. That'll show
them.* She gathered up her classic handbag, replaced her Velcro
sneakers, and happily sauntered to the blue-and-white tile room
that was there to greet us. Vitals taken, and then the door closed,
enveloping us in an unnerving quiet.

"Why are we here again?" Mom asked. She didn't seem particularly bothered. Maybe she would have preferred a walk along
the river. The sun was out, the breeze gently blowing the trees. It

truly was nice outside. Last week we had spent a great afternoon at Barnes & Noble. She still loved to read. In fact, she still suggested books to me every once in a while. The only difference was that now sometimes they were titles she had suggested previously.

I remembered my grandad exclaiming once, quite happily, "You know the best thing about losing your mind? You can read the same Agatha Christie murder mystery and receive the same pleasure in the end. You still don't know who did it until you've read the last page!" He was certainly not a complainer. He was too English for that. Fortunately, his daughter was not dissimilar.

"How's Meredith enjoying school?"

"You know, Mom, I think she loves it. She's quite a talker and now has so many new kids to be her audience. She will still talk my ear off, and Carl tries to be patient."

"Well, I look forward to our next full day together," hinted my mom.

You don't need to be a psychologist to get the full sense of this off-the-cuff remark. And it wasn't as if she didn't plan it for when we were alone. Carl positively went ballistic when she crashed her car into a mailbox a couple years ago, and he still imposed his will and a strong helping of guilt upon me as Meredith, only nine years old then, was in the backseat. I was no lawyer, but I did think he coerced her to testify that she didn't have her seat belt on in either. "Never!" From that point on, that was his viewpoint on everything about Mom. She wasn't to drive Meredith anywhere again. She shouldn't be driving, period. She wasn't to watch her unsupervised again. He wouldn't even let Meredith eat any food she brought, reminding me of the time she got sick after eating who knows what out of her refrigerator. It was amazing he let them be in the same room together.

So, where did that leave me? Switzerland. I was the neutral country between those at war. I was either denying my mom's right to enjoy the wonders of being a grandma or I was cavalierly playing with our daughter's life.

A knock on the door saved me. Mom would forget for a while, and maybe I wouldn't have to endure her begging me for some alone time with Meredith.

Smiling as always, Dr. Metcalf entered breezily. Though he was calm, I could tell he was in a bit of a hurry. Little passed in the way of introduction, and he just got right to the point: "I think we need to start medicines, and today is probably as good a start day as any." There was probably an eight-second gap where I was supposed to have made my comments, but he continued, "In the end, we would like her to be taking two different medications. The combination of Aricept and Namenda seems to work well and is the best tolerated. As the saying goes, we start low and go slow. This helps prevent side effects. We will begin with—"

"Excuse me," I finally managed. I paused for a bit to emphasize that this hadn't been a conversation, certainly not with Mom involved. He hadn't even really acknowledged she was in the room. He had this way about him. A stare. No, more than a stare. It was this intense eye contact. I guess this meant that he was very focused and caring. But it could be a little unnerving at the same time. And as Mom began fiddling with her handkerchief, it became clear that the stare and concentration were just directed at me. I was the one for whom he was providing the information; she was sitting like a child at the adult table.

"What side effects are we talking about? What should we be looking out for?"

I quickly learned that I didn't quite have his same intensity because he must have been halfway into his answer before I distinctly heard him say, "Diarrhea and vomiting. I would say those are the most common side effects. If significant enough, there can be weight loss." It wouldn't be hard for anyone to surmise that Mom was no longer the housekeeper she used to be. If there were going to be foul-smelling liquids coming out either end, it would certainly be me doing the dirty work. And though I'm not too squeamish about crushing a cockroach or above taking out the trash, vomit—that induces a whole different reaction. I think somewhere along the line in medical training, the nurses should take a day off, hand the mops and bedpans to the physicians, and say, "It's your turn; this is the other half of caregiving that you may wish to see."

"What am I to expect? Not tomorrow, or even next month, but maybe later this year and the next. What am I in store for?" Was I pleading? I think I might have been. If I thought he was in a hurry before, this question definitely got him shuffling toward the door.

Before he left, Dr. Metcalf sighed a response. "It's hard to say. She's in quite good health, really. Her ability to live alone will decline more quickly because of her mind than any physical ailment. You may wish to look into a long-term care facility. Let's talk about this more in a couple months when I see you back and see how she is progressing." And then he left. *Swoosh*ed away, it seemed. We had received what Western medicine had to offer. Top-of-the-line facility, an accurate diagnosis, and the best pills money can buy.

And now, after only fifteen minutes with the doctor, Mom and I were on our way. Not only out the door but off to start a new chapter in both of our lives. She as the one being cared for, I as the primary caregiver—and yet only one of us really understood this arrangement. How much Aloysius Alzheimer was going change our lives, I now realize, neither of us understood.

14

May 2019

THREE WEEKS AFTER JANINE AND I MET FOR COFFEE, I FOUND myself being confronted by the gang. Not everyone in our circle of friends. But enough to make me ask aloud, "Is this an intervention?"

Megan, Andrea, and Janine all laughed. We were at our favorite hangout, a local burger dive that made the best milkshakes in town. A guilty pleasure.

I don't think any topic has ever been sacred when we all get together. Wouldn't our kids love to know everything that we have said about them? Though it is probably our husbands who we hold up against the most scrutiny. Many times we debated the possibility that one of them was cheating. And the good news is that, so far, we have been wrong every time—except once. That's another story and quite a long one. Megan and Tom are still married, though. You might even be able to say their union is stronger than some of ours.

I had been expecting Janine to bring this up again. I'm sure I would have too if I were in her shoes. So, I guess I was prepared. I was out of the closet, as it were, and ready to defend my newly discovered beliefs, along with my half-pack-per-day nicotine habit. And my conviction had only grown the more I looked at things.

"OK. Enough of the chitchat," began Janine. "Allison, you know I love you. This is why I can't stop thinking you are making a horrible mistake. I'm not trying to be mean, but I can smell it on you, so I know you're still smoking. I just want to ask, do you have any doubts?"

The good news is that I was still enjoying my favorite peach milkshake. But it was clear to me that things were about to get uncomfortable. I focused on Andrea initially, as she was the last to look away. Or maybe it was because I saw a softness in her brown eyes.

I began diplomatically: "It's so easy to judge in this internet age. We have become accustomed to angry tweets, memes, and other behind-the-scenes accusations that we are desensitized. So, thank you, my friends. I really mean that. I can tell that you aren't trying to humiliate me and chase me from our circle. It seems that's all I notice in the news these days. Another prominent person taken down in public to the delight of all."

"Oh, Allison, you know we would never do that!" Andrea said, truly coming to life. "Who are these people? What possibly could they have as a goal?"

"Well, then, now it's my turn to ask the tough question: What is your goal? To understand my mind or to change it?"

"How about both!" Megan laughed. "When Janine called me, she tried to explain your position. It sounded so ridiculous that I found it hard to believe. Yet she couldn't stop talking about your conviction. How you created such a strong argument by reducing it to such a simple position—why die unpleasantly if you can choose another way? Clearly, no one could argue against that. But are you really trying to tell us that you believe dying from tobacco use is a pleasant way to go?"

"Well, I'll tell you that the surgeon general is not subtle. Each time I buy a pack, I can find a different warning—smoking causes cancer, causes death, destroys teeth, causes kidney and bladder cancer, causes blindness, harms unborn babies. And the list goes on and on. I can't tell you why anyone else ignores these warnings. But I know why I do. I don't want to live long. So, in a way, Megan, you're right. It is somewhat simple."

"If this weren't so serious, if we were talking about a football game, I really would just continue to laugh and enjoy my fries," said Janine. "But can I ask again, might you be having some doubts? When you read about all the misery on the side of every carton, do you wonder if you'll have any regret? You say you want to die 'early,' but what age are you really talking? Haven't you realized that now, in our fifties, age seventy doesn't seem all that old anymore? Who would want to end when you've finally got it all together? Soon the kids will be gone, and we can travel more, have fun, and feel on top of our game at work."

"So, how much longer?" I asked. "Seriously. Five, ten, twenty years? When might you start to think life isn't worth it any longer? You see, I've been giving this a lot of thought lately. And you'll laugh, as you know I'm not the most ardent sports fan. But I started to think about Mohammad Ali. How do we remember him? The best boxer ever, right? But wouldn't he have been even better and also not brain damaged if he had stopped when he was at the top of his game? Instead, he started to lose. Over and over again to random nobodies. I was watching a *60 Minutes* interview with him, and I started to cry. It got me thinking, as I sat next to my mom, who, like Ali, was just sitting and staring ahead.

"I had originally only remembered his brashness, his larger-than-life personality. What I saw that day was a man with dementia who could hardly care for himself, could hardly stay awake. He had dementia. Diagnosed with Parkinson's just a few years after his last fight. Might he have remained charismatic if he had quit before those last several fights? He won sixty-one total—yes, I looked this up—and he lost five. Three out of his last four were losses where he was pummeled.

"And this got me thinking. We don't like to think of the end of our lives as a series of lost fights. It's not that we have to be remembered for doing spectacular things, but the pain, the chemo, the surgeries, the hospital. These aren't what we look forward to when we are in high school. Lying frail, wasting away, trapped in a hospital bed is certainly not how I want to be remembered."

"Come on, Allison." Megan clearly felt compelled to interrupt. "Your children's graduation, their weddings, the grandkids. I think I can speak for everyone here—we have looked forward to those days. Maybe not since high school, but soon after having kids of our own."

"And I'm going to interrupt too," chimed in Andrea. "My bladder is about to burst, so I'll be back in a second."

We laughed, and Janine said, "I'll join you."

After Janine left with Andrea, Megan and I were alone. I was feeling a little tired. Mentally taxed. I felt every word was being scrutinized

At times like this, I often retreat to music. On this occasion it was Bob Seger's "The Fire Inside" that began to go through my head. No one can talk about how fleeting youth and beauty are like Seger can. No, not just fleeting—how they crumble and scatter.

I loved this song. Partly because it is his best song that no one knew, but it is also because of the lyrics. Lyrics can make a song and give it the everlasting poignancy of poetry.

I must have been staring into space when Megan suddenly broke my reverie. "I don't think you're crazy." I'm not sure if this was supposed to make me feel better, likely because I didn't know where it was going, but she continued, "I've seen old people get really lonely. Then depressed. All of their friends die, and family may be around, but the visits often can feel like a chore. They can then act like zombies, just waiting to die."

"And they are the lucky ones!" I exclaimed, finally feeling I had an ally. "The unlucky ones can no longer care for themselves. They end up with their butts being wiped by total strangers. They may even have to be fed—soft foods so they don't choke. Yet when you come to visit, you can see what they had to eat because half of it is on their chest. And the truly unlucky, they don't remember any of it. I wonder what they are actually thinking. Is anything going through their minds, or are they just registering pain and discomfort? Certainly the only thing that Mom seemed to notice was discomfort. It made me feel horrible to clean up after her. She would scream."

Andrea and Janine returned to find us quite animated. I think we all wondered if this was like one of those political discussions, one where there were clearly two very different camps and you were trying your best to get your point across but not belittle or hurt your friend who happened to be a Republican—because as soon as they rejoined us, things got kind of somber again.

I intuitively realized that what we were saying while they were gone was not going to go over well if I didn't strike a different tone. So, I made it more personal. And I was not trying to make a decision for everyone anyway. I was just hoping to have people understand my new goal: to live life now to the fullest and hopefully die before I lost my mind.

So, I went to my conclusion. This really was becoming a speech, similar to the State of the Union address—only this time, no one was clapping every time I made a comment. "Can I just sum up my thoughts? Because I'm getting tired of being the only one scrutinized. I fear losing my mind more than anything, more than death itself. My dad died quickly from a pulmonary embolus. But he still got to seventy-nine, and I'm telling you, he was getting dementia. We never had to care for him, but after caring for my mom for five years, I know he had the early stages. And then we get to my mom, diagnosed just months after my dad died. I cared for her for years until I couldn't manage any longer. She then lasted more than a year being cared for in a nursing home. I don't think I ever told you, but I insisted that she not be treated or even fed at the end. Hospice helped; they were my savior. We all knew she was no longer living a meaningful life. You all know—you saw her.

"What does this mean about me? The experts say that I'm not more likely to develop Alzheimer's, even if both parents had the disease. Yet I know that I will. I just know it. In the end, I don't want anyone having to clean my sad, puckered butt. I sure know it won't be my husband, I don't wish it to be any of you, and I definitely don't want to rely on total strangers. So, I'm going to smoke. I will die of cancer or a lung infection or something. I refuse to be a burden on anyone. And I want to remember my life for being great. And one thing smokers don't get to say often enough... It feels good. Remember those ads of couples smoking after sex? It can feel that good. So, I'm going to smoke. Enjoy the now and avoid later misery."

Silence.

"Well," Janine managed after what had seemed an eternity. "I see."

Silence.

After more than an hour, slurping the final bits of our milkshakes, seats started to move back as Andrea and Janine suddenly had somewhere to go.

"Me too," added Megan. And like the others, she was grabbing her purse and getting ready to leave. Usually we share, but I think everyone hoped that nothing more would be said. Andrea just paid for everyone, and I was soon in my car. Exhausted. I thought they were going to leave me and my craziness alone. So, I lit up my Marlboro and took a deep drag.

15

May 2019

Probably like every smoker, I had air fresheners everywhere, and my well-used Volkswagen Jetta was no exception. The last thing I wanted was for my daughters, Meredith and Sloane, to learn that I'd been smoking. Clearly this was somewhat ironic, because if I thought it was such a good idea, why wouldn't I want them to follow in my footsteps when they got older? I was sure my friends would use this as ammunition: "You're just not thinking this through." Yet, as is the case with most life-changing decisions, the path wasn't obviously black-and-white. I wished it were; it would lead to much less torment.

The intervention with my friends had left me shaking. I could barely hold the cigarette, let alone walk. In my car, my cigarettes and me remained. I was beginning to feel like an outcast, and yet I knew I was right. At least for me. I was not trying to religiously convert everyone to my opinion. It was just that once I started with an idea, if it felt better and better, then it was probably the right one.

Perhaps the strangest outcome of feeling like life will be shorter is that I have started to cherish moments. I have wept like a baby at movies where the main character has someone close to them die, and they replay over and over the final, mundane conversation in their head. *Why couldn't I have told them, "I love you," one last time?* My life isn't so dramatic, but since I took up smoking, there has definitely been a change. A soccer game, ballet recital, dinner with my husband—all became more poignant just because I have started to think these might be the last. OK, maybe not the last. I don't think I am going to die tomorrow. But since I have begun to think that I am going to die earlier, I have been getting more out of everyday life experiences. And so, while on my second cigarette in a row there in the car, I reminisced about my final vacation with my mom. A memory that helped stop me from shaking and brought the smile back to my face.

As Mom was getting older and harder to care for, I thought, *Let's make a memory. One that she and I will remember forever.* I was guessing about twenty-four years in my case and perhaps six months for her. We would go to Hawaii. She had never been. And who doesn't like Hawaii?

It had been about a year since her diagnosis, and she was declining. Who knew how long we would have to do things before they became more difficult than was practical. Looking back, it was also the start of me relating to her in a different way. No longer just her daughter but her caregiver as well.

It's a little strange packing for your mother. Though I was still helping my kids pack, they did almost all of it at that point. Mom was a much greater challenge. What did she really need? I had to plan.

When I entered her closet, I was struck first by the smell. *What happens after about age seventy to cause this odor in the home?* Invading her space more than previously, I began to notice things like a potential buyer of her house would. Everything was old. The radio was old. The fact that she had a radio in the first place. The phone on the wall was the green push-button variety. No prospective buyer would ever keep the wallpaper that lined the hallway and the bathrooms. And I recalled each burn or nick in the linoleum kitchen floor. Fortunately, the carpet had been changed from that "only in the seventies" shag to a neat, flat, gray. But where did the odor come from? Was the air still hanging around from the seventies too?

The dimly lit closet surrounded me now. It was a little suffocating, actually, and I made a mental note to bring some Febreze the next time. I also made a New Year's resolution. Maybe a New Decade's resolution. With every passing decade, I would try to rid my closet of everything I had owned in the previous ten years. There were a few recent things in Mom's closet, some with the tags on them, likely the Christmas presents Sloane and I gave her, which were well-intentioned but less well received. This colored my choices right then and there.

Really, there was little point in trying to dress her as if we were sisters, something she used to love doing during my college years. Nothing flattered her more than when someone asked if she was my sister. But those days had clearly passed, and I began to notice that her repertoire of clothes she wore was much smaller than what I was finding in this archaeological expedition. Did she throw anything away? There were shoes, I'm certain, she had had from before my brother and I were born. But this was the most obvious thing I had to pack: the can't-possibly-go-wrong choice—her Velcro white sneakers from Payless.

I grabbed a set of blouses and slacks that seemed to fit the bill. Shorts seemed an obvious choice for Hawaii at any time of year. *When was it, though, that I last saw her in shorts?* I was thinking at least ten years ago. So, no need to push the envelope now. We were going for memories, not to experience all the island had to offer. Certainly we weren't going to be booking any snorkeling or ziplining adventures.

"Mom," I shouted. "Let's go to the store."

"What in heavens for?"

I had burst from her closet, desperate for fresh air. I hadn't begun to search through her semihoarding existence for a bathing suit. And I'd had enough of that closet to realize I didn't want to spend another minute looking for one.

"We're getting you a new bathing suit," I said in as upbeat a tone as one could muster after being in mothball prison for twenty minutes. I had begun to realize that her moods reflected my own. Enthusiasm could be catching. Plus, I needed a break anyway.

After backing out Mom's aging silver car, I turned and hit the gas on the way to the mall. No need to worry about a speeding ticket; it was a Prius, after all. We made our way through traffic to JCPenney. Mom would feel more comfortable in a store she had gone to for decades, and I knew that there wasn't time to browse from store to store without her wearing down or demanding to go home.

Men will never understand how agonizing buying a swimsuit can be for a woman. You would think there would come an age when it just doesn't matter anymore. Well, apparently, seventy-four is not yet that age. She tried on perhaps fourteen different one-piece styles. We ignored the two-piece section.

"This is just not my style," Mom proclaimed while I rolled my eyes. We were starting to see more plus-size models at that time, but those past their seventieth birthdays were still not the demographic the designers were trying to impress.

Mom never liked to feel she was being mocked, and seeing me roll my eyes was her last straw. She was done and began to walk out of the store more quickly than I could have expected. Panic filled me, along with that hot feeling of nearing anger. After spending more than two hours coaxing and cajoling, I found the thought of walking away with nothing unacceptable.

But those early days of dealing with my occasionally irrational mother were teaching me to change. I was no longer a child trying to get my way. I had had to become the parent and be creative. It was becoming clear that she could turn into an obstinate child pretty quickly, and what seemed to work best was redirection—basically, parenting 101. Sister steals brother's toy, and he begins to cry. You work on being rational, and an hour goes by, and you have two angry kids. Instead, start playing a game with your son, and in two minutes, nobody is crying.

"Mom, I'm starving. Do you mind if we get something to eat?"

"That sounds like a good idea—plus it will take my mind off of those ugly swimsuits." *Did I just catch her rolling her eyes?*

And after, I excused myself to go to the bathroom. I ran back to JCPenney, bought the black one-piece that covered up enough to prevent any stares, and tossed the bag to make an easy fit in my purse. *Voilà! Kid 1, Parent 0.* Or was it the other way around?

16

December 2013

THERE WERE FEW AMERICAN FAMILIES WHO DIDN'T GRIPE about the cost of their health insurance. And if they weren't griping last year, they would certainly start whining about the rate of increase to this year.

Thirty-five dollars per month. For the four of us, that was what we had been spending on our medications. The kids didn't take any. Carl's two blood pressure medicines and my generic birth control had been my pharmaceutical experience thus far.

So, it was hard to describe my disbelief when I heard that for Nancy MacPherson's two bottles of pills, the bill came to $514.27.

Initially, I assumed that this cute pharmacy tech in her short blue jacket was not too good at math. I'm not proud to report that I demanded to see the manager after she began to explain that Ms. MacPherson had yet to meet her deductible for the year. "You see, that's why the price is so high." She smiled brightly.

How the hell was Mom going to afford $500 a month extra? True, she had no house or car payment, but she still had to pay for taxes on the house, food, and utilities. They all ate into the $2,275 she received monthly. Sure, she had some money saved but...$500 a month!

"Hello, Ms. MacPherson. I'm Dr. Gopal, the pharmacist. Is there a problem or concern I can help you with?"

"I don't understand," I began. "My mom pays insurance premiums every month so she won't have to spend the full cost for doctor visits, surgeries, medicines. So, how is it that just two pills can cost $514.27?"

As Dr. Gopal explained, he was calming me down. He had a soothing voice and was kindly taking his time to talk me off of the ledge. "It's truly complicated, but the reason why you are confused is that the medicines your family has been taking are generic and thus cheap. They're manufactured by literally any factory that wishes to make the pills. But the medicines your mother was given are both protected by patents. The pharmaceutical companies are allowed to recoup their costs of developing these drugs by being the only ones allowed to sell them. And they can thus set whatever price they wish."

"What if someone can't afford their medicines?"

With a smile, he left me with a line he had probably told countless others like me: "We may all wish to buy a $100,000 Mercedes, but most of us leave with a used Toyota."

I half smiled while pulling out my Visa card, thinking, *Well, there goes Meredith's birthday present this month. Then there will be the next month, and the month after that.* Sweat seemed to be forming under my armpits, and I felt the entire pharmacy staff was staring at me. I had to get these medicines for her. Was there an alternative? What if the cute tech had said $1,500 instead? Did I have a breaking point? And I'd have to tell my husband. I couldn't just expect him to look at the Visa bill without blowing a gasket and giving me some of the choice words I felt like telling this nice pharmacist.

I needed time to think. I didn't need more convincing about her diagnosis. With just a few short tests, Dr. Metcalf had helped confirm she was losing her mind. How could I deny her the medicine to stop this from happening? In the end, there really wasn't a choice. She was my mother, and I was going to do all that I could to provide for her as best I could. We would make it work.

Six weeks had passed since our last visit with Dr. Metcalf. Along with her blood pressure and thyroid medicines, there were now these two pills of gold that had to be changed every week. "You must titrate them up," the pharmacist said. "Otherwise she won't feel very good." So, each week we seemed to be doing something different: five milligrams of Aricept, then a week later, ten milligrams. A week after that, seven milligrams of Namenda, the following week fourteen milligrams, then twenty-one, and finally twenty-eight. Six straight weeks of changes. Seriously, someone with dementia was supposed to remember this? I wondered if they were trying to test me for the disease. *And can we just call bullshit on the side-effect thing?* It seemed that every time I changed the dose, something happened. At first, she was dizzy. Then, she got constipated. Her appetite stopped for a while, followed soon after by stomach cramps, which seemed to inevitably lead to diarrhea. And I was sure I had missed a few. So, I was more than anticipating this next visit; I was preparing for it as if I were still in the debate club. I was more than $1,000 in the hole, and Mom was definitely not better; she was worse. When was this investment going to start paying off?

My coworker Amanda usually made it easy for me. I would leave the office for a few hours, and she would cover for me. With my personal doctor visit and now three for my mom, this made the fourth time in three months I had asked for her help. At twenty-six, Amanda never seemed to get sick, and she had no kids. What she did have was resentment, and it was building. Trying to avoid eye contact, I rushed out at nine forty-five, a little late, having done as much paperwork as I could.

Easing onto the highway minutes later, it seemed my luck was about to change. My white Jetta gliding rather than plodding like

Mom's Prius furthered my good mood. It didn't hurt that I was accompanying Elton John, singing "Tiny Dancer" at the top of my lungs.

If I could just gather Mom up and be back on the road in five minutes, we would be fine.

Seeing no lights on in the kitchen was the first ominous sign as I walked up to the front door. That was quickly followed by silence upon entering. Where was she? Four minutes. As I was briskly walking down the hallway, my heart started to run.

Mom lay in her bed—awake, smiling, and reading *People* magazine.

"Mom! We've got to go. Your appointment with Dr. Metcalf is in twenty minutes."

Was this because of the diagnosis? A prophecy fulfilled. Once she knew she had memory loss, was she suddenly worsening? Or was I just becoming more aware?

"We talked about this appointment at least five times this week. You knew we would be in a hurry. You were to be ready to go at 10:00 a.m. What happened?" I whined. Three minutes.

"Was that today? Oh, Allison, don't worry. I'll be ready in a jiffy."

But it was not a jiffy. Everything about her movement was becoming slow. She could take twenty-five steps just to get from her bed to the bathroom, shuffling the entire way. I became demanding, handing over the toothbrush, helping fix her hair. My five minutes were up before I realized she had soiled herself. Not a lot, but how had she not noticed? There was no time! Forget the shower, Clorox wipes were the first thing I came up with. True, not a pretty cleanup, but soon she had on fresh underwear and slacks. Bra, shirt, sweater—and back to the awaiting Jetta, eighty-five agonizing steps later.

More steps, waiting room line, and then us. "Nancy MacPherson," I panted.

"It's 10:52, you realize," came the curt voice of Miss Know-It-All. "Her appointment *was* at 10:30, and—"

I cut her off with a smile and—*Did I just curtsy?*

"It's a long story, but let's just say we've kind of been on the struggle bus this morning." My cheeks would soon hurt if I didn't stop smiling this way.

I needn't have worried, because before I could go on, her hand went up to shoosh me. "I'm sorry, as she is more than half-way through her appointment, we will have to reschedule. Are Tuesdays good days for you?"

There were so many off-color remarks I probably should have made, but "Yes" was all that I came up with.

Two weeks later, we would be doing all this again. *Groundhog Day*, I suppose. Another morning missed from work. Cashing in another favor with Amanda—maybe I should get her some booze. Again finding Mom completely unaware that she had a doctor appointment. I couldn't wait.

17

June 2019

SAY WHAT YOU WANT ABOUT STARBUCKS, THE CONCEPT TOTALLY rocks. Before Starbucks, if you went somewhere to eat, you knew you were supposed to leave after a while. Within ten to twenty minutes of receiving the check, it was expected that you would be on your way to make room for the next customer. So even if Starbucks' coffee were bitter, I think people would still come to buy it because you could sit and talk for hours. Or work on your computer, listen to a podcast, or meditate. Whatever you wanted to do, for as long as you wanted. It was like being at home but not having to worry about the dishes or the kids.

I had already dropped the kids off at school, gone grocery shopping, and started some laundry to prevent any guilty feelings creeping in while we talked. It was one of those rare days where I had a day off but the kids still were in school. Just after 10:00 a.m., I set out for coffee heaven down the street.

After placing my order, I wandered past the inevitable few young people with piercings and tattoos to settle at a comfortable table with a view of life walking by.

In an earlier life, I used to resent waiting, even for five minutes. Now, after children, I equate waiting with complete relaxation, and it has become something to be cherished. The only downside is that sometimes I fall asleep. But that wasn't going to happen at Starbucks.

Soon I had settled in with a tall french roast and one of those apricot scones that could marbleize fat on your hips. I promised myself to try just a little bit harder at the gym later because you only live once.

"Have you been waiting long?" Megan asked as she pulled up beside me.

"One or two pounds at most." I smiled.

"Have you tried every last thing on their menu? I've kind of wanted to do that," Megan proclaimed. "Kind of like that guy who made the movie about McDonald's, where he would eat nothing else for a month except food from their menu. He had to try everything at least once."

"So, where else would you be willing to try everything on their menu?" I asked, now thinking this was kind of interesting.

"How about a breakfast diner?"

"Oh God, no. Denny's, IHOP? Would you seriously want to try every gelatinous thing on their menu?" I exclaimed. "I'd have to go with an upscale restaurant where the chef tried with every dish. Somewhere like Ruth's Chris Steak House. How about I pay for you to try everything and Denny's, and you treat me to all kinds of steak and lobster."

"Allison, does your husband ever win an argument with you? You come up with things so fast it's like you have already been preparing for days."

"We actually don't fight that often, and it's usually about money. I'm more willing to borrow if it's vacations or for the kids. Maybe I got this way because of my parents. I don't want to only know the world that is within one tank of gas. I love adventure. I would rather save for an entire year and go to France once than have four vacations at the coast. Actually, who am I kidding? I want to go to France *and* have the four weekend vacations at the coast."

At that moment, an irate, rather entitled customer took our

attention. His two shots were definitely not present in his coffee, and no apology or offer to fix the perceived error was going to be good enough.

Megan laughed. "You couldn't pay me enough to work here. I just can't figure out people and their relative importance. If he's screaming about not having enough shots of espresso in his coffee, how mad will he be if he gets a nail in his tire?"

"Or he misses his flight due to traffic from a car accident," I added.

"I think that would cause his head to just pop right off." We both started laughing quietly under our breaths. But really, why should he care about us? He seemed plenty self-absorbed. Something that really stops when you have to care for someone.

Suddenly, with no preamble, Megan began, "My experience was with my grandad. He came to live with us a few years after Grandma died. It was awful at first and only went downhill from there. And now I feel kind of guilty having those feelings, but they were there for everyone to see and hear. My parents made me share a room with my younger brother because we didn't have enough space.

"My dad and mom had one of the worst fights I can remember when she suggested that Grandad go to a nursing home instead. 'Are you telling me that I don't love my dad?' I think I heard him say a version of that more than a hundred times. But this love made the rest of us pretty damn miserable at times."

I nodded sympathetically.

"By the time Grandad took over my room, he was in his eighties and hardly could move out of there. My brother and I would joke that when we got in trouble, one of the quick punishments became 'Go keep your grandad company.' Again, I'm not really proud of my attitude, but at twelve years old, I had a personality that was pretty transparent. I would go back to *my* room and hate every last minute. It smelled, for starters. His teeth were often floating in a cup beside his bed, and conversations with him were too much effort as he could hardly hear anything. This was long before cell phones, where I could have ignored him and no one would have been the wiser. I just had to sit there in silence. The only thing that saved this from being worse than a dungeon was that we convinced our folks that he liked old TV shows. He probably didn't really hear any of them, but he seemed to smile when we would laugh, and it definitely made that time go by faster. I even got to like some of those shows like *Gunsmoke*, *The Waltons*, and my favorite, *The Big Valley*.

"It took three years before he finally passed away. As I grew older and he feebler, I had to do more and more to help him. Even though it was my dad's father, it was Mom who did most of the cleaning up. In fact, she did all of it until one day." Her voice wobbled slightly.

"I was doing my homework, and there was a loud noise. One of those noises that you know just can't be good, so you run rather than walk to the source."

I shuffled around in my handbag, sensing the tears that were about to come. I proffered a Kleenex and waited. I had become better at waiting for responses since having kids. I wondered how many times I had tried to break the silence only to crush the conversation.

"I found my mom and grandad tangled on the floor. It seemed that there were feces everywhere. In less than a second, I was overwhelmed. Grandad was flailing; Mom was hurt and crying. The sheets, along with Grandad, were on the floor, and the smell... I'm not sure I would have tried to get help even if someone else were at home. I just had to be the one. I rushed and somehow got them separated. Mom was crying even harder then, but my instinct was that it was more from being overwhelmed than hurt.

"I went to the sink maybe one hundred times the next couple of hours. I got new sheets, made the bed, sponge-bathed Grandad, still on the floor. Then I got him tucked in. You might think I had great strength to get him back into bed, but that wasn't it at all. I had never seen him naked. He looked like he was a concentration camp survivor. I don't think he weighed much more than a hundred pounds.

"I threw everything out. Every last stitch of clothes that both of them had been wearing. I did this when Mom was in the shower. My McClatchy High T-shirt suffered the same fate. Then Mom and I sat, like coconspirators to a crime, for a long while. And our relationship changed. I joke that I became a woman that day. Mom treated me differently from that day forward. She never punished me again for one single thing. She also counted on me to help, which I did until the day he finally died."

Transfixed. There was no better word I could use to describe myself at that moment. "Megan, I don't know what to say," I finally said after what seemed like minutes. Not an awkward pause, just an appropriate silence. The cool iron of the chair, the slight breeze, the sounds from the street. All of my senses were starting to wake up. For the past several minutes, my mind had been on Megan and her story. I could envision the scene completely. I could understand her fear and even imagine that smell. The emotional bond that she suddenly created with her mom, and the need to not say anything.

"Isn't it strange that, if this were your child, you would have retold this story—with detail—to laughter and applause a hundred times? We all have those stories, don't we, Megan, where you are in a hurry; you've got the wet wipes out. Another explosive diarrhea comes out like a scene from *The Exorcist*; you slip and fall, to continue the horror-movie theme, and you realize the cleanup will take you long past the start of your meeting at 9:00 a.m. Not to say that one truly enjoys an experience like this, but we've all had them with our children, and they are like a badge of courage. Something to be proud of. Something we do laugh about and even tease our children about as they get older."

In a tone that was perhaps flatter than she was expecting, Megan said, "But there is no fear. I never felt fear with my child like I did that day. I feared everything. I was convinced one of them had a broken bone. I feared dropping my grandad, getting him back to bed. I felt the pain as he struck out at me—likely because I was causing him pain lifting with all my strength. Did I tell you he bit me once? He certainly tried more than once, but that first time, I was just not expecting. I had been reaching over him to pull up the bedsheet, and he clamped down on my arm."

As tears fell, she continued, "I didn't know what to do except to start hitting him. Not hard, but over and over until he finally let go. The skin was torn a little, but the bruise on my arm came up before I even got to the sink. I lied. I told my friends it was a hickey. I know, stupid, but it was the first lie I could come up with, and I couldn't back out of it."

"But why the shame? Why is it so different?" I queried. "All you were doing was caring for your grandad. Why can't we talk about it? Why do even our best friends not seem to want to hear these details?"

"And what about men? Not only won't they talk about it, they don't seem to acknowledge it happens in the first place. I don't know about your dad, Allison, but mine never acknowledged what we were doing. Once my grandad became confined to my old room, I don't think he ever set foot in there again. Why can't a man, that strong and mighty man who would gladly put up a fence all day long, ever ask what they can do to help?"

"You are so right, Megan. My dad would never have helped with my mom. And my brother, though he had sympathy, would only help by arranging things. Helping hire someone to assist me or proudly bringing a bunch of Ensure he had bought from the store. It's not that he didn't love her as much as I did. I saw him countless occasions read to her, spoon-feed her, or simply sit by her when she was sleeping."

"But no cleanup, right? None of the 'messy details.'" Megan sighed. "Do you really think you will end up like Nancy?"

I think I stood up before I got the words out. "I'm going to have another coffee—would you like one?" I bounced from my chair as if she had struck a nerve. But it gave me time to think in any case. To think about a subject I have faced head-on and yet continued to try and avoid—*How to not become like my mother.*

I returned with two coffees in hand. Purposefully, I sat closer. What I was about to say I didn't want to broadcast for the world to hear. "For those last few years, I would wonder so much what she was thinking, what was going on in her mind. It's like there is a light that we all have. We don't notice it because everyone has one. It shines from our eyes. It shows that we are alive, aware. When it goes, it is eerie. Not vampire or evil-dead scary, just strange. As the months went by, the time when she was aware continued to drop. Precipitously at times, until one day she stopped really recognizing who I was. For a while she would call me Jan, which was her mother's name."

Despite not having direct eye contact, I felt Megan's sympathy as she squeezed my hand.

"I guess it was like talking to a robot. They kind of make sense; there just isn't the expected emotion behind it. Then there would be a day where everything seemed fine again. Maybe not a whole day, but a few hours. We could be laughing and reminiscing, and her light was back on. Inevitably, as the sun would go down, her light would fade out. It's funny how often I think of parallels to a horror movie. I think, like you said, there's a definite difference between raising an infant and caring for your parent or grandparent: there is a fear. You know that you are starting to lose control, and there isn't much you can do. Your grandfather sounded like he was bedridden early. My mom would just leave—always at night. The panic. YI'd drive by in the morning, and she'd just be gone. Not there. No note, no clues except an open front door. How I never got fired, I'll never know. Another morning where your heart pounds after every turn, worried that you'll see an ambulance—or worse, her lying in the street like a stray dog struck by a car.

"After about four or five of these episodes, we began to lock up the house from the inside. My husband was totally against this at first. I had to agree; trying to remember to unlock the deadbolt at the top of the door was about as annoying as the gate at the top of the stairs we used for our kids, and now for her. And if there were a fire... So, at first, we tried to lock her in her room. It worked until she started to scream every night. It was worse than having a puppy, because eventually a puppy gets used to things. I wanted to train her like they do chickens—have a bright light on, so they think it's daytime. It doesn't seem to work so well with humans, though. Am I boring you?"

"Oh no, not at all. I'm just thinking of so many things about what you are saying. And I'll be laughing about your chicken comment all the way home. But did you notice that, as time went on, you started to use metaphors? Like, she was an animal—a dog, a chicken? Is this what you mean by the light not being on?"

"Wow, Megan. I've never consciously thought about that. What's funny is my first instinct is to say there was even less light than that at the end. But maybe you are on to something there. It was as if she had been going downward along the animal kingdom. I remember when I was an undergrad, I worked at the National

Primate Research Center. My job was to evaluate how well these rhesus monkeys could learn. I would place food treats in certain parts of their cage, and they could get them if they were able to learn a specific task. What was uncanny was watching them think. I would tell my friends that you could see them thinking. So many would tell me that only humans have that kind of intelligence. I stick to my beliefs: they were smart. Definitely brighter than dogs I have had, but not by much.

"But you're really right about animals and the light. It almost felt, as the months went by, as if she were changing from a human to a rhesus monkey to a dog, a pig, a deer, a cow. Yet the light would then sometimes come back on fully."

"Did the medicines help?" asked Megan. "And by the way, we can keep the animal analogy secret. I don't think the world is quite ready to compare humans to dogs."

"So true. I don't think I have even thought this through. It was your fault, Megan. You brought it up and caught me off guard."

We both had a good laugh at this. Painful memories can bring on laughter. It's probably what keeps everyone sane. Shared memories are really what keep us functioning. Which makes me wonder, why is it that we are so unwilling to share what we do when we take care of our parents?

18

April 2014

YOU ARE GIVEN FAMILY LIKE YOU ARE GIVEN CARDS IN A POKER hand. And hopefully they give you a good chance in life.

Somewhere along the line, however, you actually choose your spouse. I met mine when I was on vacation. It wasn't one of those love-at-first sight things, but he was definitely my type. It's a little strange to count how many lovers you have had before you find the one. Were they all necessary? Does one need that much practice to know who is the one?

For all I know, my dad was my mom's first and only. She was completely devoted to him. They would argue from time to time, but there was never a doubt that they would stay together "till death do us part."

Although, in retrospect, I don't know if my dad could have handled all the changes if he had lived long enough. Before her diagnosis, he seemed to do fine. They had what most would define as a traditional marriage back then—he worked hard, came home, and expected the housework, meals, and kids would be taken care of by his wife, though she worked too.

But that may be why he never complained about all that he must have done for her as she became more forgetful. Maybe it was payback for all of the help she had given him over the years. He took over the shopping, the chores, the taxes. Pretty much every complex task, he was doing by himself. True, he would joke about things like learning after forty-five years how much money she spent on makeup and shoes, but he had unlimited patience. He never seemed angry.

I'd like to think that Carl will be that way for me. Yet how much can we expect someone to do for us "in sickness"? With my dad, we'll never know. Officially, at 4:34 a.m., he was pronounced dead on July 14, 2012. He was seventy-nine years old.

He had woken Mom up suddenly that night, unable to breathe. By the time paramedics came, he was blue and unresponsive. I have wondered if he heard any of the full-code proceedings. They certainly did everything they could: IVs with fluids, heart-stimulating medicines, shocking to get him back to a rhythm, CPR cracking most of his ribs. They worked on him the entire ambulance ride and for some time once he was in the hospital. Massive pulmonary embolus was the diagnosis. With the sudden loss of a vibrant father and husband, we were devastated in one day. After forty-seven years, Mom was alone.

It's hard to say how much grief, reliance on someone else, or other factors played into it, but Mom's decline seemed so much more notable after that day. Still, she was nonetheless pretty functional at that point. Dad was never burdened with true caregiving.

I truly believe my husband, Carl, is much like my father. It's not that he dotes on me, but he seems as much in love with me now as he was fifteen years ago. We first met on a deep-sea-fishing expedition. It sounded like a fun thing to do while on the coast. I was wrong. I turned green about one hour in and for the next six and a half hours found myself begging for mercy. If I had been independently wealthy, I would have offered everyone $1,000 to return me to shore.

It was in this less-than-sexy state that I met Carl for the first time. He really seemed to care about the fact that I was debating whether my entire stomach could actually come up out of my mouth. It's so common to search for that man who seems strong, confident, and athletic. Carl actually is all of those. But my experience was that these aren't the only traits one needs in a partner. In retrospect, I know that his caring for me when I was feeling miserable was the most important quality of all. So, when he called me the following day to see if I was all right, I knew.

Fifteen years and two children later, we had been through a lot together. I had always felt that we supported each other very well. Yet this seemed to change after my father died. As the months went by, I found myself needing to spend more time with Mom. My dad really had been doing a lot.

I wonder, had I chosen something that Carl found more noble, like going back to school to improve my career, if he would have been more supportive. He didn't actively argue with me about my diminishing time at home, but he didn't help, and I would get the cold shoulder as well. I picked up on his resentment about the increasing things he had to do around the house or with the girls. He felt he was picking up my slack.

As time went on, I found myself steadily sliding my way down an abyss of more and more time caring for my mom, making the next move in our game of chess almost inevitable.

"Hey, Allison, just wanted to remind you about poker night this Tuesday."

"Do you mean tomorrow? The night that I cook at Mom's house every week?"

"I didn't mean anything other than that it's this Tuesday. I haven't seen the guys in a while, and it came down to Tuesday or Wednesday because no one wanted to give up a football night."

"Are you saying that you forgot that I cook for Mom on Tuesdays? Because I've been doing this for the last few months. It seems the only way to get her enough food to last through the weekend until I see her again."

"What do you want me to do, cancel just so you can cook for your mom? I've been taking care of the girls more and more on my own, and I'm just asking for one night with the guys. Why can't you do it on Wednesday?"

I'd like to say that I recall how this particular passive-aggressive argument came to an end. But it's hard to remember because it wasn't the only one. There were many, many more that felt much the same, just progressively more biting over time. It's not that I didn't see his point—I did. As a family, we were all having to sacrifice in some ways to help my mom, who steadily required more caregiving. I was putting in enough time to get a master's, maybe even a doctorate, in Alzheimer's. But rather than a degree with accompanying pride and sympathy, I was getting a husband who was treating my time away from home as an affront to our union.

I believe that every marriage suffers at times. An incident will make you wonder who it is you've been married to all these years. Why aren't they being more supportive? Accepting of some necessary change? Looking back, I think it just took Carl longer to believe there were no easy answers. And when I think critically, I feel my mistake was not getting Carl involved sooner. He wasn't so sympathetic because he felt my time away was a choice. Like I had become addicted to some video game and wanted him to do all the chores while I scored extra points in *Call of Duty*.

Instead, I just forged ahead, largely on my own. Kicking the can down the road. He went to poker night on Tuesday. I cooked for my mom on Wednesday, and we both complained bitterly. I'm sure all his friends got to hear how intolerant and selfish I had become. And me? I really needed to talk to more people. I had plenty of friends but had begun to shut them out. Not having enough time was part of the problem. Yet even when I engaged with friends through work or had coffee with Janine, I divulged little.

I guess I simply wasn't proud of what I was doing. My husband was right; this didn't seem like a noble pursuit that I wanted to brag about. Imagine at a party being asked, "What's new in your life?" Admiration would focus intently as you told them you restarted the cello with the goal of playing in your local orchestra. Curiosity would abound if it were returning to school to get a master's degree. But mention that you were spending all your free time taking care of your mom after her husband died and you would be the proverbial conversational sponge. All of the life would be sucked out of the party, and no one would have anything further to say.

My whole life was beginning to feel this way. Carl had been hinting about going on a family vacation. We sure could use one. But what would I do with Mom? I felt bad just taking our dog to a kennel for a week. I didn't even want to contemplate the idea of Mom being home alone for spring break. Carl's solution was to get enough TV dinners and frozen waffles to last her until we got back.

I won't say I wasn't tempted. But the likelihood of something bad happening seemed high. It would be like trying to enjoy a date with your husband while leaving your nine-year-old home alone. All would probably work out, but maybe not. And that "maybe not" is so scary you just can't go, can't leave your nine-year-old by herself, pretending that all will be well. I guess the only difference was that if Mom caught the house on fire by not taking the Hot Pocket out of the package before microwaving, we wouldn't go to jail. At least, I didn't think so.

19

May 2014

IT HAD BEEN SIX MONTHS AND $3,000 IN PILLS WHEN MOM AND I shuffled back to the neurologist's office for a follow-up. The goal today was to evaluate the efficacy of her medicines and see if anything needed to change.

I was prepared. I came armed with a notebook of thoughts, facts, a diary of what we had been going through since the previous summer.

I had grown even more ready for my speech when Mom made it clear she had no idea where we were going. During this stage, I would argue with her to get her to understand the obvious. In a rather clipped tone I would say, "Mom, we've been here before—it's Dr. Metcalf's office." I'd continue with things such as "I don't know how you don't remember coming here—he's the only doctor you have been seeing lately," followed closely by, "No, this is not where you get your mammograms!"

Luckily they didn't have to take my blood pressure when we arrived, because I was frustrated and quite ready for my speech.

Then the wait came. It was not as if we hadn't waited before. This time, it was more than forty-five minutes before we got called back into the room. Another twenty before the doctor finally came in, and by this time, Mom was done. Some of it was that the room was small and claustrophobic. But she was already a bit like a child at this point. She wanted to be somewhere else, and I could only distract for so long.

I was all ready, but I heard myself answer his query, "So, how's everything going?" with just a polite, "Pretty good."

His questions were short, yes or no types of questions like "Chest pains?" "Shortness of breath?" "Leg swelling?" "Does she still have some good days?"

Suddenly, within five minutes, he was about to leave the room. My polite, ladylike manners had to vanish, and fast, because there was definitely a problem.

"She's not getting better!" I blurted.

He stopped.

"It's been six months, and I not only have to make sure she takes her medicines every day, I have to shop, plan meals, and I think, soon, do her laundry. And I don't think she's safe to drive, but I know she does on occasion."

That last declaration seemed to have been the decisive one.

For the first time that afternoon, Dr. Metcalf addressed her directly. "Nancy, are you still driving?"

"Of course," she replied, as if it were the most obvious thing in the world.

"Do you ever have trouble finding your way back home?"

"I don't believe so," she replied. She sounded so meek, uncertain. Watching them interact made me think of a schoolteacher and pupil. Teachers have a different way of talking to children. Their vocabulary, body language, tone of voice—they are all different. This was how Dr. Metcalf sounded, like he was speaking to a third-grader. I presumed this was what I sounded like as well.

It was funny how his visits terminated. More than body language—he would rise to leave. This time he came close to me and whispered, "You must take away her keys. I'll fill out paperwork for the DMV. But the suspended license she won't remember. You have to prevent access."

And then he was gone. He left the door open, and I saw him and his white coat quickly dashing down the hall to another room.

I had failed. Sitting beside my mom, I wanted to cry. Instead, I stared at my shoes, which were no Louis Vuitton, but they still proclaimed "professional." My gaze unhurriedly eased to my left, first resting upon her contrasting white Velcro sneakers. As my eyes traveled north, I took in her beige, unable-to-be-wrinkled slacks and a daring paisley blouse of startling orange and black accented by a pearl necklace that my dad had given her. She was fidgeting; I was spent. Mom's agenda, my agenda were never addressed. If I wasn't getting answers from her specialist, where would I find them? Was it worth coming back?

I had practiced my speech for Dr. Metcalf as if it were a forensics competition. Upon leaving, I wondered aloud to myself, "How is that possibly the best I could have done?"

20

May 2014

"Why the hell don't you know?" That wasn't the first thing my husband said to me that evening, but it's what I remember. Carl wasn't one to mince words, especially when it came to money. Practical to a fault, he literally couldn't bring himself to spend money on, for example, bottled water. "It's just the same as out of the tap, and that's free."

Typically, he was the most upbeat person I knew. That was what attracted me to him more than anything. No matter how down I was feeling, he could always make me laugh. And he really never swore or raised his voice. So, with both in one sentence, it didn't take a psychiatrist to know that he was not happy with me.

"The primary reason you went to the doctor today was to find out whether the medicines made any sense to continue. I think it's bullshit. Look at her. You see her almost every day. Is she any better? And yet every month, another five hundred dollars on our Visa bill. This is no longer a game. This is our retirement and our kids' college savings going out the window. And what are we getting for this king's ransom? Are you able to stop going over there to help her every day? Are you able to spend any more time with your family? No, no, and definitely *no!*"

He was getting red now. My heart was pounding, and I wanted to scream back. I just didn't know what to say. I felt as if I were falling down a rabbit hole and there was no way back out. Like a rabbit's, my legs were curled up under me. I sat there on the bed just wanting this fight to end. How could it end? Was there a right decision to be made?

"Hello," he gently taunted.

I returned a haughty silence. He was starting to get mean, and I hadn't done anything wrong. What did I do to bring this on? I wasn't the cause of my father dying the year before. Dad could have allowed me to stay at home most days, prepared her pills, and ensured she ate. I hadn't told the neurologist these were the best pills for her. And I certainly was not the greedy drug company asking five hundred dollars for these stupid pills that hadn't done a damn thing.

"I just can't fight anymore," I replied. "I'm tired, I'm confused, and I'm just not able to make a decision right now. "

"Can you just tell me why?" Carl pleaded. "Why on earth didn't you ask the question that we both agreed you had to ask? Each month that goes by, we are further in debt and...hell, you know the rest. Just tell me why you are ignoring your family and all that we have been working toward financially."

I wasn't going to cry. And I guess I could say I didn't cry. I sobbed. I already had the guilt of missing out on so much. I'd forgotten things for dinner and packing up the kids' lunches. I had originally been the homework queen, the one Meredith would come to for help, but I was gone so often at Mom's, she stopped asking. And I had been the one feeling a visceral pain every time they swiped that Visa at the pharmacy. Now my rock, the one who had complained so little this last year or so, was cussing and yelling at me. He was highlighting my failures as a wife and a mother. The fight was over. If this were a boxing match at Madison Square Garden, the victor would be obvious. Carl, like Mike Tyson standing defiant. Me, curled in a ball and crying my eyes out on the pillow.

Consciousness came slowly. Confusion was first. The room was dark, and I was cold. Where was I? The La-Z-Boy recliner in the corner was my first hint of orientation. The shutters gently knocking against the half-opened window. My left arm asleep, garnering my first moments of clarity.

Long before my arm and I were fully awake, I realized there was no one else in the room. The clock shone 2:13 a.m. at me with dull, red numbers. Drool, bad breath, a makeup disaster on my face, as I could imagine that the tears had left furrows of black from my eyelashes. I didn't need a mirror to know that I probably looked like a clown from a Stephen King movie. The thought that things couldn't get worse lasted just a few more seconds, and misery suddenly compounded as acid burned in my throat. The first of the sickness came several steps before the toilet. And then, heaving over the edge of the toilet bowl, I started to descend into complete misery.

To summarize my life so far, things had seemed quite ideal. My personal CV would have read something as follows:

Allison L. Raney, DOB: May 12, 1970
Graduated summa cum laude from Parkside Elementary
    (I liked to say that, as I felt people got so pretentious about all of their achievements when they were young.)
Gibson High School honor roll, lettered in soccer, three pictures in the yearbook indicating I was at least average on the social scale, though far from prom queen
Colorado College School of Business with a 3.4 average

Accounting firms for five years, which were generally
   miserable
Career change to working for a smaller nonprofit as their
   auditor
Married: August 14, 2001, at the age of thirty-one
Meredith born two years later, now about to finish sev-
   enth grade
Sloane two years after that, finishing fifth

We bought our first house and had had several cars. We even had two cats to complete the picture of the perfect American family. And now, here I was looking like a drug addict who was deep into withdrawals. My husband pissed at me. Meredith feeling neglected and letting me know as well as a twelve-year-old girl can with all manner of tantrums. Sloane starting to act out at school. My dad had already been gone for two years, and so there was no one to really turn to. Whose shoulder was Allison going to cry on? My mom's? Right now, it was just the impersonal, cold porcelain that was just a shade less disgusting than I was.

Something had to change. My clothes, the vomit, and my mascara were the obvious choices. But deep down I knew that things had to change. I was on a fence, balancing, trying to keep my family happy, take care of my ever-dependent mother, and avoid getting fired. And this was against the backdrop of spending an extra $500 a month. It felt a bit like a game of chess where you knew at some point you were going to lose. It was my move, and none of my options were good. This was not a game; I couldn't just concede and knock over my king. I had to keep on playing and somehow find a way.

21

June 2014

"HAVE YOU EVER NOTICED THE DRUG REPS?" I BROUGHT UP casually. "You know, those all-too-pretty girls who parade into the doctors' offices with their things? I never really paid attention before. They just seemed to come and go sometimes, and at most they stirred a slight bit of jealousy. I was never going to be that young again, never that pretty. But after that meeting with the pharmacist where I found out I was going to be paying for the equivalent of a nice Mercedes, yet receive just two pills instead, I started to do some reading."

"'Have you ever noticed?'" mimicked Andrea. Smiling, she continued, "You sound just like your mom. I remember how you used to warn us, 'Don't bring politics up at all—it's not worth it.'"

"Or the death penalty."

"Republicans in general."

"Abortion."

"Nuclear war."

"OK, OK, I know. You've made your point. Come on, am I really getting that bad?"

"Well..." squealed Andrea and Megan at the same time.

Then Megan said, "No, we're kind of kidding. But you do get on your soapbox every once in a while. And you know what you used to tell your mom: 'Have you ever changed anyone's mind?

Has someone just slapped their knee and said, "By golly, you're right—I guess I'm ready to give up my guns. Fuck the NRA."'"

At this, we were all crying with laughter. We were laughing so hard, people started to stare. Andrea literally slapped Carol's back. Even the kids on drugs seemed to enviously wonder what we were doing. But what did we care. It was summer, we were outside at my personal favorite brew pub, and generally... life was good. True, the staff here could improve their customer service. Yet who among the five of us really needed garlic cheese fries served faster.

"I know you will all doubt what I say, but I've been sleuthing, and I feel like we are all being murdered by a thousand cuts, and we don't even know it is happening. While I was sitting next to Barbie at my gynecologist's office, I looked into her bag. Boxes of Vimovo. She wasn't that talkative with me, but she sure knew how to flirt with the doctor. Anyway, I looked it up. It's Naproxen and Omeprazole. Quick *Price Is Right* quiz. How much for a bottle of Naproxen, which is the same as Aleve—ten dollars, right? What about a bottle of Prilosec for heartburn? Maybe fifteen dollars."

"Is the punch line coming? Because I'm getting bored," sighed Andrea.

"OK, Debbie Downer. How much would you spend for the convenience of two drugs in one pill? Come on, guys, I'm ready to blow your minds. How much is the most you would spend?"

"I'd say forty dollars, and not one penny more."

"Oh, hell no. Are you rich or stupid? I wouldn't spend a dime over twenty-six dollars. It's not that hard to swallow two pills."

"Are you ready for this? The cheapest I could find—with a coupon—was $2,236 for a one-month supply."

Boom.

I'd made my first point. If this were a boxing match, they would have all been looking up from the canvas, kind of dazed. They were ready to listen.

And when I thought about it, I had taken a few weeks to really start to understand what was going on. And I had pursued these concerns with a fervor. I had needed to know if there was a way out of paying $500 a month for my mom. It was crippling my family and throwing lighter fluid on the already-charged frustrations Carl had with me spending so much time caring for her.

So now, when I resumed my position on my soapbox, I was ready with examples that they would understand.

"Cialis. You all know this drug, right? Advertised like crazy. Remember that funny one where there was a man and wife holding hands, and they were both in separate bathtubs? I guess this was supposed to make us long for sex. Well, the price tag for one month of happiness: $358."

Andrea hooted, "Seriously, $358 a month for sex? That had better promise the wife an orgasm every time! I'd be hornier had he just gone out and bought me a Jaguar."

I was trying to educate a bunch of comedians.

Moving through my notes, I came up with a few more.

"Truvada to protect against HIV. I know this sounds great, but it doesn't protect against any other STD. So, your choice is fifteen dollars a month for condoms to protect against everything or Truvada at $1,667 per month to protect just against HIV.

"Jublia for toe fungus: $600 a month, and you have to take it for a year. Do you know how many mani-pedis you can get for $7,200? And no, I didn't do the math, but I'm sure it's a lot."

"Ha-ha!" exclaimed Janine. "I no longer feel bad about adding the massage to my pedicures. But seriously, Allison, how big of a difference can this all really make?"

"I'm glad you asked, because I'm trying to tell you. There's many more. In fact, the examples never seem to stop. Remember Enbrel—that golfer Phil Mickelson talks about it in ads all the time, saying how much it has helped his aches and pains for arthritis. But did you have any idea it costs $5,000, each and every month—forever?"

Andrea said, "OK, Allison, it's not that I don't believe you. Though... all right, I guess I don't really believe you. I find it hard to believe anyone other than Phil Michelson could afford $5,000 a month. No one could pay that."

"See, you are kind of right. No one could or would pay that. No matter how gnarled your hands were getting, you couldn't spend $5,000 a month on a drug. In fact, who would pay more than about one hundred dollars for any pill that they had to take off the shelf at Safeway? I can see the checker quickly scanning the items: four-dollar gallon of milk, one-dollar head of lettuce, three dollars for the dozen eggs, $600 for your toe fungus pills, and $5,000 for your month supply of arthritis pills.

"But would you pay forty dollars? Of course. 'That's one hell of a coupon,' you would say, bringing it down from about $6,000—with tax, of course—to only forty bucks. So, who pays the other $5,960?" I quietly and conspiratorially said, "We do!

"Just like a nuclear submarine—none of us can pay for one, but taxes from all of us can. But instead of taxes, it's our premiums, rising faster than a $400-a-month penis on Viagra. And we had no idea why they were going up so fast. Now we know. Each time our premiums go up fifty dollars a month, a few hundred of us can buy Enbrel for one person."

"Do you know I was given a choice recently?" chimed in Andrea. "I hadn't really given it that much thought. I've been a little embarrassed to tell you that Zachary got diagnosed with ADD this past year."

"Andrea, you don't have to be embarrassed," interjected Janine. "I'm sure all of us have had one difficulty or another raising our kids."

"Thank you, seriously," Andrea said. "His third-grade teacher kept pestering me to go to the doctor and get him treated. I am still not certain I believe the pediatrician, but his grades have not been so stellar, and he keeps on getting sent out of class, so I reluctantly agreed to start him on Adderall. Like you, I had sticker shock. It was something like $250 a month. I would cut off my arm for Zach if I felt it were necessary. But it seemed like a lot of money. And it was expensive, for sure, but I also was just not convinced there was anything wrong with him. The pharmacist was the first to inform me that there was a cheaper generic. It's funny; it sounds like what you were saying at the start. The generic was twice a day instead of once a day, and it was covered by insurance. So, he's on a ten-dollar-a-month medicine now. Why would I spend an extra $240 a month so he has the convenience of taking one pill per day instead of two?"

"How's he doing?" Carol asked.

"Honestly, I don't like it. He is more of a zombie at times, and then a starving, raving Mr. Hyde later in the day. It kind of feels like the teachers are making it convenient for them, and then he is more of a horror at home. I've wondered at times if this was because I just bought the cheap medicine. Maybe I haven't tried the expensive one because I'm afraid that it will work better. I'm working myself up to try just one month and see. Yet in my mind, I find it hard to conceive that something works twenty-five times better. I even go cheap with birth control. All of a sudden, one will stop being 'preferred,' and the price will go from ten dollars to thirty-five. Maybe a few of you are on high-class birth control, but my ten-dollar generic has worked just fine, so I'm not a believer that you get what you pay for when it comes to medicines."

"Do you all remember Karen, Jessica's mom?" asked Megan. "She was diagnosed with multiple sclerosis. But you've brought back a memory. I remember because it was just so shocking, it made me think for a few days what I would do in her situation. Karen told me that she takes a drug that costs $1,000 per *week*."

"Oh no," Carol said, her lip curled.

"She said it stopped the double vision, and she was eternally grateful. It came up when we were talking about how much she hated her job. But she's too afraid to quit because if she loses her benefits, even for a few months, they simply will not have the money. She literally has no idea what will happen to her if she stops that drug. Lose her vision, end up in a wheelchair."

Carol said, "You are all scaring me now. I guess I've never had to pay for medicines other than my ten-dollar birth control, thank you very much. How on earth does a company come up with a price tag of $52,000 a year? It seems even more cruel when you feel you must pay for it or possibly die. I was kind of rolling my eyes at the Viagra thing because, in a way, who cares. But I have heard of multiple sclerosis, and that can be pretty damn scary. I'd want to pay for a potentially lifesaving drug, but there really is no way that Darryl and I could swing $52,000. Would I just be left to die if I didn't have insurance? And I see your point: if I had insurance, it almost doesn't seem fair that I would've just raised all of your rates one hundred dollars a month forever just to pay for me."

Megan, Andrea, Carol, Janine, and I just sat there, staring for a moment. A long moment of silence. No one had died, but the comedy with which this had begun was now long gone and the mood somber.

22

July 2019

I LOVE CARL. PERIOD. FULL STOP. NO QUALIFIERS. WHAT OTHERS might value would include the fact that he is fit and clean-cut. In fact, he is GQ-model, rock-hard-abs kind of fit. He also has a steady job, helps with chores, and loves our girls. Watching him focus is one of my favorite things. When he is unaware someone is watching, he is intense.

Now, with reading glasses, his eyes seemed even larger, and brow furrowed, he bit his lower lip. And then he noticed me. His features softened. That intensity that had been focused on the page suddenly shifted and bored right through me. If he was in the mood, I could get wet just from that look alone. But the reason why he was the best partner I could have asked for was that he made me happy. At times, it seemed that was his primary goal in life—which was fine by me.

On this rainy Saturday, Carl was sitting with his laptop in his favorite spot. During downtime from pecking at the keyboard, he would stare out the bedroom window, sipping his bitter black coffee. A photo would suggest serenity; I thought this would be a picture you could place in an advertisement to sell our house as he gazed out the large bay window.

But I knew something was amiss. There was something incongruous with his emotions. Moments later I knew why.

"It's already taken!" he randomly exclaimed. "Our yearly

camping spot is booked, and it's not even February. It seems the only available spots this summer are in Wyoming. Here we come, Equality State."

"You're joking, right?"

"About which part?"

"All of it!" It was my turn to turn up the volume.

"I actually looked it up. Wyoming's nickname is the Equality State because it was the first state to allow women the right to vote. And yes, every single spot we have camped in the past is already reserved. We try to go on vacation to escape all the bustle of city life, and even in the campground, too many people. This planet is being overrun."

We had been down this road before. Though not as worrisome at parties as my mom was, Carl could alienate people with a few touchy subjects. He would avoid conflict with heady issues like abortion or the death penalty. But what got him to wind up even at a party was discussing any of the consequences of overpopulation.

I don't believe anyone likes traffic, garbage on the streets, or the inability to find a camping spot. However, there is a visceral difficulty in realizing, by definition, that you are part of the problem. Not just you, but the children you chose to have. And ever since he read a book on the topic, he made comments at every opportunity. Even our girls knew about the Great Pacific Garbage Patch.

"What do you think about Grand Teton National Park?" asked Carl between sips of his coffee. "There's a camping spot not far from the Snake River. I know it's new and a long drive . . ."

"Book it," I promptly agreed.

I knew what he was doing, and that is why he makes me so happy. Carl sensed what it would take to lift my mood. It was coming up on a year since Mom's passing, and I needed to get away.

Meredith and Sloane seemed just as happy for the Grand Tetons — or as they started preferring to call it, the Three Boobs. It seemed young boys weren't the only ones fascinated with anatomy. Plus, they would have gone anywhere other than summer school.

We were still close as a family, but independence and secrets were starting to creep in. Idle chatter between them was more guarded, and so I wasn't too surprised to find notes about boys I had never heard of in Meredith's backpack.

At my insistence, we went on several separate hikes. Carl would take Sloane, and I would try to break through Meredith's fast-growing wall of silence. Ironically, she learned more about me than vice versa. And she found out my biggest secret of all.

"Mom! You're smoking!" broke the silence so profoundly it seemed to echo throughout the entire park.

In retrospect, I shouldn't have tried to sneak one. But I needed them—physically and emotionally. That pack of cigarettes was beating like the Tell-Tale Heart as I reached my second day without smoking. After ushering her ahead so I could have a supposed bathroom break, I lit up.

The first drag was like heaven. My cravings were satisfied, and I felt so alive and thrilled that I was denying the grim reaper any sense of agony. All of this made her rebuke that much more jarring. I had been almost in a trance when the brush moved, and I saw that she had doubled back to find me. Tears welled up in her eyes so quickly that I had to stop. For the next few hours, we wandered. Aimlessly, it seemed. Because the journey was truly our destination. And meanwhile, my task—to convince my now-seventeen-year-old why I didn't want to live forever.

We stopped and sat on a rock, and I began. What I took most from the conversation was the visceral pain Meredith showed. I had never felt so loved by her.

After a good, long cry, we began our hike anew. Halted conversation had given way to an avalanche of words. It was she, however, who made the connection first: "Mom, we are saying the same thing. We agree. "We both realize that if you continue to smoke you will die at a younger age. It's just that I want you to live forever, and you want to die. The more you smoke, the sooner you'll get your wish."

Meredith didn't need to complete her plea for me to quit. I saw where this was going, and it seemed like there could be no reason good enough to change her mind. A casual observer might have presumed I sat on a shaded log because I needed rest from the steady climb. But it was my mind that needed to catch up. "Honey," I began tentatively. "We all are going to die sometime. But things have changed for humankind. People are living so much longer. I know you've heard your dad talk about this a million times, and he's right."

"So, you're just going to kill yourself?"

"Meredith, no. That's not what I meant. To put it bluntly, I want to die before my mind goes. It's that simple. Did you know that if we were living a few hundred years ago, we would have probably died in our late thirties? Everyone died too early to get dementia. Yes, I want to see you graduate from high school, go to college, get married, and have children. I want it all. But life doesn't offer a guarantee even if I live as clean a life as possible. Both of my parents lived to see all of those wonderful things. My dad remembered it all happily up until the day he died. Mom, in the end, didn't remember you, my wedding, my graduation day. By the time she passed, she didn't even remember me."

I stood up to walk farther, but Meredith collapsed onto the now-vacated log. To avoid this looking like a lecture, I squeezed in beside her, only partially avoiding a somewhat unpleasant knot pushing into my thigh. Hugging her eased both this physical discomfort and the sadness I was inflicting upon her.

"Do you know what I had to give up to take care of my mom? Do you have any idea how jealous I was that your dad took you to so many of your practices and games? How frustrated that I was no longer 'homework mom'? How many times I microwaved meals for my family rather than cooking at the end of the day? And where was I? Day after day, I was with your grandmother in the early evenings. I'd leave right after Dad got home. And this didn't go on for just a few weeks or even months. It went on for a few years. Do you realize how many fights I had with your dad about not spending time with you two? About spending your college tuition on medicines and treatments?

"I loved your grandma and would have never resented helping her. Even the gross stuff like cleaning poop out of her bed."

"Mom, that's just disgusting."

"It's true, though. All of that I could have lived with if she would have remembered any of it. If she had been able to show some type of gratitude or understanding for what I was giving up. But those last several years I was missing out on your lives, I felt like I was gaining nothing in return. I was sacrificing the happiness of my family to care for someone who no longer acted like my mother. It bothers me so much that what you remember is this confused, cantankerous old woman. She was a warrior. A woman so proud she should have been in Congress to make this world a better place."

We were ready to move on at this time. Partly because my thigh had grown numb but also because we needed to eventually get back to the campground.

"If she hadn't been demented, would you be smoking now?"

"Meredith, for not spending time with you, I would have had regrets. Same with your sister and your father. But it's more than regrets with my mom. I grew to hate having to be with her. I can't believe I just said that, but it's true. She wasn't there. And I did it solely out of obligation. As the months passed, I vowed one thing to myself: 'I will not make my children do the same thing for me.' And so that's when I started. I'd light up right there in front of Grandma, and she didn't care. She would have killed me if her mind were still sharp, but she didn't raise an eyebrow. Remember Grandad smoked and what happened to him? He died quickly—no one suffered taking care of him. Well, that's what I want for both of you. To remember me for who I am and allow you to spend your time with your family."

"Am I the last to know?" Meredith asked somewhat forlornly. "Does Sloane already know?"

"You're going to laugh but...almost nobody knows but you. Not even your dad has seen me smoke. I smoke at the office; I smoke when I go 'running.' I know, kind of nutty to go running to smoke, but it is the best way to hide it from everybody."

"That's why you've suddenly become a fitness freak. I thought you were just upset about Grandma dying."

"Will you keep my secret, Meredith?"

She stumbled a bit suddenly, which may have slowed a quicker reply. As we descended into a shady spot on the trail, I was beginning to wonder why Meredith was keeping me in suspense. I waited patiently, walking a little faster to keep up with her now-purposeful strides.

Finally, she just stopped. "Mom," she said as she turned to face me, "you're wrong. I would never hate you. And I don't think that just because Grandma had dementia it means you're going to go crazy."

She turned and began to walk further. More suspense. This time when she turned around, she was smiling, "But I'll keep your secret. I'm good at keeping secrets." And with that, she seemed to glide away from me. I would have had to run to keep up that speed. And I knew she had nothing more she wanted to say. So, I did the sensible thing, knowing I couldn't catch her before we got back. I had another cigarette.

23

September 2014

MY DATE CARD WAS FULL. MOST OF WHAT MANIFESTED AS little green dots on my Google calendar had been typed in weeks ago. There were so many this month. I liked the comfort of nothing planned, especially when I was slammed at work, but some things I was definitely anticipating. Meredith's first play was coming up. No soliloquies, but she did have several lines, which she had practiced for weeks. Further fun would be had at Carl's annual softball competition for his office. I didn't play, but I loved to cheer. And it was September. For an accountant, September is almost as bad as April. This was not the reason, however, that September 6, 2014, turned out to be such a horrible day.

The call came at 4:30 a.m. The rings likely began a full minute before I groggily came up with "Hello?"

"I'm trying to reach Allison Raney," said the authoritative voice on the other end of the line. "Is someone there?" he continued.

"Yes, yes, I'm still here. This is Allison."

"I'm sorry to have to wake you, but your mother, Nancy MacPherson, is here in the emergency room. She seems to have fallen and injured her hip. It's likely broken, actually. Would you be able to come down?"

"Who is this? Where did you say she was?"

"My name is Saechao. I'm a nurse at Parkfield West hospital. It's not urgent, but she seems very confused and probably would like to have someone comfort her. In fact, we had to sedate her. More for her outbursts than for her pain."

"What's wrong?" whispered Carl.

"OK, I'll be there as soon as I can. Thank you."

My mind screamed through sleepiness. I was in total panic mode. "Fuck!" I exclaimed, having knocked over my water glass that sat uncharacteristically full.

"Don't worry. I'll clean it up," Carl said warmly. "Go ahead and turn on the light."

I'm not sure if it was me trying to be the martyr or I simply didn't want a bright light to wake me up sooner than necessary, but I continued stubbornly in the dark. I was able to feel for my jeans, but that was about all. Though the visitors in the ER probably couldn't care less if I was mismatched, I relented and assaulted my retina with light from a thousand suns. I was awake now.

"She broke her hip, Carl," I forcefully responded to his earlier question. Anticipating further inane questions, I added, "And I don't know other details, all right? You know what just happened, you know it's 4:33 in the morning, you know she's losing her mind, and now you know she's in hospital with a broken hip. So, what more is there to say? I failed her. I should have been there . . ."

The rant continued. Maybe he was too tired to yell back at me, though I deserved it. I was not exactly being kind. "We should have moved her here once I knew she wasn't safe. The nurse even said she's having outbursts! What does that mean? He had to sedate her just to calm her down."

I'm not sure why I was putting earrings on at this moment. But the look I was getting from Carl was "I think you've gone completely mad." He just didn't say it out loud.

Then I was gone. After a quick mug of Starbucks, I quietly led my angry self through the garage door. *Why did this have to happen today?* As soon as I asked myself that question, I realized that there would never be a good day for my mom to break her hip. The problem wasn't just that I was overwhelmed at work. Nor was it that I had promised to watch the kids while Carl played at his annual company softball game. It was just that some things seemed to signal the end, and a hip fracture was one of them. From the hospital to a nursing home, then back at home for a while, and then... *I just don't want to think about this anymore. Where did I go wrong? I'm so tired.* I had gone to her house before coming home every single day this week. She seemed to be walking OK. I wondered if she didn't turn on the light and suffered the same middle-of-the-night fate as my water glass.

Parkfield hospital was generally about twenty-five minutes from our house. With no traffic, I arrived before 5:00 a.m. The lights, once I was inside, made my bedroom lights seem subtle. My pupils squeezed even tighter.

"Can you sign your name and put on this visitor badge?" greeted the clerk, Judy, who clearly had the most enjoyable job in the world. "She's in hallway bed five," Judy loudly stated while the doors she had buzzed opened up beside me.

It was not hard to spot Mom. She was lying, not completely covered, in the middle of the hallway for everyone to see. I guessed emergency rooms were so used to being overrun that they didn't mind referring to your location as "hallway bed." On this day they had eight people, including Mom, lined up in the corridor with the hope of getting an actual room. I wondered which patients got the coveted private rooms. Was it the luck of the draw? Or maybe it was related to being contagious? But I thought if I asked someone, they would think I was just being bitchy. Which, of course, I was.

"Mom, hey, it's me," I nudged after walking in front of her. She jumped a little at my touch. She then winced as the movement triggered some deep-seated pain. Her eyes didn't open. Her face quickly went slack. I had forgotten she was being sedated. In moments I had assumed the position I would remain in for several hours, a backbreaking lean over the rails while holding her hand. Chairs weren't allowed because they further clogged up the hallway in the event of an emergency. I smirked, thinking, *Aren't we already in the emergency room?*

By 8:00 a.m. I realized I couldn't stand this way forever, and progress was exceedingly slow. About the only thing I had achieved with this three-hour vigil was procuring a warm blanket that fully covered her. Still, one thing this sedative did allow was peace. I hadn't seen her this calm in months. Dementia had not only left her confused, she also always seemed agitated.

At this moment I could imagine Meredith stumbling downstairs in her pjs asking Dad where I was. Though she tended to act aloof, she seemed to suffer more than Sloane with my absences. Her grades had come down, and she knew how to push our buttons. Carl often would be agitated in the evening, dealing with her at the end of the day.

Now she would be at it again, wondering why I wasn't there to make blueberry pancakes on Saturday like I often did. I could see the conversation going something like this: "Daddy, where's Mom? I've looked everywhere, and she's not here," Meredith would ask as soon as she got downstairs.

Carl would likely hesitate a bit before replying.

"I'm waiting," Meredith would fire off. Does that statement require an exclamation point? Maybe another form of punctuation invented for girls who felt they had it all figured out. A "sassy mark" that lets the reader know that this child was working her way up to know-it-all. Anyone who has been a parent to a girl will sympathize. The only question is at what age this begins. For Meredith, it was about age ten. Now in junior high, she would sometimes add an exclamation point to the sassy mark, as she had done in my imagination just there.

Her sister, Sloane, nine, had kept more of that adorable daddy's-little-girl style. Sloane would more likely take her padded-feet-pajama self and curl up into his lap.

After the girls learned that Grandma had broken her hip, breakfast would be strangely quiet. They loved their grandma but hadn't seen too much of her lately. Which I readily pointed out was Carl's fault.

No one had ever had to tell Carl how much he loved Meredith and Sloane. They were his two beautiful daughters. Yet the day he found out that Mom had crashed while they were in the car, he changed. It was just a different love, I suppose. If he were in the Secret Service, I'm sure he would expect to take a bullet for the president, but maybe he would, maybe he wouldn't. He might even hesitate if it were his own mom. But if it came down to his girls, he would be begging to get shot if it increased their chance of making it out alive.

So his reaction when he felt Mom was a danger was not too surprising. We surely had had our fights over the last ten years, but nothing like that one. It felt to me that Carl was banning the girls from seeing their grandma, which seemed ridiculously unfair. We didn't have sex for three months. Not that sex was the only thing that went south during that time. We couldn't talk to each other, and even the most minor thing could bring on instant anger. On one occasion, I began yelling at him for buying the wrong soap. Even the therapist got me to laugh a bit about that one. "Are you actually admitting that you yelled at Carl because he bought Coast instead of Ivory?"

In retrospect, maybe the Alzheimer's diagnosis saved our marriage. It seemed after Mom got diagnosed, I softened a little. Life seemed to be scarier. I became more vulnerable in so many ways, and I needed Carl more. And we finally started to make love again. Prior decisions had generally been mutual. As my confidence retreated, Carl began to feel like the Man of the House, and the decisions started to be more solo. There were fewer discussions, and deference became the norm. And the biggest change was that I now agreed in spirit with what Carl had known deep down all along. The girls were just not safe alone with my mom.

Alzheimer's certainly didn't look good on a caregiver's resume. Now, we could add fractured right hip. Any chance that I was going to get Carl to soften in his approach was truly out the window. Or, if you prefer a better metaphor, crumbling along with her bones.

What was frustrating is that she was fine some of the time. Her poor memory didn't stop her from loving and knowing how to care for the girls. She was still the queen of the snacks. She could come up with the most imaginative games that had them laughing for hours. And yet even I recognized that there were times when she didn't notice the danger. The danger of an iron that was not yet cool. Getting caught up on the phone with a salesperson while the girls got into some mischief upstairs.

In some ways this reminded me of a dilemma that my friend Rachael had had to face with her dad: when do you stop him from driving? True, the majority of the time he would be completely fine. But when the consequences are so dire, must we not insist on near perfection? We have all heard of those seniors who mistakenly press the accelerator instead of the brake. In the next heartbreaking half minute, multiple people die, several more are injured. The senior is soon to be arrested. Panic and remorse at levels that we could never imagine. Then again, we could never imagine making that mistake in the first place.

It was now nearly 9:00 p.m. I had shepherded Mom through the entire day in the small hallway, with the exception of food breaks.

I'd downed a caesar salad and a tuna-fish sandwich that seemed past their prime.

Nurses had come and gone, explaining in great detail what to expect next. In somewhat stark contrast with the nurses, the doctors gave us little time. Dr. Bregman, the orthopedic surgeon, would hopefully compensate for his personality with stellar hands. All I gleaned from our conversation was that the operation would be on Monday morning. She would be up and around by midweek and likely spend a few weeks in rehab at a nursing home. He was definitely not lacking in confidence: "She should be back to normal in six to eight weeks." Naively, at some point I went up to the nurses' station to ask if I could talk to Dr. Bregman again. Though they didn't exactly laugh, I could tell from the glib response, "We'll certainly pass along the message," my request was going to be dropped the second I turned around.

I returned to hallway bed five surprised that the railing wasn't still warm from where I'd been leaning on it. Mom was quietly snoring. She had been tired the entire time, even when she was awake. Likely from the stress and calming medicine.

Whatever they gave her sure had worked. *I think I need some of it.* Though not now; I was beyond tired. I contrasted my emotionally charged day with that of Carl and the girls. Talking occasionally through the day with people outside the hospital, mainly with Janine, I learned they had a great time. It was one of those perfect California days. Carl had had his company softball game and apparently played great. The girls got to hang out with Janine, who stood in for me. Janine was certainly more fun than your typical babysitter. Though I knew I wasn't being replaced, there was an inexplicable jealousy. Here I was spending all day in the hospital with my mom. Carl, Janine, the girls, and everyone else seemed to be going on with their lives as if nothing had changed.

When I spoke to Carl around dinnertime, I heard him excuse himself from a restaurant. I was not sure if he took the call outside the Red Robin because of the noise or if it was then easier to downplay his happiness and pretend to be appropriately sympathetic. He was probably thinking, *Deep breaths. Sympathetic tone. Don't fuck this up and make her get mad. Don't let on that I had a spectacular day with our kids and her best friend. And definitely don't gloat about the triple I hit to put our team into the lead.*

What he got from me was months in the making. Months of wasted time away from him. Months when, even though I was present, my mind was elsewhere, trying to organize my mom's schedule. The stress of so much money being poured into her care culminating in this broken hip—a glaring example of our lack of progress. So many missed days at work, so many late nights and early mornings used to catch up with clients. And now, a perfect Saturday had eroded away. A day I should have just enjoyed. Instead, I heard myself getting out of control. I couldn't stop.

"I hate this place. We are still in the emergency room. Can you believe that? It looks like a scene from *The Walking Dead* out there. You know I don't like the smell of vomit. Well, it's everywhere. I go to get some fresh air and then have to pass the 'walkers,' who are loitering with their saggy pants or sweats looking like death warmed over. Then the smoker area that is definitely not fifty feet away from the doors. I can't hold my breath long enough to get past the fog. But I can't stay long for some fresh air because Mom is crazy. I don't think it's even the drugs, because she was like this before any pain medicine. She's talking nonsense. I think she's hallucinating. Once I came back, and I'm certain she thought I was the nurse. At least for a little while. And to get any help down here—you might think we were in a war zone. And she will suddenly begin to cry. She's in pain, and I had to wait forty-five minutes before her nurse came back to give her some pills. She's finally sleeping for a little bit, and so I called. But I have to go back soon; I don't want her being alone in there. It's too scary. And I've got work! A mountain of it, and I'm stuck here. I left my laptop at home. I look like a mess. I thought it would only be a few hours, and we are still down here in the ER."

"What's going to happen next?" Carl asked with probably more fear than I realized.

"Surgery. She's going to surgery, probably Monday, though it may be tomorrow morning. No one knows. And since they don't know, she's not allowed to have anything to eat or drink. They have given her nothing but ice chips since she arrived. I've had nothing but graham crackers since lunch. That's all they seem to have down here. And even those I eat around the corner because I don't want Mom to see me eating."

I was panting. On the phone I could hear nothing but audible breathing, as Carl was likely too afraid to speak.

"I guess I should go."

"Are you planning on spending the night?" Carl asked.

"I think I'd shoot myself first. No, I will be home once they get her up to a room. OK. I've got to go, bye." I stood there holding my phone. Looking around, the world came back to focus. I had just hung up on the normal world that I enjoyed so much. Behind me, the bright lights of the hospital. *Maybe this is what soldiers feel like when they have to go to Afghanistan or some other war zone. Your spouse continues to lead a perfectly normal American life, and you can't really convey all that you are going through.* The problem with my life now, though, was that I had no idea if this tour of duty would ever end.

In retrospect, I also had no idea how bad things could become.

PART 2

PART 2

24

September 2014

WHEN I WAS SINGLE, THERE WAS SO MUCH TIME. I'M NOT SURE we realized how easy life was in college. It was not that college didn't require effort—far from it. College, though, is a specific pursuit, and getting good grades is your primary focus. Having a job as a single person isn't that much different. You still get to do so much on the weekends, really, whatever you want. Even during the week, it's easy to say yes to just about anything. Softball league, no problem. Who cares if the games start at 9:00 p.m. Friend getting married in Hawaii, you take a few days off, and you're there. The only times you say no are when you really don't want to go on that blind date or something equally miserable.

A serious relationship starts to change things. It's your first realization that you can't just do whatever you want, whenever you want. All of a sudden *he* has things he wants to do on the weekend, and you are expected to be there. Still, this isn't so bad. If you really wanted to miss his cousin's bar mitzvah, you could still go to Vegas with your friends and make it up with some good sex later. Sometimes all you had to do is let him play golf—now that's a win-win.

Then true adulthood happens. You get married, and you buy a house. You owe thousands on your student loans, and there just isn't time anymore. It's not that you don't love your spouse, but sleep starts to become more than just something that happens between 11:00 p.m. and 6:00 a.m. It becomes a coveted time period. So important that you start to look forward to it like a minivacation. This is because you now have responsibility at work. People are depending on what you do, and there is so much more on the line than when you worked at In-N-Out Burger.

Friends? What happened to your friends? We'll start by recognizing that you aren't making any new friends. You have no time. Do you even know the names of three couples on your block? Have you been out to dinner with anyone in your neighborhood in the three and a half years that you've been living there? The good news is that you do still make time for your college buddies, your relatives. You still can plan ten-day vacations and say to your spouse, "Isn't life wonderful?" This is when you look into each other's eyes and wonder why you don't get away more often. And this is probably when you do the deed that costs you your sanity—you decide to have children.

Every parent seems to act differently than their childless friends. In fact, childless couples so don't get it, and you kind of just stop hanging out with them. They still think you can just have a beer whenever you want without planning this out with your husband a week before.

There are two easy ways to tell a new parent from one without kids. The parent will have small bits of spit-up on each of their shoulders and not really care. The parent will also have absolutely nothing else to talk about other than the cutest baby that God has come up with thus far. Once you have kids, you give up and stop talking to your not-as-enlightened single friends. Which is probably a good thing, as you've got to cut your circle even further at this point because, as you already know, there is less time.

The only sliver of hope regarding this terrible transition from all the free time in the world to every minute of your day having something going on, is that it takes years to happen. People get really good at organizing over this time and somehow still seem to enjoy what life has to offer. There is sometimes one partner who wants more kids when the other is already waving the white flag. Typically, though, the decision to get "fixed" is mutual. The only not-mutual part is that the woman usually gets the short end of the stick...again. As if using birth control for twenty-five years weren't enough, now she must go through the more complicated surgery. I bet I could do a two-week course and learn how to do a vasectomy. How hard can it be? They're just hanging out there, waiting to be snipped. And I roll my eyes every time I hear a man groan about how much it's going to hurt. Five minutes a side! That's it. Try having a baby suck on your nipple every two to three hours for six months straight.

And now, at forty-five, my life had been going as follows:

Every day I woke up at 5:15 so that I could spend half an hour running on the treadmill. I might not be considered obese, but the writing was on the wall. I had about twenty pounds to lose, and though I hated getting up earlier, it was still more palatable than reaching 160 pounds.

I could be mostly ready about an hour later. This gave me about forty-five minutes to prepare for my day at work, usually getting together the things that I had to leave the night before because of some crisis.

At 7:15, ensured the girls were awake. Alarms were not quite as good as Mom pulling off the covers. Prepared breakfast while packing lunches. Coffee and the news all getting thrown into the mix.

Dropped off Sloane and Meredith at school at 8:30 a.m. Actually, 8:20 a.m. because with traffic, I otherwise would not be on time for my 9:00 a.m. meeting at my office.

Most days I would leave the office at 4:30 p.m. to get the kids from child care by 5:00 p.m., but some days I would also then swing by basketball practice to pick Meredith up—another mother would bring her to the middle school gym.

If I had a maid, then I wouldn't have had to worry about getting dinner ready. But since my job didn't pay me $300,000 a year, I would get dinner while trying to help the kids with homework. Carl would get in about this time and had been trained to do the dishes.

By 8:30 p.m., after doing some chores, I was really tired. The kids were down by 9:00, and we finally had a little time to ourselves. You spend your life with someone, and the reality is that out of twenty-four hours, you might have just thirty minutes before one of you is dozing off.

Alas, what I hadn't realized was that those were the good old days. Life was just about to get more difficult. Much more difficult. When Mom returned from acute rehab after her hip fracture, she was much less mobile. And she seemed so frail. There was no way she would be able to manage everything on her own. Somebody was going to have to give her a lot of help. It turned out that somebody was me.

"Carl, I really don't have another choice. I'm going to have to go over there every day. I'll still try and get things ready by the time you come home, but after work will probably be the best time."

"I just don't see why it must be each and every day—what about twice a week? That's a good compromise. If you haven't noticed, Allison, we like having you around."

Shaking my head, I felt defeated but resolute. "She's really losing her mind now. It's definitely worse since she broke her hip. There's no way, for example, that she would take her pills every day. I've seen it actually go both ways, when no pills are gone after a few days and when the entire week's worth is missing and it's only Thursday."

"How much does it cost to hire somebody to do just those few things every day? It can't be much, can it? And what if..." His question trailed off, but I knew what he was about to ask. The dreaded nursing home question. What most of the world probably referred to as us sending our loves ones out to pasture. We paid somebody else to take care of our moms because we didn't have the love to do it ourselves.

"Do you think I haven't looked, Carl?" No matter what we chose, other than me, it was really expensive. We would just see how this went for a while. I would try to make it back home by about 6:30 each night.

I lasted about a week before I thought I was going to go insane. I'm not sure I ever got home by 6:30. I was truly exhausted every minute of every day. My girls were beginning to whine about everything not being quite right. And to get them to do any homework while I was preparing a meal at Mom's house was literally impossible. Carl had this passive-aggressive attitude, making me feel guilty as hell. But it was Mom who was truly driving me insane. She seemed bothered that I was there to help. "That lasagna yesterday had too much salt; I could hardly eat it. And it took me days to find my colander. I have no idea why you put it with the spices."

Some days I shrugged it off. Other days I wasn't so proud of. "It was *you*, Mom, who put the colander in the cupboard, not me!" I would leave frustrated with myself. Why would I start a fight of recall with a woman with dementia? Why did I let her get under my skin? A therapist would say it was because I wanted her to feel grateful. Which I think hit the nail right on the head. But it was more than that. She seemed to have no idea of the potential consequences. She didn't seem to realize that every minute I spent with her was time away from my life. Jesus, I sounded like a selfish bitch.

She couldn't walk well yet with her new hip. She just didn't have the strength or the balance. I wasn't sure she wouldn't fall with the front-wheel walker, the silver one with the torn-out tennis balls at the bottom so it wouldn't slide. But she so often would forget and try to walk alone. One would think with high-tech medicine we could come up with something a little less tacky than two busted tennis balls. Even though these would stick on the carpet all the time, it was still better than her roaming the hallway like a drunken fourteen-month-old. After about the third fall in a couple of days, I started to do what has probably saved countless babies from injury. I put a diaper on her. Actually, I gave her a double diaper, thinking that it might cushion her falls. Bruises and skin tears began to accumulate. I then bought a second walker and more tennis balls, so she couldn't help but notice one and might start to use it. Yet by the end of that first week, twice I arrived after work to find her on the floor.

"Mom! How long have you been here? Are you hurt?"

"Oh, I think I'm all right. You don't need to worry. I'll be fine." But her face was streaked with tears. Stoic perhaps, or had she just forgotten? Had she been down there all night?

"Mom, how many times am I going to have to tell you to use your walker? You're going to end up back in the hospital. Can't you do it for me? Please."

"It's so good you're here, darling. I was having a little trouble making it back to the bed. I'm pretty tired. I think I'm ready to sleep right now."

"Let me get you something to eat. What about some eggs on toast?"

"Allison, you're the best daughter I could have ever had. That sounds great. I'm suddenly feeling very hungry."

I realized that there was little point asking her when she last ate. Lately it seemed she just forgot to make something. It was not that she had no appetite. In fact, she was often ravenous, eating everything I put on her plate. Yet there were no dishes in the sink, no empty containers in the trash.

"Mom! What are you doing?"

"I'm about to make myself some lunch. I'm getting kind of hungry."

"I already made you an egg-salad sandwich."

"You're kidding. That's what I was thinking of making for myself. When did you get here?"

I started to learn that to challenge her with every forgotten statement was completely pointless. Or maybe I hadn't really learned because it still drove me crazy. I was just worn down. It was just easier to smile. So, we sat in her kitchen. At the same table and chairs that had been there a hundred years. She probably fed me as a baby in the same spot and marveled how it could take so long to shovel just one jar of Gerber sweet potato into my mouth. Now it was me watching her take about five minutes per bite of sandwich, adjusting dentures slightly before the next one. Thank heavens I didn't need to burp her.

My eyes wandered around the kitchen where we had spent so much time growing up. It really was hideous. I couldn't imagine selling this place without either doing a remodel or apologizing profusely to the would-be buyers. What did the seventies have to offer in the way of fashion? The colors still made me want to vomit. Yellow-green oven and stove. Orange-and-brown linoleum tile. Were there no other colors in their Crayola box?

I recalled my parents proudly stating that in 1954 they bought this house for just $17,500. It was a huge deal for them, and more money than they thought they would earn in a lifetime. It took thirty years to pay off the loan in its entirety. We had a huge party after they sent off their last check. It was much more than having another few hundred dollars every month that they could keep (or spend on us). Their pride of ownership was palpable to everyone who came through the doors that evening as they danced the night away. As we all could see, this was not a mansion, not even a nice house. But it was a good neighborhood, and it was their house that night, for the first time in thirty years.

It was strange to think about actually selling it one day. So many memories we had shared...

They say that grief is like this. One moment you're fine, and then *bam*, it hits you like a wave. This gut punch came out of nowhere. I started to cry and just couldn't stop. My mom's memories were fading so quickly. It was like termites were eating at this house, and in a few years, it would be withered down to nothing but a few random walls with no connection. But instead, the termites were working on her mind, and one by one the rooms were beginning to fade, the ochre colors of the seventies, the stucco ceiling disappearing. The laughter, the games, the friends and parties that came through here. The countless hours of homework, Thanksgiving meals, Christmas presents, gardening. I could close my eyes and start to reminisce, even smell some of my memories. And then I stared into hers—vacuous, concentration focused just on finishing the last few bites of her sandwich that had long gone cold.

I had to get out of there. I had done my daughterly duty for the day in any case. She was off the floor, she was fed now, and I had given her medicines.

This weekend I would have to do some shopping for her. The laundry also needed to be done. But for now, I was going home. I might even be able to help the girls with their homework. This thought actually made me smile.

25

November 2014

"HAVE YOU THOUGHT ABOUT LOWERING THE BED?" CARL ASKED. "I bet if there was just a mattress on the floor, she could crawl right up onto it and fall asleep in comfort. Actually, thinking about it, you probably still need the box springs—otherwise she wouldn't be able to stand up."

Carl, your typical man, liked to solve problems. He actually seemed to be pretty good at finding practical solutions where others would have been stumped. And so, this was a welcome evening. Not only did we not have a fight, he gave me a great idea. It had been gut-wrenching to find her on the floor. And scary.

After returning from the hospital, she was weaker and more confused. My logical mind wanted to scream at her for not using her walker every single time. *Why would you risk such misery?* Every time I found her down, sprawled on the floor like an unwanted doll, my mind would go through a horrible progression. *Is she alive? Did she break a bone? Did she have a heart attack or stroke? How long has she been lying there? Has she been crying because of pain or loneliness?* Only after talking to her a few moments and helping her to her feet did my anxiety start to drop. Maybe Carl's solution could work.

It was a Saturday, and the girls agreed to come with me to help Grandma. Now three weeks after she had come home, and more than two months postsurgery, she was walking pretty normally. No more diapers needed to cushion the falls. It had been me pretty exclusively those three weeks. Not a single day off. Carl did come once to help me break down the bed frame. It was then I started to notice that, one-on-one, she would continue to engage in conversation, but if there were others around, she would retreat into her own world. It reminded me of my earlier thoughts about how tired my brain would get when I was in Spain, thinking in Spanish. If the conversation drifted a little or I had trouble understanding, I would start to sit by myself and think in English. A welcome vacation for my overtaxed brain. I would never have done that when I was only with one other person. But once they had another Spanish speaker to talk to, I could relax and let them go on by themselves.

Mom seemed to be doing the same thing. When you would then ask her a question, she would act completely confused, as if she hadn't processed a word that had been said the last fifteen minutes.

The girls had clearly not adapted to this change. They had loved being with Grandma before, but lately it was not as fun for them. Like Janine, Grandma had treated them like they were the center of the universe. She used to engage with them 100 percent. Who doesn't like that kind of attention? But this Saturday was different, and Meredith was the first to notice.

"Grandma! Earth to Grandma. Don't you want to go for a walk?"

"What were you saying, sweetheart?"

"I said"—sassy mark—"why don't we go outside?"

"Of course you did," Mom finally replied. "That sounds like a good idea. Let me get my shoes on."

Unlike Mom, I was paying attention the entire time, even from the other side of the house. "Meredith, Sloane, remember to go slowly. She isn't long back from the hospital," I yelled from the laundry room.

It became quiet thereafter, and I started to think about this more while finishing folding the whites. *Mom won't know when to turn around*. Panic began. An odd, prickly sweat that seemed to come out of every one of my pores. I knew the girls would never leave her to get lost. But they could run around her for half an hour easy.

Down to only mismatched socks, I tried to calm myself. Yet the image of her teetering wouldn't get out of my head. I had already seen her physically fatigued from just walking around the house. I would never forgive myself if she fell on hard cement—this time with no diaper or carpet to help her.

I ran. My entire being began to scream. My muscles on fire, my lungs burning,

How did they get so far? Or was I just that out of shape? I think I had only been running for five minutes when I saw them in the distance. Fear is still one giant motivator because when I finally got close enough, I realized Mom was really limping and was able to speed up more. The girls, oblivious, about thirty yards ahead, were playing some type of tag.

Was Mom actually going to fall? She was limping perilously close to the top of the levee. A fall would have her rolling into the river for sure. That last hundred yards I think I did in ten seconds flat, crashing more than I had planned into her back. If I had done that to Carl, he would have just laughed, and I would have bounced off of him. But Mom and I were like an ice-skating couple that barely managed to stay on our feet. That sure got her attention. My heart was probably going 180. This was definitely not what I had envisioned when I was debating which would be nicer, chores or a walk outside.

Five minutes probably went by before I positioned Mom on the nearest bench. My heart was still pounding. We both desperately needed a rest. But by the time the girls circled back around to us like a couple of buzzing bees, she seemed to have forgotten the whole thing. She was certainly stunned for a few moments after I had first pushed her, then enveloped her to prevent her from falling. Now, she simply exclaimed, "Guess who I found? Your mom decided to come join us."

What was even funnier than the fact that she had forgotten that I almost pushed her into the river was that the girls had noticed me right away. Once they knew I was with Grandma, that extended their leash significantly, so they hadn't bothered to come circling back until now. By the time they returned, I had been on the bench for long enough that my lungs no longer burned. The panic sweat and the real sweat had dried and mingled in my purple Lululemon hoodie. It was good the breeze continued to blow steadily through the trees.

Our return trip was uneventful, which made it glorious. The sun was shining, the girls were laughing, and Mom was clearly very happy. She had missed companionship and seemed to brighten with all of us around. She became quite chatty, wanting to know every detail about the girls' activities. Even at the time I recognized that her focus was unusual. She had become clear, and no one watching would have ever suspected she couldn't last a day without some calamity happening. This was definitely not the meek woman I would bring to the doctors' office who hardly said a word. This was Mom. She was back.

"How long has Sloane been playing the flute?" she asked.

"This is her second year, and she really likes it. She picked it up quite quickly. I tried it too for a while because the awful noise she made at the beginning was giving me headaches. But I was no better than she, and in weeks, she was able to make a crystal-clear sound. I still look and sound like a kid blowing on the top of a Coke bottle to make noise."

"Oh, I bet she's just wonderful."

"At the end of the school year, she's going to be part of the orchestra doing a recital for the parents. Would you like to come?"

"Do you have to ask? I'm so excited I think I just peed a little."

I must have given her that look. I tried to not do it, but Carl would say that I scrunched up my nose and rolled my eyes a little even when I didn't notice I was doing it.

"That was actually a joke," my mom said to defuse my unhappy look. "But it does embarrass me. I know you help with the laundry, and you must smell that I do pee a lot. I just can't help it, and those pads aren't all that amazing." At this, she grabbed me by the shoulders and with clear eyes exclaimed, "We could become millionaires if we came up with a tiny little urine tampon! How hard could it be? Why not get the urine at the source so it doesn't have to dribble into your pants?"

The laughter started slowly but couldn't be held back. Maybe it was the subject matter or the visual of a little tiny tampon. Whatever it was, we couldn't stop.

At this, the girls came running back. We were laughing so hard I think I might have peed my own pants.

"What's so funny?" they asked in unison. Which, of course, made us laugh even harder. Neither one of us was prepared to tell them. We looked at each other as if we had just been asked what sex was like. Mom was back. And we continued to laugh the entire way home.

On a recent visit, Dr. Metcalf had told me that Mom's progression with dementia was more rapid than typical. A visit where he also added the scary parts that I was learning on my own. Dementia is not just about forgetting things. It is so much more all-encompassing. It plays with their emotions. It steals their judgment. It removes their personality.

I hadn't realized how bad things had become until this sudden light—that was the only thing I could call it. Her eyes were bright, she was laughing, she was alive again. Maybe it was the sunshine, the briskness of the breeze on this California winter day. But I needed more of this. "It's the drugs!" I suddenly exclaimed, surprising everyone. "Did I actually just say that out loud?" The girls probably thought I was going batty along with Mom.

Just hours before, Mom had seemed lost in her own world, but now we were having a full-on, adult conversation. And for the first and only time she let me know she was scared too. I got the feeling that she knew what was happening to her. She described all too vividly the sounds she heard after the lights went out in the rehab facility where she was recovering from her hip surgery. The moaning, the blaring TVs, the caregivers shouting—perhaps to be heard, maybe from frustration. There was almost never quiet. When there was, a certain dread would develop because nothing good ever really happened. Days would just bring one crisis after another, one death after another. A place so full of people and yet the loneliest place you have ever been. "It was like a Stephen King hotel, where residents would come for a while and only the lucky would get out alive."

This was the last insightful, clear statement that Mom ever made to me. She did have little jumps back to lucidity after that. But none as long or remarkable as that one. And maybe it was this horrible image that changed me, made me so stoic. How could I ever send her back there? A place she didn't simply dislike because it wasn't home. A place where she actually felt dread. I vowed that no matter what it took out of me, I would take care of her. I wouldn't force her to go back.

26

March 2015

A FUNNY THING HAPPENED ON THE WAY TO THE FORUM. I HAD been settling into my new life as a caregiver. A word that sounded so nice but now left me feeling the same way I did when I heard the phrase *happily ever after*. Those fairy tales and movies make it seem like every day after marriage is going to be blissful. *Caregiver*, similarly, is a word that invokes positive emotions, a sense of altruism, warmth. But the truth is that it is soul sucking. At least when it comes to caring for someone who is only getting worse.

It had been seven months since Mom fell and broke her hip. It seemed just as long since she had said anything lucid. I tried to re-create our recent walk alongside the river, but...her vocabulary was starting to seem like a looped recording. If we were outside, she talked only about the weather. No matter what music was playing, I would hear some story about Frank Sinatra. The smell of food would get her going about cooking and holidays. All of which are fine as topics the first thirty-seven times you heard them. I felt like I had to act surprised or pretend to be attentive when I heard once again the story of her ruining the first Thanksgiving she was hosting her in-laws.

Carl was the one who heard most of my whining on the subject. I had become so self-absorbed that my friends and colleagues were starting to avoid me. It seemed that I, too, was sounding like a loop. An endless stream of whining. I was starting to hate myself. But if I were to head to a confessional where I could say what I was really thinking, all others would join the bandwagon to start calling me a witch. Or another rhyming word.

What I would tell the priest would be related to my father. He was still alive. At least according to Mom, and that was what affected me the most. It had been more than two years, yet my grief was only slowly fading. The way I would have preferred to deal with it would have been random, rare, nostalgic thoughts. Like when I walked into my old room and remembered him coming to comfort me at night. He hadn't been a storyteller. He didn't try and ease my teenage angst with a similar story. He just listened and cared. And at the end, he would give me a bear hug so comforting, so loving, that I would just fall asleep.

I thought, *I could really use him right now.* To listen to me. To remind me how lucky I was and all that I had going for me. To force me to see all the positives and just to laugh.

"When your father comes home, will you remind me to ask him to fix the sprinklers?"

I might be in the middle of doing the dishes when she would turn from the TV to shout at me. Wherever my mind was, I would suddenly get pulled to thoughts about my dad. Initially I would try and reason with her. I'd be gentle and sweet, letting her know that Dad wasn't coming home. The first several times I did this, she burst into tears, "learning" of his death. More recently, they it had led to arguments, with her insisting something random like that he was away visiting his family in Colorado. I would like to say that I never argued with her about his death, but that would be untrue. I had learned that if I just agreed with her, she didn't get bothered at all. Yet I still stewed. Part of my problem was that I needed to be right. But it was more than that. Every time that Dad came up in the conversation, it opened up my grief.

Megan was the only one who seemed to understand me on this

one. Carl thought I was a lunatic for challenging her on any fact. But every time she made Dad seem to be alive, it was a reminder of what I had lost. I didn't want to be reminded, and it was happening every single day.

All of these emotions were what probably set us on the path to one of the funniest, most unexpected days we had had as a family. Well, funny in retrospect. Like most disasters, it wasn't so funny at the time.

It all began simply enough. "Carl, can I ask you a huge favor? I need a break. Even if it's just one night. Janine texted earlier and asked if I would go out for drinks tomorrow, just to catch up. So, I was wondering if you could stop by Mom's after the girls are somewhat settled. All you have to do is warm up some dinner and give her her medicines. Don't worry about the dishes or getting her ready for bed. She can sleep in her clothes for one night if she forgets to undress."

My husband, staring at the TV, didn't answer.

"Carl?"

"Sorry, lost in thought there for a while. I was thinking for a while that I've only got a few seconds to come up with an excuse."

"You are wicked!" I exclaimed.

"No, I'm not. I said yes. I'm not wicked; I'm just a little slow in coming up with a good excuse. Must be getting old. Allison, of course I'll do that. Just don't be mad if I screw anything up."

After a quick peck on the lips, I was at my phone texting Janine, smiling from ear to ear. It made me feel a bit like a kid who had been told they didn't have to go to school the next day. As for Carl, I'm not sure what he felt, perhaps a little altruistic. His task would be simple enough, I told Janine.

When I got home, I found out I had been wrong. Carl's night didn't go so well. He had meant to leave the girls alone for only half an hour or so. It didn't seem like a big deal, as they were thirteen and eleven by this time. That half hour had stretched to almost two by the time he came home, which can get you feeling that the worst has happened. It's easy to imagine so many possible things that can go wrong when you leave your kids alone. Fortunately, other than being very hungry and having skipped homework, they were fine. They had gone straight to their favorite antidote for boredom and watched Netflix the whole time.

Carl wasn't so lucky. He had been attacked by the police! My couldn't-be-more-law-abiding Carl. And he was the worse for wear. His glasses were messed up, he had a bit of a shiner, and he swore that his wrists were killing him from the handcuffs.

"What happened?" yielded a story that was hard to believe. One that would make the likelihood of Carl watching my mom alone again pretty remote.

She hadn't recognized him.

It was true, since the hip fracture, he hadn't seen her much at all. But she had known him for more than fifteen years. It all started to seem strange when she didn't answer the door.

I began to shake. Though I might have had more wine than advised, I was suddenly sober. Falling into the couch with my coat still on and my handbag tangling under me, I stared at Carl, incredulous. I had never considered anything going wrong. "Why didn't you just call out? Surely she would have recognized your voice."

"Allison, you're not getting it. She didn't recognize me! But that's not the point," continued Carl. "I stopped shouting, 'It's me, Carl' because it was so quiet. There had to be something wrong."

I imagined him walking through the door. Nothing making a sound, no TV, no radio, no noise from the bathroom. "Allison, I went from getting prepared for small talk to complete fear in about five seconds. I was convinced I would find her down somewhere. The only thing missing from my personal horror movie at that point was the eerie music."

Now my scary movie had begun as I sat, unsure whether to take off my coat. It was true that I had worried about finding her down. But the eerie quiet experience, the one where you think she might be dead—I don't get that often. And it somehow seemed worse hearing it from Carl. The only good news was that I already had a spoiler alert. He hadn't started off with...those words you just don't want to hear.

"I found myself actually creeping around now, not knowing what to expect. Each corner I turned, I would call out her name. Silence. My heart was pounding as I opened up her bedroom door."

"Oh God, please just tell me," I yelled, unable to contain myself any longer.

"I'm sorry, honey. Don't worry. Nothing bad happened to her," Carl said with a little foreshadowing. "Though she may have gotten a sore throat from screaming so loudly.

"'*Get out!*' she yelled over and over. And then came the shoe. She winged a loafer at me so hard it might have put a dent in the wall. I would have checked, but I was busy dodging the second one coming for my head. There was no point in trying to convince her she knew me. She had terror in her eyes."

"Oh my God. What did you do then?" I implored.

"I shut the door as fast as I could. That's what I did. My heart was pumping pretty fast, and I just wanted to get out of there. Which would have been my best move, in retrospect. But I couldn't disappoint my wife. I came to help, so I figured I might as well get her dinner. She was clearly too afraid to come out of her room."

As Carl continued, I imagined him banging things around just to make enough noise to let her know that he was still there. So that he didn't get something worse than a shoe thrown at his head. And it was hard not to forgive him for simply making peanut butter and jelly sandwiches. That was more than probably most would have done under the circumstances.

"As I opened the door to go, I was feeling pretty good about how I had handled myself. That is, until I got tackled by the police." Carl emphasized that last word rather dramatically. "I think I saw the police car only a second before the tackle, which sent me sprawling. Handcuffs and a knee to my back came next. The only thing missing was the taser—and I hate to say, but that is probably only because I am white."

"She must have called." I spoke softly, the fact suddenly dawning on me. I grasped his hand at this point. Carl's eyes indicated he was a little shaken. Definitely not the confident blue eyes that I typically see staring back. I could imagine her 911 call, quickly convincing the police of a home invasion. Poor Carl, walking out the door, seemingly caught in the act. It was hard to blame the police.

"But they didn't exactly have to jump me! Whatever happened to diplomacy? Couldn't they just have said, 'Sir, we have a few questions for you'?"

I finally started to remove my coat, mainly because I needed something to do. Carl clearly needed to tell an adult his story. When he had returned, it was only the girls, and the last thing he wanted to do was retell how he was attacked by Grandma and then almost arrested. But he was also angry at me. Somehow this would become my fault. The humiliation he had felt while lying facedown on the front lawn in front of looky-loos from the neighborhood—that was something he would not forget.

"Do you realize it took those officers about fifteen minutes to figure it all out? Listen to my story, grab the front door key out of my pocket." Carl continued, more exasperated by the minute, "How many burglars are going to have a copy of the front door key and a wedding photo of themselves on the mantel?"

I had to confess, I wouldn't have thought this investigation would have taken more than a minute or two. My mind conjured up the video: white guy, fifty-one years old, mop of dark-brown hair, six foot two, 190 pounds, coming out of house from *That '70s Show*, quickly being subdued on the front lawn. Two white officers with pistols drawn, making it clear that Carl was supposed to remain motionless after they tackled him. Handcuffed out front for all the neighbors to see. It sounded like the only thing missing was the yellow Do Not Cross tape and the helicopter. I didn't dare tell Carl that the song that started to play in my head at that moment was the theme song from *COPS*.

It sounded like the police left as quickly as they had come. With not much of an apology either, according to Carl. Apparently, Mom thought they were wonderful. They got her out of the bedroom, reassured her nothing was wrong. They even helped her get a drink to take the pills that Carl had left out for her. I was sure she offered them supper. Obviously, while one officer was playing out this Andy Griffith scene inside, the other was still kneeling on my husband's back. Fifteen minutes of discomfort that must have felt like hours.

"So, were you actually arrested? Will this go on your record?" I asked, fearful of the response. Fortunately, the answer was no. But I knew I was going to be making this up for a long time. This was going to require more than a back rub. Let's just leave it at that.

Even worse, this felt like the incident with the Pearson family who lived down the street from us. I remember when they asked my brother to feed their dog while they were away. We all knew their dog, Jasper, a large, generally friendly rottweiler. Without his owners, however, he wouldn't let my brother—or any of us—into the backyard. The only way he survived that week was the food we threw over the fence. Luckily, they had a swimming pool for his water. After that incident, they had to board their dog every time they went away. Nobody in the neighborhood would dare try again after that.

I guess I was back to my analogy with the animals; yet it seemed I was similarly trapped. If I were the only one she recognized, then I would need to be on a 24/7 vigil as the only one who could help. Unless, of course, I sent her to her own kennel, a skilled nursing facility. Something I just could not bring myself to do.

27

March 2015

MEANWHILE, WHILE CARL WAS SUFFERING THROUGH HIS rather unfortunate night, I was dancing and singing in my car to "Stressed Out" by Twenty One Pilots. A little ironic as, for the first time in a while, I was feeling happy on the way to giddy. I was using my Get Out of Jail Free card and flying like a bird out of my cage, a feeling that didn't stop when I turned into the parking lot.

That blue Toyota RAV4 with the 26.2 stickers—yes, more than one—I would have noticed it anywhere. Janine was here first. She was always so organized and punctual it was hard to believe she had so much clutter in her car. If Janine arrived anywhere and there were some athletic event, she would be prepared. Not only would she have her bike helmet and shoes, yoga mat, Clif bars to feed an army, and rain gear, I bet she would also have a tent, sleeping bag, and snowshoes in the backseat. *Where does she get the time?* I felt guilty saying no to at least half of the things she invited me to even before the start of my caregiving gig. Not to mention the minor detail that I sucked. If I ran a mile in under ten minutes, it was a miracle. At the finish she would always be looking fresh, congratulating me profusely while offering me a sampling of all the treats she had gathered.

Now, inside Zinfandel Grille, it would probably be the opposite. As I wouldn't be spending unnecessary effort trying to just breathe, I would be the one talking. For this was my element, with a credit card at my favorite spot. I liked the patio best because it felt like you were the only ones out there under a cool canopy of jasmine.

"Allison, I'm so glad you're here. I was starting to think you were avoiding me."

"Like that time you kept insisting I would do fine running that full marathon," I said with a smile as I sat down. "Janine, if you only knew how much I would have rather been doing just about anything else these last few weeks. I'm mentally and physically spent. It seems like I had to move heaven and earth just to get this time with you. You should have seen the look on Carl's face when I asked him to be with Mom tonight. If I ever doubt that he is in love with me, remind me of that face. He looked like a basset hound who realized he lost the bone he had buried. And he still said yes."

She added, "When you're getting married and the priest is giving that whole speech about 'to honor and cherish,' maybe he should throw in, 'to do something you really, really, really don't want to do but your partner needs it more than anything else in the world.'" We both laughed.

"You can always make me laugh, Janine. Yes, that's exactly what it felt like. And you know why he doesn't want to do it? It's awful. Everything about it is becoming a nightmare of a chore." Janine made a sympathetic face. "As soon as I walk through her front door, it hits me. That smell is indescribable, but now I know where that nursing home odor comes from. At least once a week, something is soiled. Poop in the bed, in her pants, down her leg. I think I've found urine in every room of the house at some point. On the chairs. It's not a doctors' office where every surface is plastic or vinyl and you get all of it out. And you can't just replace a couch, bed, or carpet after every mess. So, you invest in hundreds of dollars of cleaning products. I've bought more rubber gloves than a veterinarian. And yet…"

"The smell."

"Yes," I reply faintly. "I've cried trying to teach her to use her bedside commode. It's just not going to happen. Not 100 percent of the time. And, in this case, 90 percent is not an A. A five-minute cleanup thus becomes half an hour. Her mind just thinks of the real bathroom, and I can't teach her anything new, like using a commode. I imagine her trying to get to the bathroom as fast as her legs will shuffle her along. And then…"

"What does she say?"

"She's not ungrateful, if that's what you mean. At least, I don't think so. I feel a sense of embarrassment from her. But what she actually says while I'm on my hands and knees? It's usually small talk, where she repeats probably twenty times, 'Don't worry, Allison, I'll get to it later.' Do you see my hands? I'm done with manicures, and it's killing me."

"Oh, Allison, I don't know what to say. My parents really didn't convalesce; they both died in the hospital. My experience was so much more sterile than yours sounds. The flip side is that I didn't have much time to grieve. For Dad, none at all. I just got the phone call. Remember that song 'Dance with My Father'? I loved and hated that song at the same time. It's maybe the most beautiful song I've ever heard, but when it was popular, I had to buy more makeup." I didn't know what song she was referring to.

"You're giving me that blank stare. You can't be serious that you don't know that song."

I said, "Please sing, Janine, you have such a lovely voice. I'd really like to hear something beautiful."

"Are you going to make me sing it? I know you've heard it before. I haven't decided what you will owe me if I start to cry in the middle of it, but believe me, I'll wring something out of you."

And there under the jasmine, my best friend sung me a few lines of the most beautiful song. I could feel my own father lifting me in his arms as the father in the song spun his child around till she collapsed into sleep.

"Allison, that's absolutely not fair. You aren't the one who should be crying. You made me sing it. Do you know how hard it is to make it through that song without your voice cracking?"

"Janine, that is the nicest tribute song I've ever heard. And I'm not lying; I don't know if I've ever heard it."

"I still think you must have heard it. I just don't sound like a man named Luther."

"Ladies, what would you like to order?" politely interrupted the waitress. "And can I just say, I couldn't help but hear you sing. I will gladly bring you an extra dessert on the house. And I know you haven't been here long, so I can come back in a bit if you like."

"We've been here so often I can not only order now, I know what she will want too. I'll have the mustard chicken, but can you leave off the lemon? And my friend, Allison, will want the grilled salmon...and you can just go ahead and put my lemon on top of hers."

Sipping my water, I could see Janine's eyes contemplating a question. No matter how friendly you are with someone, how many years you have known them, there are some topics that are touchy. And I could tell she was about to start talking about one. So, I just waited.

Finally, while I was busy soaking up the oil and vinegar on my focaccia bread:

"Have you ever considered a nursing home?"

Another slice of bread.

"Well, yes" came my delayed reply. "But I don't think I ever could."

Thinking about it absently, I redipped my bread into the oil and vinegar.

Janine seemed content to wait at this point and gave a half smile.

"Have you ever been inside a nursing home?" I began. "They are beyond depressing. I just don't think it is something I personally would ever want. So, why would I send my mom to one?" The bread seemed to stick in my throat, demanding water before I continued.

"I will never forget visiting one. Years ago, I think I was in my twenties—I recall it vividly but can't remember why I was there in the first place. This one patient started to wail. Quietly at first. As time went by, more earnestly. 'Help. Help. Get me out of here.'

"With the first cry, I got to my feet but soon realized there were staff around, and so I sat back down. What did I know? But he just kept on going. 'I'm not supposed to be here. They just dropped me here. Help. Get me out of here.'"

"That sounds horrible. What happened?" Janine prodded.

"That wasn't the worst part. I would have come to his aid if he were choking or something serious. But what he clearly needed was comfort, and there was no one. I mean, there were people around, but no one was doing anything. Lights and buzzes were also constantly going off for those in their rooms who similarly were needing attention. But clearly this scenario was not new to anyone working there. I gathered that if they went, the call button or the screaming would stop for a short while but then restart as soon as they returned to their desks. So, the nurses just sat.

"And still that was not the part that made me never forget the whole affair. It was the sudden and awful truth that came from another resident, who yelled '*Shut up!!* You're never getting out of here. You're going to die here, just like all of us. So, just shut up and eat your food!'

"And then there was silence. It was deafening. About twenty people all sitting, eating their lunch, waiting to see what was going to happen next. And about three or four minutes later, once again came the plaintive cry of that first man: 'Help. Please help me get out of here.'

"During the entire thing, I don't think the nurses even looked up once. I swore to myself that I could never let my parents live like that. Alone. Living just waiting to die."

Our conversation, which was worse than a funeral, was thankfully interrupted by our food. It smelled great, as usual. And I would have been happy if oatmeal were being served to change this topic. I'd have bet Janine was sorry she had asked.

She did change the topic. "How are the girls doing? How's Carl? I had such a good time with them at the company softball game."

"They're fine. Doing really well, actually. Sloane joined a soccer team for this year and is loving it. It's not that Meredith is bad at sports, but Sloane is so much more athletic. She's a running machine. The coach has tried to keep her in one position, but she's on a mission once she gets out there. One time he had to actually pull her out of the game. We were up six to zero, and he gathered all the girls around and said, 'We aren't trying to score anymore, so if you get past halfway, just kick the ball forward and come back into your own half.' The other girls seemed to get it. Not Sloane. She was dribbling around like Brandi Chastain even though there was no one to pass to. All the other girls were standing back in their half of the field. After about the third time, he just had to replace her. She couldn't figure out what she was doing wrong."

"Is Meredith jealous?"

"I would think she would be, but... How old was your daughter when she started to think about boys? It seems that her friends talk about boys as much as they do anything else. She and her friends will sit around for hours looking at teen magazines, commenting about every single photo. By the end of an afternoon, they will have debated the best dressed, best hair, and cutest smile categories, and *WINNER* will be printed in red. So, jealous? No. Completely preoccupied, yes. And the drama. It seems at least once a week I have ruined her life. It's so easy to do. Her favorite socks weren't washed before Friday. Asparagus, 'Yuck.' Reminding her of the orthodontist appointment. In her mind, I've killed her so many times."

"Isn't she just twelve?"

"Thirteen, but close."

"I don't think I had my first serious crush until I was in the eighth grade. Oh, now that I think about it, that's when you are twelve or thirteen."

I nodded.

"They just seem so young, I guess. Which probably means we are getting old!"

I chuckled. "Speaking of old, Janine, I can't tell you how tired I've been lately. Every time the alarm goes off, I want to just throw it. I'm literally in a fog the first few hours of every day. And during the day, I yawn over and over. I feel like I have begun a second job as a full-time maid and cook for my mother. You could probably throw in personal trainer as well, because she doesn't really go outside unless I take her."

"I may not be the best one to give you advice, but perhaps you could consolidate things by bringing her into your home. You would have more time to spend with her, you wouldn't have the commute time, and the rest of the family could help with some things."

"Is everything tasting OK?" said the waitress out of nowhere. We must have been too engrossed in our conversation to see her coming.

"Yes, it's all good as usual. Thank you," I replied. "You know Janine, I have thought about that. I haven't even broached the subject though. It seems so hard on so many levels. The first problem is where to put her. We have a three-bedroom house. There's no den or library. I can't see trying to convert our garage. And so the girls would have to share. My ears just cringed a little, anticipating the whining. I even though of selling her house and using the money to put a mother-in-law quarters outside."

"That's a great idea. I like that a lot."

"But there's no time. That would take months, and I think she's already unsafe. And it seems like I need to do more for her every day. Sometimes just emotionally. She calls all the time to discuss the most random things. The other day it was a plea to help her invest in windmills. Don't laugh, I'm serious. I know it sounds a bit like Don Quixote. She started going on and on about the new way to harness energy that will take the place of coal and never run out. At first she sounded somewhat knowledgeable, but then I realized she was reading from the email scam directly. They actually promised that they would engrave her name on one of the windmills if she acted now. All she needed to do was to wire them $10,000, and she would get a monthly letter with how much profit she made from the wind. I looked up the company online, and there were so many 'danger' responses that came up. Also, some sad stories of seniors losing thousands. I made a note to myself that I will have to formally become her conservator. I wasn't waiting, though, I cut up all her credit cards and grabbed all of her checks. No need to donate money to Operation Windmill."

"What? And lose out on the opportunity to have your names engraved. Sign me up! What was the name of that company again?"

I grimaced.

"Don't scrunch up your face like that. You've got to admit, it's kind of funny."

And then I did laugh. It had been a long time. "Janine, we've got to do this again soon. I needed to get out, have a little wine, and relax. You two are empty nesters. Just come over one night soon, make us all dinner."

"If you keep up with those stories, I bet even Tyler would help with the cooking. I miss you, Allison. And let me know if I can help. I don't want you jumping off a bridge. But you look well, anyway. You've lost some weight."

"I don't know if it's stress or just not enough time to eat. I wish it were exercise, because that always keeps me sane. Still, it's nice to lose a little weight. But that reminds me of a joke. Are you ready?"

She nodded, looking slightly worried.

"Life is like a box of chocolates… Neither lasts long if you're fat."

"Oh, Allison, you had better not tell that at your work. You accountants aren't exactly known for your nice bodies. Have a good night and keep on smiling."

After a hug that probably only lasted twenty seconds but felt uncomfortably long, we parted. Still, I needed that touch. She kept me grounded.

I opened my door. Whereas Janine's car was filled with clutter for adventure, my wagon for the people was filled with what most parents might expect. Suckers that lay stuck to the carpet, dolls with limbs askew, crumbs surrounding Cheerios like orbiting satellites, and a whole host of other discards that become difficult to even name. Every month or two I would spend the twenty bucks to go through a car wash. Carl seemed to enjoy washing the outside, but the inside would start to look like a mosh pit at Chuck E. Cheese if I didn't pony up the money once in a while.

Now, as I entered my car, I realized my salmon leftovers would just mingle with all of the other odors that I had grown to ignore. I thought, *Surely it won't be too much longer before Febreze calls me to be in their commercial.*

28

March 2015
Nancy

OH, THAT SUN FEELS GOOD. LYING IN HER BED JUST FOURTEEN inches off the ground, Nancy felt at peace. Quiet. The house was practically soundless. A large, three-bedroom ranch-style house in what had become an old neighborhood. There were no children running up and down the streets as before. Drifting in and out of sleep had become quite easy.

Nancy still inhabited the master bedroom, as being close to the bathroom was a must. The room had been modified to a Scandinavian minimalist style. No clutter to trip on. Dressers moved to other rooms to afford more space for bedside commode and front-wheel walker. A dry-erase board, another idea from Allison's husband, where she left notes, reminders. Adjacent was a calendar with a huge month and day currently displaying flowers indicative of spring. The TV stand sorely missing an actual television hung on the opposite wall. When it had adorned this part of her room, she never left. Appetite and thirst seemingly were not as important as *Good Morning America* or *Oprah*.

Pain. This was probably the first thought that entered her mind every morning. Back, knees especially. *Young people have no idea how long it can take to just get out of bed in the morning. Everything is stiff and sore. In fact, you know you have become old when you wake up feeling more pain than when you went to bed. How can that be? All you did was lie there. It's like the marrow in your bones congeals like bacon grease left in the pan overnight.*

Oh, but that sun feels good. It's helping to warm up my bones. It's so warm now. I must have fallen back asleep. I hope Good Morning America *is still on.*

"Larry, do you remember wanting to stay in bed all day? Larry?"

This house is just too quiet sometimes. The leaf blowers were the primary intruders in her somewhat uncluttered mind; otherwise, she had only her own voice to listen to most of the time. That and her music and TV. *It's got to be time for* Good Morning America.

And the dance began. The next fifteen minutes she would spend wandering with her walker, straightening slightly this time but never coming close to reaching her now-diminished five feet nine inches height. She would use the commode because it was higher and easier to get up from than the regular toilet. She would manage to get underwear on by rocking so much that she could have been mistaken for a marionette doll. And then finally out of her room for the first time that day sometime around nine fifteen, according to the large-numbered clock displaying brightly at her bedside.

Parched. Suddenly thirsty, she made it to the kitchen for water, trembling hand steadying somewhat when she finally started to pour the lukewarm water into her cup. Anything too cold seemed unpleasant. Shuffling more quickly, she made it to her chair: large, blue, inviting. Directly in front of the forty-inch screen with sound permanently on thirty-eight. Indelicately, she crashed backward into the comfortable recliner, exhausted. *Now time to rest and enjoy the rest of the morning.*

I really like George Stephanopoulos. He's so handsome. Oh, now they're talking about that angel, Princess Diana. The only thing she ever did wrong was marry Charles. Though maybe if given a choice...

Damn, I just peed.

My Larry is so much more handsome. He's my prince. Would have been fun to live in a castle, though. And those dresses. I think I could have accepted a little ugly to wear all those dresses. But not that much ugly. Plus, he just seems mean or maybe boring. Those ears could help him fly.

Prince Charles may not be my cup of tea, but he sure is better than Dick Cheney. Why does Larry always turn the TV down so you can hardly hear it? Richard, I could marry a Richard. But if he insisted on calling himself Dick, that would be it. Engagement off.

Always her message machine. "Allison, who would you prefer to marry Prince Charles or Dick Cheney? I don't know about you, but I think I might kill myself first. Your father is so much better. And he never would lay a hand on me, certainly wouldn't shoot me in the face. Do you remember that? Bush seems like such a nice man—did he need an attack dog? Why can't we have a president like Kennedy again? He was everything: smart, nice, beautiful wife.

"Did you buy me that yogurt? I think it was peach. It really tasted good. I'll have to get some more of those when I go shopping today. After I clean myself up, but not now. I'm resting a bit because my back is pretty sore. Will you—"

Damn beep. I hate that beep.

"Allison, like I was saying. Whatever, you get the idea. How are the kids? They grow up so fast, don't they? I remember when you and Jeremy were small. You were always so nice to him. He was like your own little doll. You liked your dolls for sure, but you preferred playing with Jeremy. I wished we had more money so you could have your own room, but you played so well together. He's grown up into such a nice young man. Why'd he have to move so far away? I never get to see his kids. Maybe Sloane and Meredith can come over this weekend. I'll make them their—"

Ugh. That beep hurts my ears. I'll just call her again later. She's always so busy.

Starving. Watching Nancy in her blue recliner would be quite unexciting. Occasional smiles, blinking, head sagging down toward her chest. If her lights were on sensors, they would almost always be off as the rise and fall of her chest would fail to trigger them back on. Hunger would be fleeting, but when it came, it was enough to propel her on the journey back to the kitchen where she had taken out a yogurt several hours earlier.

Many years ago, this kitchen was bustling. The kitchen slept only at night along with everyone else. But now the efforts were too great. Simple ruled the day, and a new favorite was the old classic peanut butter and jelly. Almost no time to prepare and just a minute to clean.

I should probably get something to eat. Am I even hungry? Of course I am—it's lunchtime, isn't it? It's funny how different things are now without the kids around. It seemed like there was always something going on in the kitchen. I was either making a meal or cleaning up afterward. And could those kids eat. The funny thing is I could have served them the same meal every day and they wouldn't have minded a bit. It was when I ventured to some real cookbook challenges that I got the most grief. A vegetarian lasagna was far more likely to get bad reviews than baked chicken, mashed potatoes, and vegetables. And Jeremy, he probably had fifteen thousand peanut butter and jelly sandwiches. The tough decisions were chunky versus creamy. Sometimes he would vary the jam. Probably a good thing. I was not the best cook in the world. No one would mistake me for Julia Child.

You know, thinking of peanut butter and jelly, that doesn't sound like a bad idea right now. That way I could sit down and rest soon. But let me get out of these clothes. Allison would get her panties in a twist if I were wearing the same thing she saw me in last night. Yikes, they smell. I better start the laundry right now.

Was it always this complicated? I thought there were just two holders, one for the soap and one for the softener. This one has three. I don't want to make a mistake. Maybe I should just leave it for now—I may remember in a bit. Why would there possibly be three holders? But it sure beats drying clothes out on the line. That really took all day, and the clothes would be stiff as a board. Where did I find the time to get everything done back then? Laundry, ironing, cooking, clearing up, cleaning the house. They all seem to be easier and quicker now. Except that washing machine. I'll have to ask Allison which hole I put the soap into. Maybe I should just put a little soap in all three of them. I don't really need the softener.

You know what I need? I need some music. That always helps make chores go faster. That's actually inspiring me to do the laundry. Nancy's stomach growled. *Maybe I should go and make some lunch.*

Oh, hey, a sandwich! "Allison, are you here? Did you make me a sandwich?" Nobody answered. *That's exactly what I need right now. Maybe she came and left while I was working on the laundry.*

Oh, I love this song. Never really knew what Roberta was singing about. She seemed so sad, though. So lonely. Nancy felt lonely too sometimes. She sighed. *The house can get so quiet with everyone gone. Maybe that's why I talk out loud to myself sometimes. Or sing. I've always liked to sing.*

But nobody beats Roberta Flack. What I would do to sing like she can. "You know, Larry, you make me hurt like she sounds in this song." Nobody answered.

She just seems so sad. What's there to be sad about? Life is beautiful. Maybe I'll go outside. It's pretty right now. I can do the dishes later.

Oh, that sun feels so good. I really love gardening. I should start doing more of it again. The flowers are still nice back here. Did I leave the music on? Maybe Larry will turn it off. I just want to enjoy the birds and the sun.

Got to run. Urine could come so fast and unexpectedly. Her feet were seemingly glued to the floor, shuffling more than walking. Minutes passed by the time she reached her commode, and by then there was little point. She was soaked. Again. Shame. Defeat. Another marionette dance for more new clothes.

The living room was bright and warm. Facing the front, she could watch what little occurred outside 1426 Mulberry. And she could rest here. Life was tiring, but this was home. Sitting in her worn and oversize green sweatpants and simple cotton pullover shirt with three buttons, she faded in and out of sleep.

A man suddenly caught her eye. Not too surprising to see someone walking along the street—but he was walking with a purpose, quickly crossing the road toward her house. Hair rose on her arms and the back of her neck; instinct told her something was wrong. Fear, such a strong motivator, helped overcome the screaming pain in her back, and she was soon out of the line of sight. And she was right, footfalls loudly echoed on the steps. A short scream escaped her lips as the door handle turned slightly. Panic glued her feet to the floor. Her heart was pounding so quickly she feared passing out. The lock turned. *Nightline, 20/20,* and countless murder mysteries had prepared her mind for the worst. She was moving as if through glue, but her mind willed her to go as fast as she possibly could.

She had yet to enter her room when she heard the door open and a loud "Hello! Nancy?" fill the house.

"How could he possibly know my name?" *He must have been watching me, stalking me.*

Terror. Physical signs of terror are familiar to us all. It's quite different from fear. Fear, you can still think. Terror leaves you frozen, physically and mentally.

Nancy cowered by the one dresser remaining in the room, holding nothing but a small clock now announcing 7:28 p.m., shaking so badly she could hardly stand. Leaning heavily against the dresser for support, she heard him hunting for her. Calling out her name, he was approaching. As fast as she could, she undid the

Velcro on her shoes, the sound breaking her attempted silence but at least giving her a weapon.

As the door opened, her senses exploded. Screaming at the top of her lungs, she threw her shoe with all of her might. The other shoe followed seconds later. Out of ammunition, she retreated farther into the corner and crumpled. Wailing replaced the scream and racked her small frame. She couldn't stop even after she saw that the door had closed, leaving her alone. Minutes went by, and her terror remained. He was not gone; she was sure of it. *Oh, 911.* She needed to call 911. The phone was just a few feet away by the bed. Crawling now, as she was shaking too much to stand, she dialed.

"Hello, 911, what is your emergency?"

"He's in my house. Someone's trying to kill me!"

"Ma'am. Is there an intruder inside your house right now?"

"Yes, please help me."

"I'll send a police unit immediately. Just stay on the phone. What's your name?"

"Nancy. Nancy MacPherson."

"OK, Nancy, are you safe at the moment? Where are you?"

"I'm in my bedroom. I scared him away, but I think he's still in the house. Why won't he go?"

"I'll talk you through this, OK? There will be someone there in just a few minutes. Nancy, can you try and keep as quiet as possible and just stay in your bedroom? Can you do that for me, Nancy?"

"Yes, I think so."

"Do you have any idea who this is?"

"I've never seen him before in my life. He just walked into my house and started looking for me, like he knew I was here."

"Have you heard anything else, any doors? Is he still inside?"

"I can't hear very well, but I don't think he has left. When are the police coming? I'm so scared."

"Nancy, they should actually be there right now. Here's how it will work. When they have got it under control, the officer will bang loudly on your door and call out your name. Don't be scared—it's his signal to let you know it's him and not anyone else. He will do the same thing when he gets to your bedroom door. OK, then you'll be safe."

"I feel like I'm going to die."

"Not tonight you won't. Hang in with me, Nancy."

And then it happened. *My nightmare has ended!* The policeman was huge. A large, burly, African American man who could scare away any intruder. *But he's my hero. And he is so nice.* He almost carried her out of the bedroom to show her the house and that all was clear. He even asked to take a framed photo of the family outside, she thought to show his friend. But the nicest thing was that he sat her down and helped her have something to eat and gave her her pills. He even left a note. Nancy hoped he would never leave. He made her lock the door behind him, and then he was gone. The house was quiet again.

29

July 2015

A NEW ROOM THIS TIME. NOT THE WAITING ROOM, THAT WAS the same. The same magazines, the same music. If I had dementia, that would not have been such a bad thing. The lemurs of Madagascar would have always seemed fresh and fascinating.

I considered telling the receptionist that this *National Geographic* was about twelve years old but worried I would set the wrong tone. Perhaps this was a survival of the least fit. The better magazines all left in someone's purse or jacket while the dull ones lived on. *Sunset, Redbook, Golf Digest,* and the ubiquitous *National Geographic* adorned the several coffee tables. *People, Automobile,* and maybe even *Playboy* never to be seen or read as those winners would walk off as soon as they arrived.

Nearly two years had gone by since we first came to see our friendly neurologist. This seemed like forever ago. There had been a few further lab tests, a few more in-office quizzes, but the conclusion was the same. Nancy MacPherson had dementia. Happily had dementia, apparently. Up until this point, at least. My personal take on the subject was that people with dementia acted like those who ingested too much alcohol. You didn't know exactly how someone would behave when intoxicated, but whatever their style, each time they drank too much, they would behave the same way. Fortunately, when Mom drank, she became happy. Though, on the rare occasion when she drank a few too many, she got quiet. Was this our future?

I even thought it might be an interesting study to see whether the happy person with dementia had similarly been the kind, talkative person after two or three cocktails when they were younger. Others perhaps would turn into the angry drunk, criticizing everyone. There would be the demented conspiracy theorist who was convinced that the September 11 attack was all staged. I desperately wanted to know how these people had acted at parties when they had one too many. Would this agitated man next to the fish tank have been the one to talk my ear off, insisting that Jews were the ones who actually planned the Twin Tower attacks so the US would attack the Arabic world?

What had changed, however, was that Mom was no longer consistent. She was no longer always the gregarious, fun person at the party everyone was happy to meet. She had become quietier, more fearful. Highlighted, of course, by when she attacked my husband and called 911. It was hard not to take my husband's side when I heard what he went through. But later I realized how paralyzed with fear Mom must have been, thinking a random stranger had broken into her house, perhaps to rape her. A scary movie can be awful, but despite your fear, deep down you know it's just a movie.

Before I could further my waiting room research, we were taken back to the inner sanctum, past the old man trying to convince his caregiver, or maybe the fish, about another government plot.

This room was different—bigger, new posters on the wall. The largest was an outline of a man and his nerves. It looked a little like a road map with yellow streets going everywhere. I couldn't believe this was used to instruct the patient, or even the caregiver. Seemed a little pretentious to me. *Damn, I'm being critical today. Maybe I could use a little wine right now.*

I definitely needed some by the end of the visit.

What transpired in the next twelve to fourteen minutes was a conversation that bordered on the absurd. After a brief rundown of how Mom was regressing, I had hoped for a little empathy from this only-somewhat-jaded medical professional. I was sure he had heard similar stories before about how tiring it is to care for someone, and perhaps I was expecting a bit of a pat on the back. Maybe even a "You've done an incredible job, Allison, made it work longer than most, but you might be ready to have her go into a nursing home."

Not only did I not get that affirmation from Dr. Metcalf, I received an economics lesson that I was woefully unprepared for.

It all began when I innocuously said, "Surely Medicare will help pay for a nursing home when that time comes. My parents paid into Medicare their entire lives. Because I don't know how long I can keep visiting her every day."

"Well, I'm sorry to be the bearer of bad news, Allison, but Medicare simply won't help you at all," Dr. Metcalf replied. "They pick up the tab only for a 'skilled need,' like when Nancy broke her hip. The physical therapy required to get her back on her feet is covered. But it's not a hotel with nurses to help when one becomes feeble."

I'm sure a little more whining occurred. Perhaps he didn't realize what I was saying. He wasn't getting the point that I could no longer keep her safe.

"What does one do when they simply can't live alone? There's no way all those people I saw there had a skilled need. And I can't believe they could afford that cost month after month. By the way, how much does it cost, Dr. Metcalf? Do you know?"

"Well"—he chuckled—"if you thought college room and board was expensive, think of a dorm that employs twenty-four-hour nursing care with a pharmacy and physical therapist. They often run about $8,000 per month, or about $100,000 per year. So, getting back to your concern about the $500 a month for the meds—if they can prevent the need for going to a nursing home for just a few months, they are a great bargain."

If I looked calm and collected, I certainly was not. In fact, I was desperately trying to calm myself down, so I didn't pass out. I could hear my heart beating in my ears, and sweat started to drip from the small of my back. A hundred thousand dollars per year! "There's simply no way we could afford that! We weren't sure we could afford college for the kids. This is like having another one or two kids at Harvard. Would the state just let her die? What happens if I get sick and can't care for her?"

"This is complicated, but it's OK. It will work out. The state insurance for the poor will take over in the end. Once her house and assets are all sold and there's nothing left, then the state pays... Allison, are you OK?"

I felt like an idiot. Did everyone know this but me? It reminded me of my first paycheck. I had worked so hard at the grocery store earning $5.35 per hour. While stocking shelves, I would be planning how I would spend all that money. I would do the mental math: $5.35 x 22 hours = $120, a fortune to a fifteen-year-old. I even planned to give a gift to my parents, thanking them for driving me back and forth. So, imagine my surprise at receiving a check for just $87.50. *What the... happened to my other $32.50!? What are Medicare, OASDI, FUTA, and all that other crap, and why should they be getting my money? Why should a fifteen-year-old be paying taxes anyway?*

This lesson from Dr. Metcalf felt eerily similar. Work your whole life. Get money pulled out of every check. Save what's left to buy a house over thirty years. Then, when you are about to die, sell your house back to the government and end up with nothing. Somehow I missed this lecture in high school. Somehow I was grossly unprepared for this new reality of the American Dream.

The rest of that appointment was really just a blur. We wandered back to the front desk and made a six-month follow-up appointment as she was "doing so well." My interpretation was not quite the same. I was definitely not doing well. My life was being turned upside down so that hers could go on uneventfully. The one bit of good news—at least I had the answer for Carl on our $500 per month bargain.

And this might have been the first time I had my dark thought. What if she just died before the $8,000 per month nursing home? Like the Tell-Tale Heart, this idea, once it began, would not go away. It became louder and louder, no matter how I tried to suppress it, bury it. Hoping for her demise was abhorrent in every way, evil. Evil, as if the devil had tuned in to my consciousness. Nancy was still my mother—no hardship could be too great. But it wasn't just me being sacrificed. My work, my friends, my husband, my kids were all receiving a hollowed-out Allison. So, I concluded like so many others have before me, *I must not be trying hard enough. I must have more to give.*

30

August 2015

THE FIRST THING I DID WHEN I ESCAPED FROM HIS OFFICE WAS call Janine. Did she know that nursing homes weren't paid for even if you had an illness? I got the idea that they weren't there just if you became widowed and lonely. But Alzheimer's was a serious disease. Wasn't that what medical insurance was for in the first place?

Janine, in fact, had not known. Neither had any of my friends—even the ones who pretended to know everything. I began to even question Dr. Metcalf, so I started to do some Google research again. This was a very short research project. I could hear in my head a peppy voice from a girl, probably named Cindy, when I read the quotes from Medicare: "We make a distinction between 'medically necessary care' and 'custodial care.' Unfortunately, most care for someone with dementia, such as toileting, bathing, dressing, and eating, is deemed 'custodial' and is not covered by Medicare."

After a near nervous breakdown that lasted for a few weeks, I realized something had to change. And that something had to be me. What was not going to change was that my mother needed even more care now. I was there almost seven days a week. I say almost because a couple old friends of hers from church would often come by on the weekends to help by giving her pills and preparing meals. Frank, a widower, was probably the most attentive of the lot. On multiple occasions he would assure me that he enjoyed the times with her. It made him feel useful. Plus, I think he might have had a soft spot for her, and she broke up his loneliness. Occasionally when I would see them together, he would be just holding her hand and talking to her. Listening to music with her. That seemed to be their favorite thing to do together.

I would watch them sometimes for a while. It was relatively easy to be a spy. Both of them had terrible hearing. She never seemed to get angry with Frank. He seemed to provide her a feeling of warmth. Maybe that would be true for me if I just recorded those kinds of moments with her so I could remember them. But I was also the bad guy. The one who made her eat, who forced her out of her clothes to clean her up, who made her get up and walk to avoid bedsores. And I'll admit, I wasn't always nice about it either. I didn't have time to cajole in the evenings; I needed to get home. Our routine had often become more of a fight than a pleasant mother-daughter moment. Nonetheless, the routine was now faster, more efficient, and it kept me sane. But there was no doubt in my mind, I would have loved to have been rich, hired twenty-four-hour caregivers, and left all the dirty work for someone else to do.

And so, the weeks dragged on. But as the days again grew longer, I began to feel better. I was getting more done in my life. I could spend more time with my family. I even went to the gym on occasion.

Laughter and love. Being loved. Exercise. A sensory delight of food. Living. I was feeling alive this week. Could having sex just once make the entire week better? Happy. Joyous. Walking into work, cheeks flushed, Cheshire-cat joyous. The looks on colleague's faces were enough. In college, they would have just said, "Ooh, Allison got laid last night." As professionals, they just smiled back and gave me a high-five look with their knowing expressions.

Had it been that long? You know you've been married too long when you have to search your mind, trying to come up with the last time you had sex. But this was a little different. Maybe a lot different. I needed to be fucked. Everything had to go out of my mind for as long as possible. I knew the second we stopped, my anxieties would seep back. Carl hardly said a word. The next day, I wondered what he was thinking, but he was pretty quiet, smiling, attentive, loving. I went from hours of pleasure to instant, dreamless sleep. If they ever invented a pill to make one feel as content as I did that morning, all human endeavor would instantly cease.

I had a supportive, wonderful family that I needed to get to know again. It had been about four months that I had been going to my mom's every evening and on the weekends. Probably what had changed was efficiency. That amazing capacity to adapt. Another child is a lot more work. Unexpected twins more than twice the effort. Taking care of your parent with dementia, just another hurdle.

My last intense memory I have of my mom came one random Saturday, August 18, 2015. What was special was that she was particularly lucid that day, and it felt good to reminisce. It was effortless, like our talks used to be. I think at the time I reasoned that my attitude was playing a role in her doing better. Or maybe those stupid medicines actually were doing some good.

We just sat on the couch, watching a lazy afternoon roll by. Late summer can be so relaxing. And then our typically one-sided conversation became more even. As I was lamenting about being the disciplinarian of the family, Mom gave me her two cents. "You realize it doesn't get any easier from here on out. Your kids think you can do no wrong now, but they're young. Just you wait, by the time you were fourteen, I was getting an earful."

"Wait for what? Meredith has already started. She certainly loves her father more."

"That's just not true. I think girls just have a special relationship with their mom. We care so much that we can smother the girl desperately trying to spread her wings. But we want those wings to spread, and when they do, we become her biggest cheerleader. I can see how much Meredith loves and needs you. The frustration comes from her wanting to think she knows it all but understanding she really doesn't."

And then it went. Just like that. I got up to get us something to drink and snack on, and she became vague and confused upon my return. The following day she wasn't even sure who I was at first. Again I was Jan, her mother. But I knew something else was wrong. At the ER they told me she had a urinary tract infection and she would be back to normal by the end of the week. They were wrong.

That Saturday was the beginning of the end. When I look back, I think of that day as the day I officially lost my mom. My confidant, my philosopher and mentor was gone.

We certainly had conversations after that, but they were different. The insight never returned. She even lost her sense of humor. As Megan pointed out to me later, she had dropped an animal along the animal kingdom. And what that ultimately meant was that the decision was now imminent. We would have to decide if it was with us or in a nursing home where she would spend her remaining days. Keeping her alone in her home though was not an option. She was just not safe alone.

Coincidence, perhaps. Embarrassing for sure. Whoever "they" are, they always say that there two things in life that are certain, death and taxes. I'd heard this line all too often. Nobody likes to pay taxes. And just in case you were wondering, that includes accountants.

What gets me frustrated is how many ways you have to pay taxes. I get the fact that money needs to be collected for the common good, but taxes are everywhere. Sales taxes, income taxes, tolls on roads and bridges, employer taxes, building permits, car license fees, and...oh, did I leave out property taxes? I think I did, because I completely forgot to pay my mom's!

The first time I realized this was with a delinquency notice in the mail. The font of the letter even looked scary. The message sent was crystal clear—pay current and past due taxes, plus penalties, of course, or the state can legally sell your house. It seemed rather draconian, but that was when I realized that she hadn't paid their property tax for two years! Now she owed $9,284, including the assessed fees. We were going to have to mortgage or sell her house just to pay this bill.

Why can't they leave old people alone? Have my parents not paid enough money in taxes over sixty years? I just sat and cried. It was a rainy autumn Saturday, after all. What were we going to do?

The thought that kept coming into my head was to just pretend like I had never seen the letter. Which was about as logical as not telling your parents that you got a D in your seventh-grade English class. Parents always found out, and so did the county. They had their ways of collecting in the end. It was just a matter of time.

I looked out the window at the gray skies. I had felt for the longest time that the government was no longer representative of the people. I thought if we were asked to pay for things we actually wanted, we might be a little less bitter. My thought was that with every return, there would be a survey. I pictured it. On the left side of the page would be the top twenty things that your tax money actually was going toward, in order. On the right side of the page there would be those same things, but the taxpayer would write down what percentage of their money they would like to go to each of those twenty things. The hope would be that when the lawmakers saw the discrepancy, they would have to start spending money more in line with what the people actually wanted. The flip side would be that the taxpayer might finally learn a thing or two.

For example, the US spends about $220 billion per year on the interest for our national debt. It is the fourth-biggest line item in our budget. Three times as large as what we spend on education. Could you imagine that the fourth-biggest thing you spent on every month was the interest on your credit card? I shook my head and watched the neighbors trying to unload their groceries.

And defense spending—no matter your politics, you have to wonder why we spend more money on defense than the next nine highest-spending countries combined. Every year. It is even more dramatic when you look at our priorities. The US spends 54 percent of its budget on the military and only 6 percent on education. If I were president, I'd take 4 percent from the military and give it all to teachers. *That would make me pretty popular at PTA meetings.*

My mind was wandering. I sighed. It sure beat facing reality. Maybe Mom was lucky in that way. As I looked over and watched her staring vaguely out the front window too, I realized she would never stress about this bill. Even if I told her that the state was going to take away her house, she would probably reply, "Oh, that sounds like a good idea."

Now I had another major headache on my hands. Realtors, lawyers, bankers all needed to be called. And I already know what Carl was going to say. "This isn't a coincidence at all. It's God's way of telling us that you need to sell the house. She's not safe there anyway."

As Mom sipped her tea, I realized that imaginary Carl was probably right—she was going to have to move. I couldn't keep up this vigil; plus, she was not safe at home. Which then brought us back to that awful question: *Do we ship her out to a nursing home, or does she come and live with us?*

31

November 2015

MOMENTS ALONE WITH CARL WERE GETTING FEW AND FAR between. I used to be jealous of my married friends, thinking, they have twenty-four hours to spend with the love of their life! But married, two kids, parent with dementia—the reality was more like five to ten minutes in the morning and again before one of us was snoring in the evening.

Carl suggesting dinner *and* a movie kind of came out of no-where. As we drove, I thought, *Maybe he's seeing a therapist. But who am I to judge?* He had not only called a babysitter, he had made a deal with Frank to watch Mom, and the next thing you knew, we were talking about Matt Damon's movie *The Martian* while being waited on at Ruth's Chris Steak House.

"Seriously, Carl, who in their right mind would want to live on Mars, even if you could get there in a couple weeks?"

"Maybe you would. Did you ever think that what looks miserable now could look more like a hotel in the future?" Carl sipped his drink, then added, "You'd even get new views that you would have never seen here on earth."

"But why would you want views if you couldn't even go outside to play without being in a spacesuit? And I could never take the risk of having our kids out playing where they might fall, rip their spacesuits, and have their faces start to melt."

"Allison" comes out in a long sigh. I love when he starts to humor me when he thinks I have said something completely crazy. He always starts off saying my name in the same way, "All-iiii-son."

He continued, "Here's the thing. We like pretending that the Earth isn't changing, but it is and very quickly. We've polluted our planet so much that all the time you're telling Meredith and Sloane, 'Don't drink that water,' or, 'You can't swim there.'" I nodded reluctantly. "How many Spare the Air days did we have last year? How many horrible fires? And we live where it's nice. Do you recall watching the Olympics in Beijing, and we couldn't believe the smog? I just think we aren't too far off from a point when, if it were possible to live in a man-made pristine environment on Mars, rich people would want to go. And leave us here on Earth to squander our last precious resources."

"Would you like to order now?" asked the rather attractive waitress. Carl wasn't so lost in thought that he didn't take in the fact that her uniform was filled out to perfection.

"Can you give us a minute?" I said. "We don't get out much, and we can't stop talking." With a knowing nod, she scurried away.

"OK. No more talking until we've decided what we are going to eat. I don't want to get in trouble," announced Carl.

"Well, I'm having the rib eye. I'm not being treated to dinner with my husband at a steak house and ordering the fish. And you can either have a few bites of my steak or get lucky later tonight, but you'll have to choose, as you're not getting both."

"Wow, I guess I had better order something that I really like. Or get you so drunk that you forget that I ate half of your steak," he delivered while giving me that smile that had kept our marriage going even when he drove me insane.

And speaking of insane, I kind of knew where things were going to go next. It's hard not to when you've been married for fifteen years. Carl just couldn't understand why everyone was ignoring overpopulation. On one of our first dates, he made it very clear he would not have more than two kids—"replacement" was what he called it. But he would have been OK with just one, maybe even none.

Over the years, I would hear him make these speeches to friends at parties. "The primary difference is that humans have been able to manipulate the environment to allow unrelenting rises in population throughout the world. We have no predators to keep our population in check. Our health care continues to improve, so we are living much longer lives. It seems everything we do is focused on not allowing babies to die and then on having them live as long as humanly possible.

"Our self-interest is so strong that no amount of data can change our need to prolong life at all costs. The military can do this to an unusual degree. One soldier caught by the enemy, and we would risk a hundred to save that life. Our entire country was on the brink of war when Iran held 444 US hostages in the 1970s. It's not just the military; it's in our culture, our DNA. Our innate need to save the youngest child, resuscitate someone over age one hundred, rescue someone no matter how long the odds can't be cured by science."

And yet, midway through my steak, which was absolutely amazing, Carl began something new. It was not like I was ignoring him, but I had heard these arguments before. But when he got to talking about the octuplet mom, I started thinking again how much he was making sense.

"Do you remember Nadya Suleman?" he asked. I shook my head. "Maybe the name isn't familiar, but she is the lady who delivered octuplets a few years back. She was celebrated. It's in our DNA. We can't help but think the best thing to happen would be more kids and longer lives. The amazing thing is that twelve embryos were actually implanted."

"Carl! I totally remember the Octomom. They implanted twelve?"

"Yeah. And you can guarantee if twelve kids could have been delivered, then she would have had a full dozen. If they need to be born at five months' gestation, that's OK. Use millions of dollars to save them. That's what we do. Life is just that precious. We have billions of people on the planet consuming more resources than we actually should, and yet we don't dare let one die that we could save. And the end of life, the same. No expense seems too great to try and get someone to live even a few days longer."

I pointed out, "But not everyone celebrated Octomom. In fact, a lot hated what she did. Mainly because she was single and on public assistance."

"OK, you're probably right, not everyone liked her. But they still wanted to save her kids, thought it was wonderful. Did you know she actually had six other kids before the octuplets? All in vitro babies."

I almost choked on my steak. Which would have been a tragedy because I had just a few bites left. "You have got to be kidding. Fourteen children! That reminds me of that off-the-rails family, the Duggars."

Now it was me teaching my husband a thing or two. Clearly, not enough husbands watched TLC. He had never heard of this family that was celebrated for having nineteen children. In fact, while telling him the story, I could practically hear him humming that Marvin Gaye's "Mercy Mercy Me" in his head.

Over dessert we kept on talking. I don't know if it mattered what the subject was. We were being a couple again. We had gone to the movies and discovered Mars and our friendship again. I didn't want to stop.

As we were driving home, Carl was still talking, and I was watching him as his eyes focused on the road. "Anticipation is not our strongest suit. Despite attributing ourselves with significant intelligence, we behave similarly to every other animal species. We eat, we survive, we procreate as much as possible. We destroy our environment. And the good news is that our planet is really massive, and we have plenty of resources to waste and pollution to make before causing serious harm. But what separates us from other animals that can have a boom-and-bust cycle in their populations is that we have never really trended downward. True, there have been wars, diseases, famines, which can locally diminish numbers. The trend, however, looks like our world population is going straight up. We aren't finding any limits preventing more humans from inhabiting the Earth—"

"And that's how we find ourselves on Mars," I interrupted, finishing the thought. Carl smiled. I laughed. And then we retreated to our own thoughts. The silence was comfortable. It had been a good night.

As I began to let myself get more enveloped by the comfortable seat, I tried to understand my own feelings. Why would we save lives at all costs when it seemed obvious that we need fewer people on the planet?

Yet, despite knowing what science has taught me, why couldn't I help wanting to keep my mom alive? *Why can't I be more content that she's led a full, wonderful life? Why is there such sadness at death?* Because if there weren't, maybe we would be OK with not resuscitating someone who no longer recognized their own children.

32

December 2015

I shouted at my brother, "You're coming out! I don't know what to say other than, 'Thank you!' in capital letters and twenty-six-point bold font."

"Sis, I'm not going to lie, Cecilia and I had a good laugh about what happened to Carl. Mom, the pacifist, hurling shoes at someone. The only other time I have laughed that hard about a shoe was when that Arab guy chucked both his shoes at President Bush. Seriously though, when did Mom get so crazy? When I last saw her, she was her normal self. Well, as normal as she's ever been. Republicans would say she's always been a little off, proudly wearing her Reagan Is Demented shirt while marching on the Capitol."

"The irony is that now she's even more demented than the man she loved to hate," I noted forlornly. "I really still can't believe you are coming."

Jeremy had bailed me out on a few occasions. Not literally, as I had never been on the wrong side of a jail cell. But he was a good person at heart, and so when I needed him, he tended to come through.

Except for that one time in high school. It's true I was a couple grades ahead, and he wasn't exactly Shaquille O'Neal. But he was my brother; he was supposed to defend me. And this time I am being literal—it wasn't my honor I cared about; it was my front teeth. I realize that sounds so high school, but that's what happens when you are seventeen.

For some reason, Carmen Maldonado decided I was going to go down. She had heard that her boyfriend liked me, and her friends let it be known that I was trying to steal him. In between third and fourth periods, Shannon rushed up to me, breathless, to say that Carmen and her friends were going to beat me up after school.

"You've got to be kidding" was my initial reply, but as Shannon explained further, the blood started to drain from my face.

It's funny, in retrospect, how you would never think to just tell a teacher about this. I think partly because you knew that the beating would only be worse when they finally got you alone. *Surely my brother will save me,* I thought.

His response, devastating and short: "Oh, hell no. A girl fight, those are the worst. You're on your own."

I still reminded him of this every once in a while. He still stood by his description of girl fights, asserting that girls were worse than boys, who would just beat you up and leave you alone. And he did have a point that there was no winning proposition for a boy against a girl. If the boy won, he'd be a jerk. If he lost, he'd be a sissy.

But now I needed his help again. What were we going to with Mom? He was not clueless, as I had given him regular updates, but he also was not expecting to hear that she didn't even recognize Carl. And worse than fighting a girl, how do you take on your violent parent? I had heard that in nursing homes they would sometimes just tie them down—obviously a better alternative than punching them back. It was hard not to wonder what people were thinking when they struck their loved ones. Were they just like someone who was drunk and no longer had their social inhibitions? Or was it fear? I had spent the last year or so watching her decline, and I was just not sure what she was thinking much of the time.

"Will you really fly out, Jeremy?"

"Allison, it's OK. You don't need to keep on asking. It's a done deal. I've talked it over with Cecilia, and her mom will be able to help with the kids while I'm gone. And you don't have to tell me how much harder it has been for you living in the same city. It's time I did something to help Mom...and you."

"Well, amen to that. I was wondering when you would come around. And since you are suddenly being so nice and understanding, maybe now is the time to ask if you will take her in to live with you."

He chuckled.

"That actually wasn't a joke. My life is bad now; I'm not thrilled to be signing up for worse."

"Do you hear that? I think I just heard a pipe burst in my basement. Or maybe it was a tornado touching down in my backyard. I'm going to have to run, Allie."

"Does that really work for you? With anyone?"

"You'd be surprised. People are pretty gullible. Hey, was this all a joke to get me out there?" I started to tear up, and he continued, unaware: "If so, you've not only learned from the best, you've taken it to a new level. Shoe throwing, cops handcuffing. That's showing some ingenuity. The sad part is that you got me. I've already bought the ticket, and you know how cheap I am! I'd never waste a nonrefundable ticket."

I sniffled.

"Shit, Allie, why are you crying? I was just teasing. I really am going to be there in a couple of days."

"You just don't understand. I have laughed at the absurdity of it all sometimes. Most of the time, I'm not laughing. I'm crying inside. You'll see for yourself. She's no longer Mom. Our caped crusader who made everything better. As a parent, you realize how much you do for your kids. And that's when it hits you. How unappreciative you have been to your own parents. But this is something altogether different. Now I'm the one who's not appreciated."

"Allison, that's just not true! I have not been there physically, but I keep on telling you how much you are doing. Those flowers I sent recently, those chocolate-covered strawberries. I don't even do that much for my wife. Really, I can't begin to let you know how much this has meant. I remember coming out after she broke her hip. That nursing home she recovered in was actually very nice. But once she got through rehab, I could tell she was so much happier at home. She could have never stayed at home alone without you."

Sobbing now, I said, "That's not what I'm talking about. It's not you; it's not Carl."

"OK, you've lost me now, sis. What are you trying to say?"

"It's Mom! She no longer... She is just existing. We are hardly talking now. She is the one who isn't appreciative. She's the one who doesn't seem to care about anything anymore."

"Why aren't you talking? Is she mad? Are you mad?"

"She doesn't talk, Jeremy. When I'm there, I'm mostly talking to myself. It keeps me sane, I guess. Though maybe I am also hoping that it matters to her. Have you ever gone to a hospital and seen someone who is not communicating? The friends and relatives will talk to the patient, thinking maybe they are actually hearing. But who really knows? Well, often it's like that talking with Mom. Sometimes she will be part of the conversation and nod appropriately. But when I'm busy doing the dishes or laundry, she kind of just stares blankly ahead. And so I find myself occasionally throwing out something totally crazy just to see if she's paying attention. You know, like, "Can't believe the president got shot today.""

"You do not!"

"I'm serious. I do that kind of stuff all the time. But it doesn't really get much of a reaction. They say that the memory starts to get eaten away going backward. The stuff that happened today and this year, gone. Absolutely no clue. Things that happened five years ago start to go next. And by the end, they start even forgetting who their family is. I think that's why she has started to call me Jan sometimes."

"You don't even look like grandma. She was much prettier," Jeremy couldn't help but say, likely smiling from ear to ear. "Do you think she will recognize me? It hasn't even been a year since I last saw her. She didn't seem nearly so bad back then. And isn't she supposed to be on medicines to make her better?"

"Whatever you do, don't ask Carl that question. It's a sore spot because he really feels we have thrown thousands of dollars down the drain. I can't blame him because I feel that way myself. To some extent, you just have to trust. You have to believe she would have been worse off if she hadn't taken them."

"Kind of like when you see my son play tennis. He can get the ball over the net for sure, but after he misses maybe twelve serves in a row, it's hard not to think, are those sixty-dollar-an-hour lessons really worth it? How much worse would he be without the lessons?"

"And you say I'm cruel? Your son is only ten. And do you actually think he will turn pro at twenty-three, win Wimbledon, and support you and Cecilia? You always were a dreamer."

"Allison. I'm scared."

"What are you afraid of?"

"I really don't know what to make of all of this. I certainly thought I knew about dementia, but I guess I don't really know. And the stuff you are telling me is making me feel so ill prepared. What if I mess up? I don't have any idea how to be with her alone. How much help do I need to give her? Do I actually have to feed her? Does she need help walking or getting dressed? And I'm sad to say I'm really feeling a bit reluctant if I have to bathe her."

"Are you through?"

"I'm sure there are more questions and maybe some I'm even afraid to ask."

"Jeremy, the bottom line is that, even though she isn't the same mom you remember, she's still Mom. Those questions you ask are a little bit like asking every conceivable scenario when it comes to your kids. Would you defend them if they were being bullied? Would you help pay for college? Would you clean up their vomit when they were sick? The list could similarly go on and on. The answer will always be the same. Of course you would. You just do. And I don't think there is any right or perfect way to do it. You just do the best you can. I've certainly screwed up plenty of times with my kids and now with taking care of Mom. But you get better. The only difference is I have had a lot of time to get used to everything and build a routine. Your learning curve will have to be pretty steep."

Steep was the understatement of the year. *Vertical* would have been more accurate. By the time Jeremy returned to Seattle, he would feel like the president after four years. You look at the before and after pictures and think that he aged about twenty years in that short period of time. Though the trip was eye-opening for Jeremy, it was most important for me. I didn't want to be the only one making momentous decisions.

On his last day, we sat on two rather sad chairs in the backyard of our old home. Probably fifteen years had passed since the last time Jeremy and I sat out here. Dad was quite the gardener. He had built small fountains and tiny bridges and set out an array of small stone animals to complete the picture. The immaculate lawn, which would have been good enough for a putting green, was now a mixture of probably three different grasses and at least as many different weeds. The color that would rage in the spring was now primarily just green. But even when Mom had been more attentive, she had neither the ambition nor the talent that Dad had had in the garden.

We really didn't see each other much since Jeremy had moved away for college. "Are you close?" is the question often asked of siblings. And I guess the answer to that would be yes. If something happened to me, Jeremy would be in the hospital before I was awake from surgery. When the kids were born, he was the first one to hold them after Carl. Another way that you could tell was that we didn't need to speak very much to know the other's feelings. And now, long stretches of silence passed before we tackled the inevitable. What were we going to do?

"What would you do, sis?"

"I'm so torn, Jeremy. It's just so hard to decide. I know that she's going to be in her own world most of the time wherever she ends up. But I don't think she would ever have wanted to be in a nursing home."

"Allie, that's not what I am asking. I want to know what you would have me do if it were you in this position."

"Oh, wow. I can't believe that's what you are asking. Do you think I'm starting to lose it or something?" My voice started to rise even further. "What makes you think it won't be me putting you into a nursing home?"

"Hey, hey, calm down. That's not what I was trying to imply at all. I'm just philosophically asking the question: should we not do for her what we would want done for ourselves?"

I said, "Oh."

Jeremy continued, "I've been thinking about this a lot and have talked about it with so many people and, to a man, everyone says the same thing. 'I would never want to end up in a nursing home where I'm just being fed and watered. No one seems to visit after those first few months, and then it's just turning the page on the calendar until you finally die. Too depressing for words. I'd kill myself first.'"

"And yet, nursing homes are a thriving business. They are everywhere. Only one in a hundred of those aged sixty-five to seventy-four live in a nursing home. But for those over eighty-five, it jumps to 25 percent. Why do you think that is, Jeremy? It's because of people like me. We just can't keep it up. We not only wear down physically and emotionally—we are faced with the grim prospect that things will only get worse."

"So, what gives? What changes between now, when we are saying that we will never be a burden on our families and we'll never live in a nursing home, and later on, wanting a stranger to take care of us until the end? You know when I watch horror movies or that series *The Walking Dead*, do you know what I think of, Allison? I quickly realize there is no hope, and I don't want the pain or the suffering. I don't want some zombie starting to chew on my arm and face while I am trying to sleep. I'd just grab a grenade, pull the pin, and rush into a crowd of zombies, taking out as many as I could in the process."

I just about exploded myself, with laughter.

"What's so funny? Seriously, Allison, you're about to fall on the floor."

"Only you."

"Only me, what?"

"Only you, Jeremy, could make our depressing conversation even *worse*. You've now leaped from living with a bunch of seniors to having your face chewed off by zombies. Remind me who not to call when I need some comic relief."

"What do you mean? I got you laughing, didn't I? If I could make this subject funny, I would kill on the comedy circuit talking about Trump."

"A perfect segue to opening up a bottle of wine. Shall I grab you a glass, my comedic-legend brother?" He just stared at me. "Oh, I don't know why I asked. I'll be right back."

When I returned, I found my brother, all six foot two inches of him, reclining so far back in that chair a gust of wind could have knocked him over. Not quite as thin as he used to be but still a force to be reckoned with playing basketball, I was sure. Well, at least in the rec leagues.

It's unfair. As long as men stayed in shape, they remained attractive no matter how old they were. "Why don't men have to wear makeup?" I asked while proffering his glass of merlot.

"Because if we did, there would need to be double sinks in every bathroom in America. Not only that, no one would ever arrive on time to anything."

I laughed.

Jeremy said, "Speaking of which, have you noticed how Mom is never ready to go anywhere? She's like my kids were when they were small. I have to remind her of everything. 'Are you getting ready to go? Have you brushed your hair? Did you brush your teeth? Are you sure you will be warm enough with just that blouse? Did you already go to the bathroom?' It's like she's getting her revenge for all the times she had to nag me growing up."

"Just to throw it out there, Zombie Boy, forgetting Mom for now, what do you think the president should do about end-of-life care? Is there something to truly change that would be politically palatable? Remember when President Obama was trying to get his health care plan passed, and the whole nation reeled over the idea of 'death panels'? The strategy clearly worked because it was easy to come up with a vision of three to five elderly men evaluating case after case and deciding whose life was worth continuing and who had passed their finer days. Or whose life just cost more than society was willing to pay."

I pointed out, "Let's just agree at the start that there is no one solution that everyone will agree on. Further, there will always be exceptions that wouldn't fit. It's a little bit like, if you have the death penalty, you will sometimes screw up and kill someone who is innocent. If this is simply not working well for society, how can we try to make things better?"

"OK, Allison, I'm willing to call you in your crazy game of deciding the fate of the United States and raise you to deciding for the whole world."

"Perhaps I could figure this out in an economic type of way. Accountants, after all, are just economists who aren't charismatic enough to be able to teach." Jeremy chuckled at my joke. "Is there a point where we could decide that the cost to take care of an individual is no longer worth it to society? We do this already for college. If a degree is going to cost $100,000, we presume that it will lead to a higher-paying job that will eventually pay off that cost. If we did it this way, then age wouldn't be a factor. A government might just say if it costs more than $100,000 to care for someone, then it's time to withdraw treatment."

"OK, Ms. Accountant, I hate to burst your bubble with the 'politically palatable' speech, but *wow*. That's harder to swallow than swords on fire. But I hate when people say, 'No idea is too stupid, and I want to hear them all'—and then they immediately berate the first idea that comes up. Because then you can't get anywhere. You can't begin to really explore your true feelings and come up with really awesome ideas if it's not safe to consider them. So, let me try another way. We don't make it so variable. The money way is not only variable in the US, but it would be crazy to extrapolate to the rest of the planet. How many families in other countries actually spend $100,000 per year on care of their elderly? And this gets a lot into the muck of life having a price and whose life is more important.

"I'm thinking this is not unlike retirement. Who came up with the age of sixty-five to retire? It's an arbitrary number. It doesn't apply equally for all jobs. Air traffic controllers must retire at fifty-six. Ditto for prostitutes." I snapped to attention, and Jeremy laughed.

"OK, I made that last one up, but I wanted to see if you were paying attention. But for the most part, we kind of assume that, once we get to sixty-five, we can stop working. It's just a known fact. What if we chose an age where it's expected we stop living?"

I said, "Oh my God, have I talked to you about that before? *Brave New World*? It's an idea I have had in my head randomly for years after reading that classic by Huxley. The focus was on the society. And living past the prime of your life didn't really make sense. Yet there seemed to be a corollary: the idea that once you know that you won't live past a certain age, there's not regret, anger, or any other negative emotion. In fact, it forces you to live your life more fully. Who hasn't had the thought that if they knew when they were going to die, they would do things differently? If I knew this were my last year on earth, I would quit my job right now and spend time with my family, travel the world, finish out all the things on my bucket list.

"I met a man once whose doctor said he had a huge mass on his pancreas and would likely die within a few months. The following week, he had another scan, and this time it showed nothing, no mass at all—the first scan was a mistake. You would think he would be furious, but he was not. He had become thankful for every day. He was living differently. He was living as if any day could be his last."

"Sis, so what you are saying is that being forced to die at a certain age might not only save the planet, it might make us happier? This does sound a lot better and less selfish than your $100,000 plan. But do you really think you would feel that way as you aged? Say if the age were seventy, would you be thinking at sixty-nine how lucky you were?"

"Jer, do you remember the movie *Blade Runner* with Harrison Ford?"

"Yes, of course, it's a classic."

"I think why it's a classic is that it is also talking about this question. The movie is about how to 'retire' robots engineered to help humans. What truly makes the movie a classic is the ending. Harrison Ford falls in love with a human...or a robot? He's not sure. If she's human, she has a human life expectancy. If she's a robot, they were programmed to die in four years. Why would you decide to spend your life with someone if she only had four years to live? The answer...I think it's the same answer we are exploring with a mandatory death age. Love and happiness aren't obtained just by reaching a specific milestone like age eighty-five. They are part of life. And just maybe, they are made more special when we know there isn't any time left."

PART 3

33

February 2016
Nancy

NANCY SQUINTED, CONSIDERING GETTING OUT OF BED. *I THINK I checked the front door. I'm pretty sure I did. It must be locked because I haven't gone outside yet, have I? Still, I should check. The wind might have blown it open.*

No, that's impossible. I'm sure I locked the bottom and the deadbolt. It's kind of scary when it's so quiet. It's always quieter in the dark. Does sunlight bring sound? Sunlight makes me want to sing. But not now, not in the dark.

I'm not going to be able to sleep unless I check that front door, so I might as well get up; no one else is going to do it for me. She rolled off her mattress. *Larry will just continue to snore, so I might as well do it myself. It's strange—I don't hear him snoring right now. He must be sound asleep.*

It's easy to laugh at yourself when you get old; you can't take life too seriously. Then, finding herself in the bathroom instead of the hallway, she thought, *I might as well pee now that I'm here.* Laughing harder, she thought of the saying, "When life gives you lemons" —*Here I am, making lemonade. But I must check that front door. I'm sure I left it open. It seems kind of windy outside; wouldn't want it to blow open.*

Phew, it's closed, let me check the locks.

What do I have for breakfast? She tried to remember but didn't think she had bought anything. *I've gotten this far, so maybe I should* go to the store and get something for breakfast. I think I need some eggs and bread. I'm wide awake, and I've walked this far—might as well get something so Larry won't be fussy when he wakes up.

It was cold outside. I don't suppose it will rain. This spring has been pretty wet so far. We need it. Can't seem to conserve enough water these days—we are always in a drought. And then you have the Robinsons down the street with the most immaculate green lawn. There's no way they are watering just twice a week as they should. I bet they even take twenty-minute showers. Doesn't anybody care about the planet?

She stubbed her toe and stopped. My feet are freezing. But since I'm halfway to the store, I might as well keep on going.

"Oh, shit, I should have brought a list." She looked around. Then she shrugged.

That's OK, I can always come back again later if I forget something. It was so quiet, she noticed. Except for that wind. It's blowing so hard I don't even hear any birds. I remember walking to the store with my sister growing up. It's always more fun to go with somebody. Larry never walks anywhere. I wonder why. It's not that he's lazy, and he was quite the athlete. To get that man to just stroll with me is near impossible, even when we are on vacation. Me, I can walk for hours. Even if I have nowhere to go. It's just nice being outside. But how can it be so cold, isn't it April?

There was almost no one in the parking lot. Lucky for me, I guess. Unless it's a holiday. They don't tell you about all the times you will forget it's a holiday when you stop working. Once you retire, every day is the same. But Safeway is looking kind of dark. Please, please, please be open.

Oh dear. The sign said Closed, and she stared at it in disappointment. I was hoping to warm up, at least. The frozen food aisle is probably warmer than out here.

Well, that settles it—time to turn back. It seemed so dark, maybe that was why things didn't seem familiar. *Hazelwood?* She didn't recognize that street sign. But it was going the right direction, so she would get home eventually.

I remember that time in Hawaii. I think I walked on the beach for miles each way. What's fun about walking on the beach is people watching. Kids running in and out of the waves up to their ankles. Others building sandcastles or digging holes. Frisbees hovering in the wind before inevitably ending up in the surf. A giggling teenager rushing in to retrieve it before throwing it again. Collecting shells. Some beaches aren't so good. A bunch of seaweed might be all you can come up with. Or a rare jellyfish. But looking for the perfect shell—I love that. The warm sand between your toes. Not now. My toes—I can hardly feel them.

Nancy was tired. She felt as if she had walked for miles. *Where is my house? Where is everybody? I can't understand why no one is around for me to ask. If I don't recognize the name of the next street I'm sitting down. I'm pooped.*

Are you kidding? Poplar Avenue. I don't think I've even seen a poplar tree. Where on earth am I? She needed to rest. She just wished she could find a warm place.

This grass is soft but even colder than I already was. I'm sure the owners won't mind if I lie down for just a while. She got on her knees. *Maybe they would even let me in to rest on their couch.* She dropped down to recline on the grass. *Oh my God, this grass is freezing, but I am too exhausted to move. Oh, Nancy, what have you done? How did you get yourself stuck out here?*

"Do you remember that time, Larry, when we got stuck on the Loneliest Highway in America? We were so cold that night." Nancy remembered how everyone had laughed at the story because they thought it was so obvious. *"What part of 'loneliest' escaped your mind?"* But this is America—we drive everywhere. *Though Larry does almost all of the driving, I love being the navigator. We had it all planned out. We were driving from San Francisco to Utah that summer. We were just kids, and so we had almost no money. The plan was to drive all night so we would stay only one night in a hotel. But that plan was shot to hell in middle of nowhere, Nevada. The sign said sixty-five miles until the next gas station. So, we went to fill up. 'Why risk it?' I said. And that was when the problem started. The gas station was closed. Larry was mad. He said,* "What the hell! Who closes a gas station at ten o'clock on a summer night?" *We told the guy we'd give him an extra five if he opened it for us, but he was on his way out and couldn't care less. Larry was so intent on driving that night that he yelled at the man's back,* "Well, we'll just take our business to the next town!" *Larry never yelled, but I was glad he did because the guy turned around. At first I thought he was mad, but he just warned us:* "Do what you want, but this road will eat up gas in them hills, and even if you make it to Tehachapi, they'll be closed too."

We were screwed either way, so we had no choice—might as well just wait out the night. The stars were so beautiful. They were everywhere, kind of like now. And why sleep in the car when you've got this view? So, we took out our blankets, and I wore about three sets of clothes, and we lay down in the dust by the side of the road, staring at the night sky. It was summer, it was the desert, how cold could it get?

I'd say a lot colder than you would ever think. We were dressed like Eskimos, sandwiched between two blankets, watching the world turn. It remains one of the most and least romantic nights of my entire life.

I wish Larry were with me right now; maybe he could make it a little less cold. I've just got to get up and go home. She sat up. *I just wish I knew which direction to go. I'm the navigator after all.*

Oh look, someone's coming! She got up and moved toward the car. *I'll just flag them down—they will know where to go.*

"Lady, get out of the fuckin' road!"

She didn't know why, but she started to cry. *Whoever that was must have had a mean mother. But that was so rude. I just wanted* directions. *Sometimes I wish I were dead. Does the world have no more use for me?*

And then kindness finally came. It was the paperboy, or really a paper*man*, driving an SUV, who approached slowly, getting out every few houses to throw papers to the porch. He spotted her maybe half a block away and looked worried. She wondered, *Do I look so obviously lost?* He stopped running about twenty feet away from her and looked a little scared of her. *Maybe I didn't do my hair before I went out.*

"Ma'am, are you OK?"

"Oh, thank you for asking. I think I'm lost. I can't find my way home. The store was closed, and it has gotten so cold."

And that was when he let her know she was barefoot. *Why on earth would I have left the house without shoes? Did I lose them along the way? That makes no sense—how would I lose my shoes? No wonder I'm so cold.*

But he was such a kind man, he brought her to his car and turned on the heater. He even had heated seats. Nancy sat there shivering while he asked her question after question. He seemed so agitated.

As she ran her fingers through her hair, she thought, *It must be how I look that he wants to take me to the hospital.* "I'm fine, really I am, just a little cold. I'm sorry I can't remember my street. It's 5981 something, I'm sure about that. I've lived there most of my life." If she could have walked any farther, she would have insisted he let her out of the car so she could find her way back herself. He had no interest in driving her around until things looked familiar. *But I can't be angry at this newspaperman.* He was even gentle helping Nancy out of the car into the emergency room. And that was when things really started to get crazy.

I hate hospitals. To start, they need a better decorator. The emergency rooms are always so white, and people act so impersonal. A little soft music wouldn't hurt either. Plus, there is no need for me to be here. All I felt was cold.

One person after another coming in asking me all sorts of questions. Am I being interrogated for a murder?! Now a policeman?! Maybe I really am being accused of a crime!

Oh, this one visitor I will not forget. Her name is… Oh shit, I think I already forgot her name. Maybe it's Brandy. She is beautiful. Long, brown hair and a smile that lit up the room. She touched me. I felt her warm hands on my shoulders and back. She plumped up my pillows and brought me some blankets from an oven. She even brushed my hair. If I go to heaven, I want the angels to all be like Brandy. She is a unicorn, as my daughter likes to say.

And for the first time in a while, Nancy had a glorious sleep.

34

February 2016

I PULLED THE CURTAIN BACK IN ONE QUICK MOTION, REVEALING an elderly woman at peace, buried beneath several layers of blankets with just her face, serene and calm, poking above. Her gray hair was matted and tangled, her eyes closed. She would be embarrassed to be seen like this, with her mouth open wide, dentures out, so relaxed a line of spittle was collecting along her left cheek. But oddly, she seemed beautiful. Maybe she was so relaxed her wrinkles were not as pronounced. Or maybe she was safe, free from whatever nightmare had possessed her to leave home in only a nightgown well after midnight. Whatever she had been thinking this evening, she was now a picture of serenity. It seemed a shame to wake her.

Quietly replacing the curtain, I returned to the chaos of the emergency room. An array of people moved around with clear assignments, but to me they were like a colony of ants. I felt just as lost about their structure as a patron of the Exploratorium watching ants rapidly moving, organizing, creating.

Grabbing the attention of a random worker clothed in faded green scrubs, I disrupted the flow. I simply asked if it were OK to leave my mom alone for a while. A minimal intrusion that was not noticeable seconds after we parted. The man in the green scrubs headed for supply, resuming his place among the rest of the colony. I watched idly for a while, realizing no one noticed or cared that I was here, certainly not my mom.

So, I snuck off to the cafeteria, allowing her sleep and myself the time to process.

The fluorescent lights buzzing overhead did little to calm my nerves or to make my gooey mac and cheese look more appetizing. Yet as I picked aimlessly at my food, I knew it was the least of my problems. I knew this time signaled the end. For what seemed like eternity, Mom had been declining. Sometimes falling but never badly. Sometimes talking, more often not. Sometimes eating, sometimes playing with her food as I was this macaroni. Sometimes soiled...no, often soiled. Happy? Was she happy to still be at home? Was Mom happy with the time we spent together? *Does she even remember what happiness is?*

Happy or not, she was no longer safe at home. I wouldn't be surprised if I got a call from Adult Protective Services. A conversation that would probably go badly if I were on the witness stand. I stopped trying to eat and leaned back and imagined it.

Attorney: Isn't it true, Allison, that you contemplated putting locks on her doors to prevent her leaving unassisted?

Allison: Yes. We were a little afraid, though, that she might get trapped and—

Attorney: Is it not true that you already have a life alert for her? And yet, despite her many falls, she has never used it?

Allison: Well, yes, but—

Attorney: And during the past year, have you ever arrived to find her soiled skin breaking down enough that you had to go to the doctor?

Allison: Unfortunately, yes. That's why I now go there every morning before work. Carl has to take care of the kids in the morning and evenings as I am with my mom — to prevent her from…

Attorney: To prevent her from what? Allison?

At this point in my make-believe trial, the jury just decides to put me out of my misery as I hear the foreman state loudly, "Guilty as charged!"

Allison: But what am I guilty of?

As my voice trails off, I realize there is no winning here. If the judge asks Nancy what is in her best interest, there will be no response. So, we are all left to guess the right thing to do.

The only thing I knew for sure was that Mom detested the idea of being in a nursing home. Would she have ever chosen safety over happiness? Would she feel different now if she realized that she could have been hit by a car?

"Paging Dr. Norton. Dr. Norton, stat to the ER."

No one moved. My heart had leaped into my throat, but I seemed alone in my fear. The cashier didn't blink. The staff and visitors continued helping and eating as if nothing had happened. But was that for my mom? With no regret, I tossed the remainder of my congealed yellow macaroni and headed back to the emergency room, hoping that I would not run into Dr. Norton.

35

February 2016

MY EYES WERE SORE FROM TEARS. MANY DAYS HAD PASSED SINCE they first began to fall. They created a look of anguish that makeup poorly masked. The hospital stay after her barefoot, nighttime walk was fleeting. We spent thousands of dollars to find out nothing was wrong. She didn't even have a urinary tract infection this time. And I had gotten called into what seemed like the principal's office, informing me that it was felt that she wasn't safe at home alone. She needed twenty-four-hour care.

Driving her home from the hospital, I began to think about what it would mean for me if someone else was caring for her all day. I told myself, *I should be so happy. I've been freed. I can come home after work. Straight home. I get to be mom again in the mornings with my family. I get to sleep in on weekends! I have my life back, and all I have to do is visit. The fun type of visits—not the cleanup-and-feed kind of visits from before.*

Back from the hospital, I stared at Mom lying peacefully in her bed. I reflected on the hard choices facing me. We needed money for her caregiving. We needed it now. We had to either get a reverse mortgage or sell her house and move her.

Lying with her left hand resting gently on her right, she was oblivious of her potential fate. Her chest rose and fell gently. Tranquility personified, she stared blankly ahead. *Where will her life go from here? Will the pleasures outweigh the pains? Will she even remember to keep score? Is there some future experience that will make her life complete?*

"Mom, are you suffering? Are you still happy?"

A year ago, I might have pursued this conversation Asked the question in a way she might understand better. But now I was more experienced. Silence was more likely to lower her anxiety and misconceptions. That was what worked now. For her, not for me.

Sitting quietly, watching her vacant stare, led me to my dark place. A place I was visiting with increasing frequency. Who would ever know? A victimless crime.

My favorite victimless crime was committed by an Englishman. He devised a way to steal money from millions of people without anyone ever noticing. And if no one noticed they had been robbed, was a crime actually committed? Like the tree falling in the forest, he stole without making a sound. Every time they bought or sold stocks, he rounded down to the nearest dollar, so $1,184.26 became $1,184.00 He just took the twenty-six cents. With millions of transactions a year, he became incredibly wealthy, and there were no losers. While I was a little horrified by myself, I was not convinced that if I held the pillow over Mom's face, she would lose out on any part of her life. She had already led the principal of life. I would just be removing the final twenty-six cents. Could I live with my crime? Would it be a crime? Can a body without a mind be a victim?

The problem with the choices confronting me was the unknown. How much longer would Mom live? The shorter the time, the easier all of the choices would be. Even a reverse mortgage would work if she died in three years.

As I looked at her dozing in front of me, I just wanted her to be happy. She had always been the world to me. I looked back and thought about how much she sacrificed to provide every opportunity for Jeremy and me. Reliving the past, reminiscing, was typically a good feeling. Something that would make me feel warm inside. But I had such different emotions when I thought of my parents.

When my dad died, it seemed as if my world had ended. It was sudden, unexpected, and for a short time, devastating. I had just come back from a run. Mom had just blurted it out in a message. She was sobbing hysterically, words unintelligible. I recall waves of utter grief for weeks afterward. Yet this was where things were so different for me. By the time the funeral happened, there was already a change. Preparations for the funeral were difficult, but there was a tremendous amount of love and support.

In the end, it was the pictures; they seemed to change everything. With each smiling photo came a memory that was happy. It was true I would never go camping with my dad again, but I hadn't gone camping with him for twenty years. And at seventy-four, with two bad knees, he was never going to have gone again even if he had not died. Helping me with homework, cheering me on at games, giving me away as I walked down the aisle, holding his grandchildren—all of these memories kept coming back, mostly with a lot of sobbing. He had provided me with countless good memories. But the fact was that these memories were simply that, memories, all of which weren't going to be re-created even if he were still alive. Lord knew there were not going to be more grandchildren to hold.

Between the tears, I found large oases of smiles and comfort. The large, framed family photo that stood proudly on an easel watching over the eulogy captured his essence perfectly. Standing tall, arms stretched over our shoulders, he was beaming proudly. He had fulfilled all of his goals—why should we be sad for him?

I can't say the funeral was a party; I envied the Irish for that. There were way too many "I'm so sorry for your loss"-es. Weeks after the event, I looked back and felt comfort. I was certain he had been remembered in a way that would have given him pride.

The calmness I displayed when it was my turn to speak can only be attributed to my years on the debate team. I had prepared for hours, rereading my speech so that tears wouldn't detract from what I had to say about my dad. This was my time to let everyone know what his life meant to me. Yes, I was going to miss him dearly. There was no doubt he could have continued to teach and comfort me if he had lived another few years. I wanted to express all of that. But the main reason I didn't want to cry was that I didn't want people to leave sad. He was iconic, at least to those who knew him, and I wanted him remembered as such.

So now, when I looked at my mom, the contrast seemed so glaring. Painful. What speech would I be writing for her? As I looked at her, staring blankly, looking right through me, I wondered. Would I be able to say, "She could have continued to teach and comfort me if she had lived another few years?" Would I miss the time we were spending now, mostly in silence? Most concerning to me: would I be able to suppress the resentment that had been building? The frustrating conversations about nothing, the missed appointments, the money I spent to keep her from harm, the missed opportunities to create memories with my family. Would these unpleasant post-dementia times start to outweigh all of the good times before?

When marriages end, they have often been bad for several years. We are freed with divorce. But were there not years of good memories with that person as well? Yet how do we remember our former lovers, spouses? I would venture to answer that almost everyone you speak with will say, "Good riddance," to the former loves of their lives. They don't seem to want to remember any of it. The anger and hatred of the final few years tip the scales far away from the infatuation stage when their partners could do no wrong. I thought, *Will this be my fate if Mom's life continues to drag on?*

The past two years had worsened quickly. She called me Jan pretty much exclusively now. Getting more than a few words an hour was becoming rare. And I hadn't realized there would be such lack of movement. She spent days on end without leaving her bedroom and didn't really seem to care. In another year, she would probably be catatonic. On the weekends, I took her outside in her wheelchair. In the moment, she seemed to enjoy that, but I never got the sense she was looking forward to it the next week.

"Mom, I've got to go. Mom?" The only response that I got was that she did squeeze my hand back. It was clearly time to go. My mind was starting to circle, and I was not sure how much I was comforting her anyway. My time with her was starting to feel more and more like visiting a grave. You would go, you would remember for a while, and then you would leave. The only real difference was that I wasn't leaving flowers for the deer to nibble after I was gone.

36

June 2016

THE CICADAS WERE OUT IN FULL VOICE, THE BACKGROUND soundtrack to the summer months. The wind was nonexistent as I strode toward 87 Arnott Drive. I had had to use my GPS, and so the address would stay in my memory for another few days and then fade quickly, as the computer is charged with the task of never forgetting.

Will computers be our downfall? I wondered. Before I had a smartphone, I had an array of phone numbers and addresses I could quickly recall. I smiled at the memory of my first boyfriend, Nate: 428-6683, 144 West Clover Lane. If you heard a number in those days, you would commit it to memory as soon as possible. To help, you might write it down on your hand, giving you a full day of practice. Now, you meet someone, you enter their name and number, and your iPhone seems to encourage you to forget it. You just need to recall their name, and the phone will dial. It's so bad now that it's not just the phone number and address that are lost in the cloud of data—you often end up with a good number of so-called friends whom you can't recall at all. These friends get transferred to the memory of each new phone, but it doesn't help you remember who they are. It's pretty much a certainty that once you get more than a hundred people in your address book, there are at least five you can't recall at all.

Knocking on the door felt weird, and I thought, *Upside down.* My life was completely changing, my thoughts stuck on things that seemed to concern me alone. But tonight was going to be fun, and I was smiling when Andrea flung the front door of number eighty-seven wide open. It was Bunco night, and the gang was already here.

"You're here!" exclaimed Andrea. Cupping her hands as though about to blow into an alpenhorn, she bellowed, "She made it. I told you Allison would come. Now you all owe me five bucks."

"You bet on whether or not I was coming?"

"Well…yes. And let it be known that I, your humble host for the evening, am the only one who said you would be here."

Sensing that I was a little miffed about being called out as a total flake, Janine came over carrying a peace offering. She didn't even say a word; she just kissed me on the cheek and exchanged my purse for a glass of red wine. And within a couple of minutes, I realized I was not only a flake but one who could be easily bought off. *I'd make a great politician.*

Andrea's home was not large, but it was welcoming. My favorite part was the staircase with family photos arranged from her wedding day to recent smiling faces of the kids in sports and Thanksgiving photos with the entire family. It made you want to live here.

One of my favorite things was an old-fashioned phonograph. Not just a simple turntable—this was the original kind with the huge needle and the megaphone to help you hear the sound. I remember not believing it actually worked and Andrea's husband proudly bringing forth the crackling sounds of a singer from the early 1900s. The sound quality was horrible, but I was simply fascinated. I couldn't get enough of him trying to explain that small vibrations of the needle were creating the sound of this soprano's voice rising and falling. Vibrations being created by the grooves on the record that to my eye all looked the same.

Suddenly an arm wrapped around my waist, pulling me toward the kitchen. Megan said, "It's time to hear about you. We've all been waiting to hear what has kept you away for so long."

The wine helped! The fleeting snarky comments that almost escaped were trapped before they could escape my lips. Yes! I was becoming a politician. "Oh, this and that. The kids with their activities and school, Carl working late sometimes, and the occasional trip to the emergency room for my mom." OK, I said *becoming* a politician. I hadn't perfected my craft.

It's hard to decide how much to divulge of your own personal tragedy. What's the goal in the end? To gain sympathy. To give an excuse, perhaps, for all the missed events. Or maybe it's a little "I've endured worse than you." We all know those women. The ones who start to divulge their horror stories about birth when you are seven months pregnant. It's not a warning that is practical. You can't turn the clock back and not have a baby's head squeeze out of your vagina in two months' time. So, why do they insist on implanting the fear of God with their stories of labor lasting thirty-four hours? I got to the point where I was having nightmares of an epidural needle being about fourteen inches long. And I even think I started babbling to my doctor, begging for a C-section because I didn't want to rip from stem to stern. I was convinced this was a phenomenon of them trying to show that they were a little tougher than you will ever be, a way to put you down. So, for all of you women who have never had a child, let me be the first to tell you, it's a beautiful experience where the pleasures far outweigh the pain.

Maybe what I needed was practical advice from someone struggling with taking care of a parent as I was. I had been thinking that maybe I should see a therapist, and now I had the next best thing—my Bunco group. These beautiful, smart women who were currently surrounding me, waiting for me to tell all so they could enlighten me with words of wisdom. Currently, it seemed they were all poised to listen to my story. It was hard to know where to begin. So, I started at the end.

"Let's just say I've been a little overwhelmed." I filled them in on Mom's nighttime sojourn with practically no clothes on and the immediate need to get a caregiver. "And that's when I met Lana. The local hospice actually had a name board to help me get in touch with twenty-four-hour caregivers. She definitely seemed caring and willing to do things that, frankly, most people wouldn't want to do. But have you got any idea how much a caregiver costs? Think of having your child in daycare for eight hours a day, and then triple it. Even at just ten dollars an hour, since it is round-the-clock care, $250 a day is quite common."

Janine, never slow with her math, let out a slow whistle before almost whispering, "That's $7,500 a month!"

"Welcome to my world," I said sardonically. "And with all that money, you would think that would be all-inclusive, but it's not. I can't say I'm not grateful for her being there—it's giving me peace of mind. But when she presented me with receipts for gas and food, I wanted to scream. Not only because it seemed petty after paying her so much money, but also you wouldn't believe how much crap she ate. Oreo cookies, Ben & Jerry's, Ho Hos. Seriously, who eats Ho Hos after age twelve anyway? The monthly food bill for just her came to almost $500."

"Wow! That's a lot of Ho Hos!" exclaimed Megan.

"Allison, this sounds partly like a joke, partly like a nightmare," added our host.

"I wish it were. A joke, that is. Because financially, it's going to cripple us. We're already working on selling her house. Whatever we do, we have to do something quickly. This can't last forever. Lana seems like such a nice person, but it's a king's ransom to have her as a twenty-four hour babysitter. But I have taken advantage to some degree, like coming out tonight. And I don't miss being there every single night."

"You went out to your mom's every night? And kept a full-time job? And had time with your family?"

"Megan, I'm not Superwoman. It's not like I was doing a good job at any of these. You just do what you have to do. I couldn't take a night off. Pretty much the first thing I did every night when I got there was change her. Some days she was more cooperative than others, but I couldn't let her go to bed with that much urine in her diaper. A rather cruel irony is that all the pills to help with urine leakage make the patient more confused, and the doctor felt it was malpractice to prescribe one of those."

"Cruel irony. That's an understatement," chimed in Andrea. "You had to choose between more urine or more confused. I think I'd go for more wine."

"Very funny. But not far from the truth," I agreed. "And along with various chardonnays, I became very familiar with the incontinence aisle at the store. I've tried them all on her. At the end of the day, it's always the same struggle. She can get pretty feisty when I take off her clothes. She's hit me, scratched me, and yelled all sorts of obscenities that I didn't think were part of her vocabulary. You know when a two-year-old is getting so strong that you have a hard time changing them when they don't want to be changed? Well, imagine an adult. It sometimes feels like a rodeo. I've wanted to take a rope and wrap it quickly around both arms and a leg, tie it off, and yell, "*Winner!*" Instead, it's like a game where, armed with a washcloth, I do the best that I can as fast as I can go. Once her pants are back on, she calms down pretty quickly."

"Do you think she is embarrassed? Like subconsciously thinking she shouldn't be naked in front of you?"

"You know, Janine, I never thought about it that way, but you could be on to something there. Because if you think that's bad—and yes, it's every night—I try and bathe her a couple times per week in the bathtub with a shower bench. Cleaning up the bathroom afterward sometimes takes as much time. There is water everywhere because she gets so agitated. Maybe she is embarrassed. That's a really interesting idea. I haven't even asked Lana how it goes for her, but she does bathe her. Oh, and lest I forget, I feel like she is being potty trained as well. I've had to clean poop from the bed more times than I can count. And maybe I'm being too much of a psychologist about this one, but I think when I walk into her room and say some curse words of my own, she walks away with shame. Bags, gloves, hot water, lots of soap, sometimes just giving up on a set of sheets. Basically, what I'm saying is that my visits with my mom are not what I thought they would be. If someone relates that I spend a couple hours every evening with my mom as she has gotten older, that sounds so sweet. 'What a wonderful thing to do for her now that she's a widow.' Reality feels quite different. It's more like a second job. Probably closer to a bathroom janitor at a middle school."

"Do you talk much? Are you still able to have a conversation?" asked Andrea.

"No. Not really at all. That ship has sailed, for the most part. She will talk, for sure, but it's not really a conversation. At best it's a disjointed story from the past. At worst she just sits there humming to herself. So, frankly, I do a lot of the talking, and she may or may not be listening. I like to think that I do make her feel better for the company. But I'm not sure she really knows. She seems surprised every time I come. And, to tell you the truth, I'm not sure she misses me at all now that Lana is there."

"Well, that's good, at least she has Lana to keep her company."

"And I thank God for her every single day. I'm starting to get my sanity back. I'm beginning to get my family back as well. And sad but true, without Lana, I wouldn't be here tonight. So, Andrea, let me be queen for a day and ask you for some more wine," I announced loudly while proffering my empty glass.

"I'll second that," Janine added while extending her glass toward Andrea, "and let's get the game started. We need something uplifting, don't you think?"

And with that, my moaning was over. I had divulged too much. When you are walking by a coworker and ask, "How things goin'?" you don't really expect anything other than "About as well as you could expect." And if you get something worse, you try and change the subject as quickly as possible. No one wants to hear about your misery. Unless it's salacious gossip like an affair. In that case, everybody is all in, wanting every last detail down to hair fibers. Not unlike politics. Ask someone Bill Clinton's achievements during his eight-year presidency, and you'll get about as much detail as you would from a third-grader summarizing a play. But ask the same person if they recall anything about Monica Lewinsky, and you will get enough information to write a few articles for the *New York Times*. I do feel sorry for that woman. We've all been hurt in love, but I would venture to say that no one before or since has been punished as much as she.

Still, I was so glad to have spent time with my friends. I didn't expect any of them to want to open up my can of worms again anytime soon. But maybe that was not the only thing I needed them for. I did need to have some fun, and lately there had been little to laugh about until tonight. Which made me wonder, *What am I waiting for? What am I waiting for to laugh and live again?*

The elephant-in-the-room answer hit me while I was driving home. *I'm waiting for my mom to die.*

37

July 2016

I was not proud of the fact that I had started to see a therapist last year. I felt even more guilty spending money on what was basically just for me. It wasn't like I was trying to save my marriage. I wasn't dropping eighty-five dollars an hour to prevent the kids from having to live in two different households. It was just for me. This seemed so selfish. Though Carl was the one who suggested it initially, I thought he didn't push it to avoid an argument.

Janine was more like a dog with a bone. "You need an outlet to be able to say whatever you want. To really explore your emotions. No matter how much you trust Carl, or me, for that matter, it's still not as safe as a stranger."

Janine had a point. It's like that person next to you on a plane. If you told them a deep, dark secret, it would be OK. No one would ever know. And even if they thought you were crazy, you wouldn't be losing a friend.

I finally brought up the subject with my doctor, and she readily agreed with everyone. Was I really becoming that obviously depressed? "Stop giving excuses," she said. And that was how I started seeing Phyllis the MSW every other Thursday.

It was a long journey. Leaving work a few times per month was a bit of an ordeal. I had to first get an FMLA letter signed by my doctor to give to my HR department at work. This gave me permission to leave twice a month to get my head worked on by my therapist.

I then had to find Phyllis. I must have called twenty-five therapists before one called me back. But I think I chose Phyllis in the end because her name sounded kind of old-fashioned. I didn't want a twenty-five-year-old, freshly minted, master's in social work person instructing me how to think about my mom. I wanted someone with enough gray hairs to know what I was going through. Not only would she have more experience dealing with others like me, she probably had someone in her family causing her similar tensions.

Our first visit really wasn't that successful. If this had been a date, we wouldn't have made it past that first one. "What would you like to talk about today?"

And the ubiquitous "How did that make you feel?" I really hated that question. You'd have a death in the family, you'd be going through a divorce, and the therapist would want to know how you felt? Was it just me who wanted to give a wise-ass comment? Something like "It made me feel like a jelly donut. Not just like I wanted to eat one, but like I was one, sugary on the outside and all warm and comforting on the inside." The sad fact was they probably wouldn't even crack a smile. They would nod and wait for a little more of your insight to your soul.

I returned probably for only one reason: it allowed me to leave work after lunch twice per month. That seemed worth it to me even though a walk around the park seemed like it might be more productive.

But then something started to happen. It took a few visits, but she began to get me to answer my own questions. I would pose a question to her such as "Do you think I am spending more time than I should with my mom?" And after about half an hour or so, I realized she had gotten me to answer my own question. Damn! She was good.

And she would make a point to ask me, right after I would talk about my guilt about not spending enough time with Carl and the kids, "Your guilt seems to make you realize that you are neglecting your family. Are you noticing how this gives you conflict?"

After a few more sessions, I got the answer to whether I was OK with putting Mom in a nursing home. It started to seem so simple. Phyllis would guide me through my thoughts and home in on the fact that I had already made a decision, right after I said something like "I began to feel comfortable with the idea once I realized she didn't really recognize her surroundings anymore." *Bam.* She would give me that look. The look that said, "You realized you have just answered your own question."

This was so cathartic. It was like climbing the mountain to speak to the guru to give you the answer to life's key questions and then discovering you knew the answers the entire time. Phyllis just allowed me to see. I thought everyone needed a Phyllis in their lives. Because Janine was right. What helped me get at the answer was the freedom to bare my inner thoughts, those ideas we keep buried because we are afraid exposing them in the light of day would make us look crazy. Or in my case, like a monster.

It was probably four months into the process that I started to let my idea escape. Not the idea that I wanted to end my life early by starting to smoke. I hadn't even come up with that craziness yet. It was my Tell-Tale Heart. The idea that, when it came, caused me to sweat. My heart would beat faster, forcefully. And I would back down. Who could I ever tell? How could I ever get the topic started?

"What have you not asked that you need to talk about?" Phyllis asked, breaking the silence. We were about twenty minutes from the end of my session, and I was feeling pretty good about myself. Yet she knew. Was I sweating? Could she hear my heart? She was daring me to get to the part of me that was causing so much anguish.

I think it was timing in the end. She had caught me off guard. Or more accurately, with the thought in my mind right when she asked. And then out it came in all its hideousness.

"I want to smother my mom with a pillow. I want to end her misery as well as mine."

Phyllis had never really reacted to anything I had said before, but I saw a flinch. Abruptly I stood up, grabbed my purse, and ran. The door swung back so fast on its hinges I worried later I had damaged the wall. I stayed focused. *Don't trip on the stairs.* Every sound suddenly seemed so loud. Head down to avert any eye contact, I rushed out the building as fast as I dared, to not attract attention. The air was stifling as I careened through the glass doors. A wave of nausea struck me as I crossed the street to my car. I jumped in and shut the door to the world.

I began to breathe again, consciously. Deliberately. It felt as if I were the one being smothered.

What have I done? What have I done? My mom had raised a monster.

38

July 2016

UNCOMFORTABLE SILENCE. LOUD SILENCE. PHYLLIS SAT. SHE was calmly waiting after a curt hello. I would have heard the ticking of her clock, had it not been digital. I sensed Phyllis was staring, but I couldn't return her gaze. I wasn't ready. I sat there, mute.

It had been two weeks since my revelation. It's not every day that you come for a discussion about killing your mother. Melodramatic—perhaps. I reminded myself, *But the cat's out of the bag—what's the point of beating around the bush?* This was precisely what I had come to talk about.

I was sure she would have seen me earlier if I had asked, but even now all I did was look around the room. If she caught my eye, she would see my shame, and I wasn't ready to be judged. The inevitable trophy case of books became my focus, and I physically stood up to see the titles, touch the bindings. There were books on marriage, books on childhood psychology, Thoreau. Alongside the books on the developing mind were old imposing texts about anatomy and physiology.

Moving along to the wall, there were the obligatory diplomas evidencing her expertise. *Master's of social work presented to Phyllis Dunmier on this 18th day of June, 1986.*

Bachelor of arts also from the University of Cincinnati. Similarly framed was a finger painting by an A. D. I wondered if the A was for Allison. Perhaps her child.

Moving completely behind her now, I arrived at the second pair of mahogany-colored bookshelves. Though this had more scholarly books as well as some journals and magazines such as *Psychology Today*, it also had some popular books. I almost laughed out loud at the title *Are You There, God? It's Me, Margaret.* Yet this wasn't the book I pulled from the shelf. That honor went to Stephen King, also because of the title. I smiled when I saw it near the bottom—*The Shawshank Redemption*—for redemption was what I needed now. I needed to be saved from my sin.

The entire fifty minutes could have been taken up with this endeavor. In my younger days, I would peruse books at secondhand shops for hours, immersed, before deciding on the few I wanted to buy. Discovering gems that the world didn't seem to know about became a passion. It was in this reverie, thinking about *Major Pettigrew's Last Stand*, when someone touched me, and I let out a scream that I didn't realize I had in me.

"I'm so sorry, Allison. I didn't mean to startle you" came her soothing voice.

Startle wasn't really the correct word. *Scared out of my freakin' mind* captured things more appropriately. I had jumped like a surprised spider. My reverie had been replaced by dilated pupils and a pounding heart. The surroundings seemed to close in around me; the room felt even smaller. Two steps, and I sat quickly back on the couple's couch. Alone. A singular figure with no one else to spread the blame.

Was I ready? After my declaration the time before, I had spent no more than eight seconds in this office. Twenty-two minutes into our session today, I had yet to utter a word. Say what you want about Phyllis, she was patient. There were a few plants I could have stood up to examine, but save those rather boring succulents, the room had no further excuses. As I reached minute twenty-three, I finally gained the courage to look into her blue-green eyes. They were smiling. Despite her completely passive face, Phyllis's eyes were accepting of me. Despite that I had showed the ugliness inside of me, she continued to look at me as a person. Did I deserve that?

The sobbing came and wouldn't stop. Surprised as I was with the first touch of my shoulder minutes earlier, I was even more overwhelmed when I felt her arms envelop me now on the couch. The irony was that this felt like the love of a mother—unconditional. This thought made me cry even harder, something I might have thought impossible.

You would imagine that at a therapist's office, a cathartic experience would be filled with words, an intense dialogue back and forth to arrive at a conclusion. To arrive at this spot might take months or years of probing, learning. Finally, guard completely down, you would begin to get at the core of your deep-seated discontent.

For me, the experience was completely different. It was true we had spoken at length in the previous few sessions. Phyllis was able to learn about the pressures I was facing that were draining my spirit. She saw the albatross hanging steadfast around my neck.

Phyllis was clearly a good therapist, and for most, she would have been certain to offer sage words of advice. Presumably, she would have been that therapist for me as well. But she turned out to be much more than that. She freed my soul. To be clear, she didn't give me a license to kill, like James Bond. She gave me license to know that the feeling I had was OK. In her eyes, I didn't see a monster reflected. That was her gift to me.

It had been thirty months, six days, and about fourteen hours since I had first learned my mom had dementia. It had taken less than three years to turn my life completely upside down. I had become a different person with thoughts I wouldn't have believed possible. I had changed as fast as my mother.

Expected to some degree was the physical aspect of caregiving. In many ways, these just became extra chores. Laundry, preparing meals, taking her to doctors' appointments, and the like. I believe I could have gone on with these forever and not had a nervous breakdown. What I had not expected was the mental aspect. I didn't really understand what it was like to watch someone's mind regress. Not just anyone's mind, but the mind of the person whom you have the most love for in the world.

The journey had begun as family jokes about her forgetfulness. We started to imitate her talking about a family friend, saying two or three times in a row, "You remember, old what's his name." If someone came up with the name, she would just smile and reply, "Well, you knew who I meant."

I didn't think we realized at the time how much Dad must have buffered these early changes. We didn't realize that he had begun to take over things that she used to do on her own. How would we have realized that she could no longer be trusted to write a check, remember her PIN number, grocery shop, or cook on her own? With each of life's adversities after that, there seemed to be a corresponding further decline. The death of my father, her fractured hip, a urinary tract infection. And with each decline, I lost a little more of my mother forever. Her mind was just not going to come back. And what I certainly hadn't known was that there was a corresponding physical decline. I truly believed her body could have been able to function better if her mind were normal. But she began to just sit. Then she stopped talking much. She could no longer dress herself or bathe herself. She couldn't even feed herself. She would have literally starved if not spoon-fed.

Those changes were so much more than just a woman who couldn't remember you. I had imagined more of the dialogues that used to frustrate me. I had foolishly believed that repeated questions would be the worst Alzheimer's had to offer. What would I have given to go back to those times where all I had to do was repeat the same thing three or four times? What would I give for me to be that naïve person again, like everyone else who hasn't experienced dementia firsthand? Let there be no doubt, I had changed. I had come to my Brave New World as fast as my mother fell into the abyss of her mind.

Watching Mom had become torture. Not just the lifting, bathing, changing sheets, feeding. Not even the mental anguish of watching my once-eloquent mom go from babbling to moaning to often nothing at all. *Torture* is a much stronger word than that. Torture was what brought me to my new world. The world that Phyllis acknowledged with her eyes was my philosophical one. The world where I questioned the point of it all. The world where I openly questioned whether she was gaining anything from being alive. The world where, if I answered this question truthfully, it made perfect sense for her to not live another day.

What Phyllis said with her eyes that day was not conspiratorial. It was not an acknowledged, "I'll look the other way if it happens." It was that my feelings were *valid*. Like a soldier who had experienced the horrors of war, I was experiencing my own traumatic stress disorder. And thus, my feelings were normal. It was OK to feel this way.

Walking out the door of my soon-to-be-ex therapist, I realized I had never said a word the entire time. She said little more than hello. It was her gaze that spoke volumes. Her deep, blue-green eyes were all that I needed. I didn't need further words; I didn't need to return.

As I left, I realized I had received the thing that I had needed most—redemption.

39

October 2016

I DON'T KNOW HOW OTHERS FINALLY END UP IN A NURSING home. The decision likely is difficult for every family. But after years of struggling, it was a single three-day weekend that completed my journey from helping Mom in her home to paying for a twenty-four-hour caregiver to her taking up residence at Emerald Gardens—a name that likely is meant to assuage our guilt.

It was strange taking a sick day when I wasn't sick. I knew people did it all the time. Euphemistically, millennials liked to call it a "stress day." Nursing a hangover, getting a massage, or even heading to the mountains for a ski trip could qualify. But I always felt too much guilt to lie to my boss so blatantly, to hoarsely call in in a thick voice, "Boss, cough, cough...I don't think I can, cough...make it in this morning."

Ironically, of course, I would have much rather been working that particular Friday morning. Instead, after dropping the girls off at school, I headed to Mom's house to relieve Lana. Weeks before, Lana had requested this weekend off to go to a wedding on the coast. Denying her request was my first instinct. But who was I kidding? I was in no position to argue. Not only had she worked for three and a half months almost nonstop, it was for her cousin's wedding. Which meant that her relatives, some of whom sometimes substituted for her, would also be unavailable.

With less comfort than I had imagined, I ascended the three well-worn brick steps to my old house. Lana was all smiles, opening the door wide for me.

As she talked, I realized I had wrongly assessed her character. She cared for Mom. Yes, she was being paid, but the details of her daily routine showed a level of caring as good as any relative's. To help me, she had written a plan for me to follow. On paper alone it seemed a little complex, not dissimilar to a *Joy of Cooking* recipe that seemed somewhat difficult upon first read. Yet when you started trying to make it, you realized it was pretty close to impossible.

An example was using sheets to roll her in bed to make cleaning possible as a one-person job. In practice, this was an hour-long job requiring feats of strength that would test anyone's back. Lana had outlined feeding schedules, how to avoid Mom throwing food, what to give her so she wouldn't aspirate. And the tutoring went on. Lana was acting as if I had never done this job. I tried to patiently tell her I would be fine.

"Mrs. Raney, I know you know a lot, but she's really declining fast. I just worry for you here three full days by yourself."

"Lana that's sweet of you, but I'll be all right. She's my mom, after all."

"Well, you've got my number. Call if you need any help."

My three-day-weekend vigil with Mom was about to begin. These last several months with a full-time caregiver had allowed me to get my life back. My visits were not so infrequent, however, to prevent me from realizing there had been a change. This was why Lana's receding figure filled me with such dread. Lana was a large person. Would I physically even be up to this task?

The house stood quietly, the air heavy and stale. Mom still slept soundly after another long evening. I only came this early because Lana had to leave by 9:30 a.m. But I knew not to visit before eleven o'clock. *Sundowning*, the obscure word used to describe nights of pure misery, had changed her sleep pattern, a joy I had yet to fully appreciate. Lana's last words of warning were to rest in the morning while she slept, a difficult task today as two cups of Starbucks dark roast had accompanied my pancake breakfast with the girls. So, I sat in the front room and waited. Watching the world turn slowly, I relaxed until my job officially began.

At the sounds of handrail rattling, I sprang to attention. "She will keep trying to get out of bed despite the guardrails. If you don't get there in time, she will wiggle her legs through and either get caught or fall to the floor." Her advice continued: "Get her out of her wet diaper ASAP, or you will soon have urine all over the floor. She hates the wet one and will pull it off as soon as she wakes up."

Sounding like a prisoner was in the house, the rattling of the guardrail carried on. It was showtime. As I entered the room, I saw Mom rocking the rail back and forth in a trance. I had seen autistic children perseverate like this; she even moaned similarly.

"Hi, Mom."

At my voice, she stopped. "Help me," she hoarsely whispered.

"Of course, Mom. I'll get you out of there." But it was harder than I had expected. She really didn't help much anymore. I had known she was having more trouble walking, but I didn't realize she was this much of a deadweight. I felt like a firefighter trying to grasp her torso to maneuver her from the bed to the wheelchair.

Breathing heavily, I realized I hadn't accomplished much. In fact, I had made the situation worse as I hadn't removed her wet diaper as yet. Back in the bed we went. Yes, the two of us, because she had fastened her arms around my neck, and I went down with the ship. No need to go to the gym after this adventure; I was starting to sweat already.

Taking off her diaper and getting a new one on felt a little like a wrestling competition. She wasn't talking much, nor did she have much strength to walk, but she seemed to be able to wriggle like a very large toddler, especially when it was something she didn't want to do. As I started to put her diaper on, I was consciously thinking I had to do my best not to hurt her. She seemed so frail. Maybe this is why I was so surprised by what came next. She spit at me! I wanted to slap her. At least that was my first instinct.

"Mom!" I yelled. "What the hell are you doing?"

And she just glared. An odd, defiant glare as if we were in a fight. I finally finished getting the diaper on and backed away slightly, wiping spittle from my face as I sat down. The staring contest continued, and I broke first, looking away.

"Mom, do you know who I am?" I began to plead.

"Hmph" was her only reply.

"Mom, it's me, Allison. Do you still know me? Do you still love me?"

And she turned away to face the wall, away from the avalanche of tears that now began to fall.

An hour passed, and neither of us had moved. The morning ordeal had probably physically worn both of us out. But I was more hurt than fatigued. What was I doing now? Was I no longer her daughter? Was I just a caregiver? Could I have been anyone? I thought of Meredith, just a few hours ago when she was so angry at me. That hadn't felt good either. Yet it was different. Meredith had, more than once, said she hated me, but she knew who she hated and why. I could reason with Meredith. I could expect that at some point she would understand and apologize. With Meredith, I was not only her mom, I was a human being. But what was I now to my mom?

As she stirred, I decided to try again. At least this time the diaper battle was over. Looking at her more closely, now that she was in her wheelchair, I could see that a new change had happened. She no longer sat up straight. I could see why the belt. Without it she would probably catapult forward even if we weren't moving.

She seemed so uncomfortable, like a young child who fell asleep in the car, with her neck at an impossible angle.

Per instructions, I brought her to the backyard, where it was so peaceful. She seemed to perk up a little, even hum to herself. I left her for a moment to get her some water with a straw, as she could no longer master a cup by herself. She drank almost half the glass in less than a minute. It felt like a huge success. I had finally done something right. I brought a chair to sit next to her. With me holding her hand, she seemed comforted. I was comforted. This was starting to feel like it should.

As I had so many times before with her, I began talking alone. Telling her stories of things that were happening in my life. I began by telling her my idea for when I next host a Bunco party. I had decided I wanted to make it a Jimmy Buffett theme. I knew that would make her smile as "Margaritaville" was one of her favorite songs.

Her favorite singer, though, was Neil Diamond. For her sixtieth birthday, I got her tickets to a Neil Diamond concert. She was so giddy the whole night. It seemed she imagined he had come to play for her just because it was her birthday—even though her actual birthday was many weeks before. My dad came too, as who doesn't appreciate "Cracklin' Rosie" or "He Ain't Heavy." Now I found myself in our garden animatedly reliving the night of that concert. I wanted to think it was more than my imagination that she was actually listening to me, remembering. After all, this was her good time of the day, as Lana kept repeating. She made it sound as if Mom were a vampire. During the day, nothing happened, but at night, beware!

Scary tales be damned; it seemed as good a time as any to go in to try and get her to eat. Wheeling her inside to the kitchen, I thought, *Time for our next adventure.*

On a good day, per Lana, it was eggs or yogurt or banana. A not-so-good day, just Ensure through a straw. A bad day... *Seriously?*

I didn't know if I had really read or comprehended this until now. On a bad day, she would throw food at you. I couldn't imagine what she would have done to us if she saw us throwing food at another child when we were kids. How did her mind change to doing something she wouldn't ever have done or condoned before? Like spit at somebody. I couldn't imagine that was fear. Tossing her cookies, figuratively or literally, was "also a distinct possibility," added Lana. So, did she have fear? I was not really sure, but as we began to eat, I was plenty scared. I decided to go with eggs, as those seemed less disgusting in my hair than yogurt or bananas. My putting on her bib made her more aware that it was time to eat, and she perked up a little. This felt like even more of a success than the water. She was letting me spoon-feed her scrambled eggs. And then yogurt for a while. She had eaten most of it when she suddenly blew hard at the spoon, flinging some yogurt in my general direction. Quite effectively, really.

It was hard, really hard, not to take offense. Would she have done this to Jeremy? Could she have ever spit on her son, who could do no wrong in her eyes? Was she showing me a side of her that she kept hidden when she had had control of these emotions? Maybe she resented me for things I had done as a child. Perhaps she had never liked Carl and subconsciously wanted to throw shoes at him. Maybe she was indeed like a drunk person, who steps easily out of social norms to comment on your appearance, pick a fight.

That is not what I believe. When I looked at her, I saw someone who was reactionary. If something bothered her, she would strike back by any means she could. It was indiscriminate. It was not meant to be hurtful. Except that it was. It crushed my soul. Not just because of the action itself, but because she no longer knew who I was. I no longer meant anything to her.

Four and a half hours. That had been my shift so far. Sixty-seven and a half hours left to go. Maybe Lana counted the hours like this with how much money she was making. But somehow I doubted it. Finding a caregiver wasn't easy, even though she earned far more than she would in many jobs, mainly because it was twenty-four hours instead of eight. But that was also why no one wanted to do the job. It didn't end. Those sixteen hours of free time were anything but free. At any moment, you could need to really get to work. The smell drifting over from Mom let me know that this was one of those times. This was definitely one of the things I was most dreading. And there was no waiting. I couldn't just leave this like the dishes that were currently in the sink.

"It's showtime!" I declared loudly. Maybe if I approached this with zeal, it wouldn't be so bad. I sprang to my feet, put on some upbeat music, and got to work.

All I really need to say about the whole poop affair is this—it took forty-eight minutes from start to finish. I had never really timed myself wiping my butt or even changing the girls' diapers. But I guarantee you it never took more than four minutes at most. So, imagine the job taking twelve times that amount. That's really all I want to say about the subject. And that was not counting the bathroom cleanup, which was another twenty minutes, or the fact that I felt compelled to take a shower afterward—another twenty minutes. From first smell to rejoining Mom in front of the TV, it took about an hour and a half. I wanted to think that I would become more efficient with practice. But what I really wanted was to not have any more practice.

The sun started to drop slowly. It now felt like a lazy, early-summer afternoon. Sleep came easily to me, and Mom seemed content with the TV or sleeping, herself.

40

October 2016
Nancy

GOT TO GET OUT. OH NO, I'M WET AGAIN. MUST GET TO BATH-room—but I can't. This damn rail won't go down. So tired. But I'm wet. If I could just get my good leg over that rail. Got to get out. But I can't move. I'm tied to the bed! Who did this to me? Am I a prisoner?

Maybe I should be quiet. I'm going to have to wriggle. Got to get out. But I'm tired. I can't move. I'll rattle these bars like I'm in jail. Someone's got to help me. Where am I? Won't anyone come. Larry, are you there?

Finally, someone. Is that you, Mom? Somehow I've gotten stuck, and I have to get out. Ouch! That hurts. Be gentle. Stop, stop, stop! Who are you? Get away! Killing me softly...killing me softly. Don't kill me. Why won't she leave me be?

Oh God, she's taking off all my clothes. She won't stop. I'll hit. I'll bite. I'll spit. That stopped her. She's back. Oh, I give up. I hurt too much. I can't win. I'm being treated like a rag doll.

Ha-ha! She's brushing my hair, just like a doll's. That kind of feels nice. And now, oh, the sun. Now that's living.

I'm feeling so tired now I could just go to sleep. Or even just close my eyes and hear the birds. It's so nice out here.

41

October 2016

DINNER WAS PERHAPS OUR BEST TIME. MOM HAD ALWAYS LOVED tomato soup. I figured this was also thick enough that she wouldn't choke on it. Dessert was applesauce with cinnamon. It was comical, thinking about regression. It really felt as if I were feeding a two-year-old. The need for a bib, the types of food, the time. It could take up to an hour feeding a child, and feeding Mom was no different. I wouldn't say she seemed happy. She just seemed neutral, content. That was good enough for me. Again, I was feeling that I had been victorious in my latest task of the day.

I figured by now it was time for another bathroom adventure, the preemptive kind. This was where I would have her torso lie on my back while I maneuvered her clothes and diaper out of the way before setting her back down on the toilet. What could possibly go wrong with this strategy?

At first, she just sat there for minutes on end. Lana was right again, however. Running her hand under warm water did the trick, and she peed. We reversed the process and headed back to the living room.

I had listened to enough music for the day. After turning off the radio, I decided to read out loud. She seemed to nod in approval. But who could be sure? It felt a little as if I might be doing the equivalent of anthropomorphizing a pet. Who cared anyway? What difference did it make if I was wrong about what she was thinking if it made me feel a little better in the end. So, I read her to sleep. A slow, deliberate-breathing, tranquil sleep.

I worried it might be too early. I considered shaking her awake, but that seemed wrong. I decided to turn the TV on, hoping the flickering and noise might waken her gently or at least cause poor sleep. But it seemed I was the only one watching the ten o'clock news. After the second or third murder they described, I too had fallen asleep. It had been a long day.

The vampire awakened. I had napped for just a moment. The news had moved on from murder but not yet past the crime and scandal. The weather and good stories were still another ten minutes away.

The sound of the vampire must have awakened me. Grunts mostly. Occasional unintelligible words. Mom was awake. Wide awake, it seemed, with eyes glazed yet vibrant. She didn't seem to notice me, focused solely on removing the belt tying her to the wheelchair. Squirming, she was wriggling downward to the floor. In anguish now, she was trapped in what must have been an uncomfortable position. I had to let her go. Picking her up from the floor, I was surprised to see her walk without a cane. But she moved and didn't seem to want to stop. She moved slowly yet in a frantic way. She seemed desperate. It was sundown for us.

I first tried a redirect, actually funneling her into her room. Agitatedly, she was looking wide-eyed, touching everything. For balance? I was not sure. The walls, the dresser, the blinds, all being touched while she walked around in a circle. I grabbed her as if we were dancing and pushed us onto her bed, where we sat. Rested. I even was able to lift her feet off the floor and get her to lie down.

Celebrating way too early, I thought I had won. She was in bed, and it wasn't even 11:00 p.m. The rails were up; she was comfortable. But she wasn't asleep. I turned off the lights, hoping. I hoped the world would be silent. No jets overhead, no motorcycles revving their engines, no barking dogs, just silence. *Let her sleep through the night. Let me sleep through the night.*

An hour or so went by. All was not well.

I wasn't even sure what woke me. It was clearly much closer to midnight than sunrise. The air was too heavy, the darkness too complete for my wish of morning to have come true. Though it was quiet now, I knew I had to get up. All was not well.

The light from the hallway illuminated all I needed to see. Nancy was caught in the railings, halfway out of bed, moving like a fly trapped in a web. So preoccupied with her task of freeing herself, she never heard me approach. I know there is tremendous controversy about physically or with medicines restraining patients. This wouldn't be a controversy at all if she were just going to read the night away in her armchair. Calming her was so necessary. She was truly a danger to herself or others.

The fact was, freeing her was going to trap me into watching her every move. Slowly, I went about my task of untangling her arms and legs. The last year I would have rushed to help her, but I had learned one doesn't run toward a punishment.

Almost like a windup soldier set on its feet, Mom was freed, ready to roam. She had had seemingly little or no energy during the day. But now, once removed from the prison of the bed rails, she was off exploring once again. Resembling a sleepwalker, she seemed to again want to touch everything. Perhaps for balance, maybe for some other unclear reason. Only her mind could say.

After she broke her hip, the combination of pain, grief, narcotics, and dementia had caused a decline that just seemed to accelerate. Having her fall was therefore the last thing I wanted to have happen.

And so, for the next few hours, we paced the house. We went from room to room, turning on and off lights as we went. At one point, during a rest, I got her to drink some Ensure. I confess to drinking a little brandy myself. Certainly, if brandy alone could have gotten her to sleep at 3:40 a.m., I would have given her the entire bottle.

They always say, "Don't try to wake someone who is sleep-walking." Why they say this, I really have no idea. I've never met someone who walked in their sleep. But what I do know is that trying to talk or reason with Mom in the middle of the night was impossible. She might have been a shell of her former personality during the day, but at night she was someone completely differ-ent. This person was unpleasant and mean. Much like the defiant person who spat on me at the start of the day. In summary, I spent about four hours in the middle of the night alongside someone with a nasty personality.

Medicare, in their wisdom, had sought to address this con-cern. They decided that caregivers had had the wrong approach for so long. In 1991, Dr. Mark Beers published a paper with a long list of drugs that should be avoided in people living in long-term care facilities. Medicare ran with his idea that these drugs were causing more harm than good and not only advised avoiding these drugs—they refused to pay for them. A Big Brother way of ensuring you don't do the wrong thing. One of the big no-nos is anything that might cause a senior to be sleepy.

When I first heard this from Dr. Metcalf, I said, "Are they fuck-ing kidding me?" Now I wondered if any of those experts had ac-tually spent a single night with a sundowning patient. If you could use a medicine that might keep them in bed rather than wandering all night in a drunken stupor, why would you not? Was I missing something really obvious here? And what is the recommended treatment? you may be wondering. *Nothing.* Perhaps the number one thing that could cause a caregiver to go crazy was sundowning, and the medical establishment had concluded that doing nothing was the best option. Ironically, if I asked for a sedative to help *me* sleep from 6:00 a.m. to 11:00 a.m., they would have given it to me in a heartbeat. Regular insurance didn't have that stupid rule, only Medicare. So, I could take my Xanax or Valium or whatever at 6:00 a.m. This way we could both become vampires.

By the end of the night, just when it was starting to get light outside, Mom calmed down. She was like a rooster with the wrong clock—crowing all night and ready to sleep when the sun came up. The agitation started to just vanish, and she made her own way to bed. She even let me help her brush her teeth.

As Saturday morning was about to start for the rest of the world, we were settling down to rest. Just two more days to go.

42

October 2016

I WOKE UP ON THE THIRD DAY BLIND WITH EXHAUSTION. RINGS under my eyes, a dour expression, and an attitude to match. It was this weekend that had changed me. This weekend, when I officially became burned out as a caregiver. And I knew I would never go back. I had learned what it was like to have Alzheimer's in the late stages. I wanted none of it. I didn't want to be a caregiver; I didn't want to be cared for. I vowed to never do that to my family or anyone. I didn't want my family to resent me like I now resented my mom. And so, Allison's Brave New Philosophy was born. It was simple really: to avoid being cared for, you had to die before you became reliant on others. Boom, a one-sentence philosophy.

My mind, punch-drunk as it were, couldn't stop at the ramifications. I bet when Darwin first thought of evolution, he saw it in one species: the finch. Once the idea began, he couldn't help but see it everywhere. That was happening to me now. The more I thought, the more obvious it all seemed. Dying early was the better choice. There were just way too many positives. It's not like I hadn't thought about these concepts before. I guess the difference is that I had never really believed I needed to change my life. After this weekend, though, I think this is what got me to truly desire the idea of a deadline. No pun intended. A deadline would completely eliminate the gray zones. I wouldn't have to argue what it meant to be "reliant on others."

My philosophy would argue that our happiness, our self-worth, our accomplishments on earth are not dependent upon a length of time lived. In short, our reason for living doesn't require us to live as long as our bodies will possibly allow. A deadline is not only needed to avoid being cared for—it can provide a huge positive to our lives and humanity. Two birds with one stone.

As I staggered around Mom's house, I thought, *If we made a cutoff, age seventy being our last day of life, what would change?*

The world would have so many more resources for those left behind.

We would live with renewed purpose. As fifty, sixty, and sixty-five years of age came, we would live with increasing vigor, striving to make our lives as meaningful as possible. Deadlines do this naturally. Our productivity increases greatly knowing that there is an end.

I continued my mental list as I tried to feed Mom. *Some argue our lives' purpose also would be heightened. Ask anyone who feels death is imminent, and their appreciation for all that they see and do multiplies.*

We wouldn't need caregivers. The memories of our loved ones would remain as they had lived.

And money goes hand in hand with resources, but so much of our health care dollar is spent in the last few weeks of life. We spend so much of our lives saving for the later years, not knowing when they might end. How freeing it would be to not worry about money after age seventy!

The only detail I hadn't figured out for humanity: How was this supposed to happen? Where was Dr. Kevorkian when you needed him?

It could be argued I was delirious at that point. Forty-eight hours with what felt like no sleep. Physically I was feeling broken. Mentally things were even worse. I could hear arguments from everyone over seventy, and those who were fast approaching. They would argue my experience was unique. They might even commiserate while gently chiding me for such a reactionary solution.

But I would counter that they were the ones being naïve. People didn't seem to realize that they too would one day die. They knew it intellectually, but they didn't really see themselves on death's doorstep. No one wanted to imagine what that step really felt like. And so, everyone erroneously believed they would one day just fall asleep and pass away happily at age ninety-four. But how many have really given thought to exactly how they will die?

It's similar to when you ask a teenager what they want to be when they grow up. Not once has a high school student said, "When I grow up, I'd like to be a homeless heroin addict who dies a meaningless death shivering next to a garbage-can fire." Despite the fact that we know this will happen to a handful, it seems ludicrous to imagine this will be your fate.

When answering how we are going to die, we leave out all the potential bad things. We don't even consider them. And yet unlike becoming a heroin addict, which will only afflict a few, every single last person will eventually die.

While watching my mother die a slow, meaningless death of forgetfulness, I began to contemplate death's choices. I began to realize they all seemed bad. Even those who "beat" cancer after going through the torture of radiation, surgery, and chemotherapy eventually succumb to...the cancer again. Or something else. A stroke, leaving them helpless, unable to talk or move one side of their body. A slow death from COPD or heart failure resulting in frequent ER and hospital visits. Dialysis where, three days a week, you would get hooked up to a machine to prolong your agony for another couple of years.

Looking at Mom, uncomfortable in her wheelchair, I thought, *My final answer: no!* I was not having a uniquely miserable experience watching my mom die from dementia. The body had found countless unpleasant ways to die. And the farther we have gone with technology, the longer we have been able to prolong these agonies. An agony, I had realized, that might be just as hard on the caregiver as it was for the dying patient.

It was during this weekend that I decided how I was going to change my course. Not only would I take up smoking, I would refuse any and all treatments. The death would be sooner and the dying process shorter.

Very early Monday morning, Lana returned from the wedding on the coast. I had mixed feelings. Not that I was sad to be leaving my mom to return home. Far from it. I was physically and emotionally spent. The last three days had been a misery I didn't wish anyone to ever go through. My mixed emotions came when I realized Mom no longer knew. She no longer knew who I was or who was caring for her. I truly believed that Lana cared for my mom. But despite her caring, I had learned that Mom didn't notice. It could have been me, Lana, or a gaggle of other caregivers. It thus made more sense to get her to a nursing home where there were more people to care for her and so that we could sell her house to pay for all of this.

Before this weekend, I had felt tremendous guilt about the idea of placing her in a nursing home. I now realized she wouldn't even notice. Hence, the only positive thing out of this whole affair was that my guilt about sending her into a nursing home could be gone. She had never wanted to be in one, but if she didn't know...

As I was walking out the door, I wanted to tell Lana that she would soon need to be looking for another job. But I wasn't ready to disappoint. I found myself walking away giving her only my thanks for all that she had done.

I wasn't sure what a prisoner feels when the gates finally open. What came to me were lots of mixed emotions with a dominant sense of relief. The breeze striking my face as I left 5981 Rosemont Lane seemed to infuse life back into me. I wanted to open up my arms like Andy Dufresne from *Shawshank* after he escaped via the sewer. I wanted to feel life again.

It had been days since I had seen the girls. Only now did I start to miss them. Similarly, I hadn't even missed Carl. I presumed my mind had preferred to shut out intrusive happy thoughts while I was there. But now I was ready to enjoy life again. And dare I say it? I already knew I was going to enjoy it more. I was going to experience more from life and be more appreciative because of my newfound philosophy.

Anxiety. Growing rapidly as I headed to the local pharmacy. Exhilaration. I was going to do it. I hoped to sound calm, rehearsed when asking for Marlboro Lights. Yes, I wanted to jump headlong into my new habit, but I didn't want to cough through the entire first pack. The full-strength Marlboros would have to wait for another day. I was sure some of my anxiety was knowing the person behind the counter was going to be the first person to judge me. But I needn't have worried. First off, she seemed to have seen more than one variety of mind-altering substances in her life. She also had about six tattoos that I could count and acted as if she had only twenty minutes left of a twelve-hour shift. She handed over the pack of cigarettes and lighter with a distraction bordering on being a robot. Was I a little disappointed the interaction was so anticlimactic? This was the first pack of cigarettes I had bought in my life, and it felt so mundane.

My next stop was the river. I needed a walk. I needed my cigarette. Maybe there was a fear that if I didn't start now, I would timidly avoid my new plan. Return to the instinct everyone else seemed to have about self-preservation. Shaking. Lack of experience perhaps. It took me several tries to light my first cigarette on this windy morning. Brave. I began.

Yes, I coughed. There wasn't an instruction manual on how to breathe in, just warning labels from the surgeon general. Still, it wasn't that hard to get the hang of, and in a few minutes, I was energized. I'm still not sure how much was the nicotine itself and how much was the understanding that I was taking control of how I was going to die, but I felt fantastic. The water seemed bluer, the colors of the leaves more vibrant. I felt the air going in and out of my lungs. My heartbeat was stronger. I was tingling. I was more alive than I thought I had ever been.

That first day was also exhilarating because I was being a rebel. I had a whole pack, a lighter, and miles of trail to be a bad girl. Doesn't everyone secretly envy the Joker for being able to revel in the idea of not following the rules? Well, for the first time in years, I was doing something gloriously wrong... and yet it felt so right.

I closed my eyes. I breathed in the smell of the smoke while listening to the wind flowing through the trees. The morning sun glinted off the snaking river, flowing with apparent slowness. Birds were beginning to sing, and I joined in spirit. Whistling was never my strong suit. Plus, it was time to return to my home. But I had to clean up first and return to responsible Allison.

I wasn't prepared to tell Carl or the girls yet about my smoking habit. When I kissed Carl, I had better be ready. I put on a clean blouse from the car and started the first of several mints for the drive home. The fresh air didn't hurt either. I just wasn't prepared to deal with Carl's judgment. Or anyone else's, for that matter, as I got more than a few glares along the bike trail. Carl had been through enough lately already. What he was sure to notice, however, was now that I was planning to die, I couldn't wait to really start living.

A start that began immediately upon coming through my front door. "Mommy, Mommy!" squealed Sloane and Meredith in unison. Carl remained behind at first, allowing the girls to smother me for a while. Soon we were in a group hug that felt glorious.

Everyone was so chatty, including me, as I had basically been talking to myself for three days.

But there was no time. It was just before 8:00 a.m.; Carl had to go off to work, and I got to take the girls to school. I noticed he had already made their lunches. I had planned for a late start as I knew I would have to catch up on things before heading to the office at ten.

I realized almost immediately that was a mistake. Not only had I forgotten what caregiving is like, it had become so much more difficult. I soon realized I wasn't simply physically exhausted, I was mentally spent. My months of just visiting mom and living my own life had removed me from that incredible stress. This weekend changed all of that. And now I had to drag myself to work in a couple of hours.

That was an error in judgment that I would regret. I should have taken the entire day off. Maybe the whole week. Because that week I spent countless hours with Jeremy on the phone and with nursing home directors at their facilities. It felt a little like deciding on which college to go to when I was younger. Similar to colleges' pamphlets, the brochures just didn't provide the real impression or prepare you for the almost-instant feeling when you walk in: "Ain't no way I'm going to let my mother live here."

What I did gain from those few weeks of deciding was a sense of the caring the directors generally showed to their residents. It's a very difficult job, which is why we pawn it off to complete strangers.

When we had narrowed it down to three, Jeremy flew down to help me decide. What persuaded him was the kindness of the staff when they didn't think we were looking. A little like the line we tell our children: "Integrity is doing the right thing even when nobody is watching."

43

December 2016

I STOOD OVER THE TABLE, SCATTERING ART SUPPLIES. "COME ON, girls, this will be fun. It's supposed to be fun," I added.

"Yeah. Well, it's not," came the response from Meredith.

"But you haven't even started. And we can get more things, if you like. I grabbed everything I could think of yesterday at Michaels." I pointed. "You've got crayons, finger paints, glitter, even some stickers. And now it's time to let your imagination run wild. A blank piece of paper. Anything you want."

"There!" After stabbing the blank white sheet with a single dot of blue, Meredith announced, "I'm done. Have Sloane do it."

"I am. Mommy, tell her I am drawing," said the ever-pleasant one of my girls.

I really dreaded the day that both of them required as much work as Meredith. If it was just the age, then it was going to be a miserable few years when they were both teenagers. But Sloane had always been easier. It wasn't that Meredith was not loving at all. Sometimes she really needed me and could hug me like she would never let go. Meredith desperately craved encouragement, wanting approval more than anything else. Yet if you looked up *contrarian* in the dictionary, there would be a picture of Meredith. When she was younger, if you asked her to clean up her toys, she simply would not do it while anyone was watching. What happened next was equally predictable: she would drag me back to the scene to exclaim, "Oh, wow! Meredith, this room looks beautiful. I love it. You even organized your room differently." In some ways they were like two cats with totally different personalities. Sloane was always running in and out of your legs, seeking attention. Meredith was happy to disappear, quick to scratch you randomly. They would both curl up with you at times, but Meredith...she could purr on your lap so sweetly words couldn't describe the feeling she gave. It made you wonder if the pleasurable times were made all the sweeter simply because they took so much effort.

"Oh, Meredith, I know you can do more than that. And remember, you aren't doing this for a grade. It doesn't matter how it turns out. Grandma will love it just because it comes from you."

"But, Mom! I'm awful at art. I would draw if I could be like Dad or Sloane, but I can't. I'm just like you. You're terrible. It's not like you play Pictionary anymore. You know, where every animal looks identical—four legs, a couple ears, and a tail. Even your stick figures look like they're drawn by a four-year-old."

"OK, OK, I get it. I'm not good either."

Sloane then started to laugh. In the middle of making what was becoming a dense forest on her multicolored drawing, she had to stop. She was laughing too hard. Soon the three of us were all laughing.

"Sloane, what on earth could be so funny?"

"Because you are really bad, Mom. Meredith is right—you are terrible." And then more laughter. I thought she might fall out of her chair. Pantomiming, they both started to pretend they were drawing like me in the air.

"You know, you two, I'm not that bad! At least I don't look like that when I draw. You act like I have some type of neurologic disease."

"Sloane, do you remember that time she tried to draw the word *beach* and the only thing she managed was a wavy line and the sun?" More laughter.

"Mom, I've got a great idea. Not just a good idea, but a lightbulb-blowing-up fabuloso idea," Sloane finally managed to say. "Why don't you and Meredith have a contest? You both do a drawing for Grandma, and then Dad can try and guess who did each one."

Like in a game of chess, you sometimes know you have lost long before the word *checkmate*. If I was going to get any effort out of Meredith on this one, I was going to have to draw. Ugh. I really did hate art. My mom used to feel sorry for me when I was a kid. It was the only homework she ever really helped me with because I would start crying. I could spend hours and hours trying as hard as I could. Eventually, she would take pity and do it for me. The irony. Now I was going to be doing artwork for her.

We shook on it as if we were about to start a duel, Meredith exaggeratedly pumping my arm up and down. "May the best drawer win!" And with that, she sat down in fierce concentration. I thought, *What is it with kids?* It seems they like nothing more than to best their parents at some competition. Though they are gleeful when you let them win at a young age, they must know it isn't really a competition. Because when they are older and can actually beat you, that's pure solid-gold pleasure.

I had little choice—the gauntlet had been thrown. The cause was also mine, so I had no excuse; we were doing this to brighten the somewhat austere nursing home room that mom inhabited at Emerald Gardens. For months I had looked upon her mostly empty walls and felt we needed to do something to make the room look happier. More alive. Grabbing my twenty-four-by-thirty-six-inch blank white sheet of paper, I joined my two at the table. For the first time in probably thirty years, I was going to do some art. Luckily, I had bought glitter.

I was sure my therapist would agree with every other therapist I had ever heard on the subject. Looking at someone's art could be a window to their subconscious. The colors they used, the subjects. Keenly aware that my mood had been quite dark lately surrounding my mom, I felt I had better make a conscious decision to make this as sunny as possible. This led me to stare at the white piece of paper for quite a while. I couldn't stop thinking of drawing the picture that came to mind of Mom, walking in the middle of the night, completely lost. So, I began with a large sun in the corner. I even gave it a face for added cheer. I might not be able to outsmart a therapist, but I could certainly fool my girls and my mom with dementia.

44

February 2017

I NEVER SENT OUT FORMAL INVITATIONS; THAT WAS WHY GROUP texts were invented. But for some reason, doing so this time seemed fitting. This night was going to be special to me. I was trying to create happiness. I sent fifteen cards and began household preparations.

Carl and the girls didn't mind, actually. They had such a good relationship. On the rare occasions that I hosted Bunco night at our house, he would treat them to something special. They brainstormed for days about what they were going to do.

The three of them would first be going to Carl's favorite restaurant, Red Robin. He was really just a big kid, so they were always happy with his choice. I hoped they didn't have too many onion rings because the true cherry on top of their evening was the swimming. The only thing the girls were talking about these days was the heated pool at the hotel. A chance to swim for hours in the middle of February seemed better than Christmas. So, guilt, I had none. Well, not on that topic. While I was trying to re-create my social life, the three of them would be squealing like pigs at the state fair. Well, probably only two little pigs—Carl presumably would be squealing only on the inside.

Typically, when it was my turn to host, I was pretty lazy about the food. I had even been known to just order pizza. This time was different. My fridge was bursting with food. I was offering three types of salad: potato, pasta, and caesar. If I were to analyze myself, I would say that I was throwing myself a coming-out party. This night was not just a get-together with fifteen of my friends, it was a referendum upon me. It was not that I didn't feel love from my family—I couldn't ask for better. But I wanted people to recognize me again. I had had these same feelings going back to work after maternity leave. I had been walled up in my house for so long with such a defined role—mom. I was the breastfeeder, cleaner-upper, soothing person for weeks on end. Tired to the point where lifting my eyelids could have classified as a workout. I no longer cared what I looked like, with bags under my eyes, ill-fitting sweats, a swollen belly, cracked nipples, and all. Yes, motherhood was the greatest job I'd ever had, but I started to miss being an attractive woman. Not that I wanted anyone other than Carl. Still, I wanted a night where I would go out and heads would turn my direction. I enjoyed twirling in a new dress, showing off in front of my friends. Hearing the compliments about my earrings or how much weight I had lost. I needed to be told sometimes that I looked great.

And just like when you are a kid, praise can't come from your family. When Dad absently says, "Don't you look wonderful," it means something…but not very much. If a kid at school, or your girlfriends, or even a total stranger says something complimentary—this you recall for days.

This is all starting to sound like I was pretty vain. Perhaps I was to some degree. But my exterior had always seemed to reflect what was happening inside my head. When I was confident, I thought I even walked more upright. There was a bounce in my step.

This all gets me to the white dress with blue polka dots and matching belt, the new shoes that I also bought just for Bunco night. I had gone shopping for me, no one else. In fact, this entire night was all about me. It felt as if it had been years since I had been so selfish. And when you think about it from that perspective, it's a little sad. More than a thousand days of caregiving, and I was finally devoting all my attention to just one night for me.

Two months had passed since we finally placed Mom in a nursing home. The guilt had yet to recede. Nonetheless, we made the decision over years, really, and only after much heartache. But the decision had led to this, Bunco night at my house. I just hadn't had the time before.

Meanwhile, Jeremy knew how difficult things had been for me, and so despite being out of town, he was the one who had put Mom's house on the market. He had taken care of all those details. It still broke my heart a little each time I drove by and saw a For Sale sign in the front yard. Still, this was yet another weight off my shoulders, and I was very grateful.

As Saturday arrived, Carl and the kids were acting like they were going for a weeklong vacation. They had even gone shopping because Sloane needed a new bathing suit, which led to several more articles of clothing. And Carl couldn't have Sloane get something without buying something for Meredith. He could be such a softy when it comes to shopping. It was scary to imagine them as older teenagers—they did such a good job of manipulating him already. Which would explain why they spent even more money than I did! This Bunco night was turning into a vacation; it even had the requisite hotel bill. But life is for living, right? And there's no point taking money with you to your grave.

The music was on, and I was dancing by myself for an hour or two before my friends were supposed to arrive. Well, dancing and making sure everything looked how I wanted. I had created a playlist for the entire evening. Two playlists, actually, just in case the mood needed to be changed. My first was more background music. Not the boring Kenny G kind of background music. Real jazz. I had a mixture of South African jazz, Cuban rhythms, and old Louis Armstrong kind of stuff. The second playlist had more vocal tracks, and they were generally a little more upbeat, sing-able tunes. These were the ones I would often go running with, earbuds bouncing as I went along. The first song on that playlist was a no-doubter: "I'm Still Standing." First of all, you can never go wrong with Elton John. If I decided that second playlist was needed to pick up the mood, I would probably get up on the table and dance, singing at the top of my lungs. I guess I did feel like a survivor. Tonight was my time to get back to living again. Because, in the end, I was still standing. And it felt good to be back.

The gang arrived almost en masse. It seemed as if they had all come off of the same bus. I guess that's what invitations will do for you.

Jessica was the only one to come fashionably late, and she looked stunning as always. This time, though, it was different. She now had movie-star looks. I certainly was not the only one who was jealous of her mommy makeover. It was hard not to stare at her flat stomach, the perky boobs. Not knowing her, you would think she had never had kids. Though the rest of the makeup and that large hoop earrings left her far from virginal in appearance. Or, as Janine would have said, "a little East of Eden." *Damn, women can be catty,* I thought. *Why can't we just be happy for someone instead of putting them down to detract from our own jealousy?*

"You've got to be kidding!" shouted Margo from the backyard. "I was wondering where everything was." As she came through the french doors, I was surprised with not only a bear hug but also a kiss on the cheek. "Allison, you really outdid my party, and yours has only just begun."

"I take it you discovered my theme. Well, don't just stand there everyone—let's go!" The rest of us headed outside. Parrots, frogs, and primary colors abounding adorned much of the backyard. And in the corner was my masterpiece, looking a bit like a lemon-ade stand for kids with a large sign above reading Margaritaville.

"I tried to get Jimmy Buffett, but he said another group offered him more."

"Allison, you continue to amaze me. Just a few weeks of freedom and you came up with all of this," Margo said.

"It's sickening," added Janine. "I'm semiretired, and I could never get my backyard looking like this. But I know the cure for my newfound sense of inadequacy, and it's got salt all over it."

"Please tell us you got a male stripper to bartend."

"That idea went the way of Jimmy Buffett," I replied. "But if we turn this into a poker night and get you all wasted, maybe I'll have enough money by the end to hire Mr. Rent-a-Cop."

And with that, the drinks and conversation started to flow. Luckily the only difficult thing about Bunco is keeping the dice on the table. Which is probably why we played Bunco instead of poker. Plus, I never really could get poker. Not only did it seem like games took longer than a melting glacier, I would always forget which hand was better. There was nothing worse than thinking you had won the pot only to find out that a full house was actually better than your straight. Or is it the other way around?

The only reason that our games took all night was that we hardly played. It was just that Bunco night sounded so much more palatable than gossip night. Let's face it, though, there was a lot of gossip to go around, more than enough to fill the four to five hours of playing time. What seemed to get all of us going was Jessica's impending divorce. I hated to say it, but the mommy makeover was a clear sign. I had even joked with Carl that the reason I looked so frumpy was that I was content in our marriage. Nonetheless, it wasn't her looks that made us all buzz—it was the money laundering. Apparently, her soon-to-be ex had tried to gift money to his siblings with the presumption they would gift him back after the divorce was final. Hearing about their drained savings was both awful and fascinating at the same time.

"Can he really get away with that?"

"Is it even legal to give away your money without your permission?"

Unfortunately, out of our jury of sixteen, we hadn't a lawyer among us. So, putting his siblings on the payroll of his business seemed fiendish, yet possibly quite legal. But what did we know? Well, enough to give all sorts of random advice while reflecting on our own marriages. It was probably sobering tales such as Jessica's that helped keep some unhappy marriages together. The divorce could seem that much worse, the inevitable attempts to hurt one another a rite of passage. The breakup of a marriage was endlessly variable in the cause of the downfall, and singularly common in its cruelty.

As the evening was coming to a close, I realized that Jessica's misery had helped make my evening that much better. Not that I was so sadistic that I wanted her to be in so much distress, but it diverted the attention away from me. In fact, it may have been the first six-hour stretch in the last several years in which I hadn't thought of my mom even once. And the cherry on top: I got to go to bed without having to help anyone but myself.

45

February 2017

CONSCIOUSNESS CAME SLOWLY. I RARELY SLEPT ALONE, WHICH added to my disorientation. The four or five margaritas from the night before certainly didn't help. As my eyes adjusted to the bright light, feelings started to accompany the headache. My emotions seemed to echo the physical, contentment and foreboding mirroring my relaxed yet hungover state. It would be nice to revel solely with the yin part of the equation. The warmth, the smiles, the memories of last night. Yet as the sun rose slowly, it illuminated those dark recessed areas of my subconscious that I would gladly have kept hidden—along with a heaping dose of nausea, which became hard to keep at bay.

My guilt, which seemed to compete with my pleasure, began to surface as well. It was hard not to recognize that my recent happiness had coincided with abandoning my mom in a nursing home. As a parent, I know I always feel that I would sacrifice my happiness for my children's. But was I making this assumption for my parent? *Mom, I hope you don't mind that I'm leaving you in the care of total strangers so that I can continue to live my life and feel pleasure again. Is that OK with you?*

I had not had many conversations with either of my parents about death. It was just not a subject anyone wanted to talk about. In fact, any mention between us could hardly be called a conversation, more like snippets, as related to a movie or some news story.

I remembered as a girl when the case of Karen Ann Quinlan was in the news. I distinctly remembered hearing the word *coma* for the first time and not understanding why some wanted her to die. For a while, I feared going to sleep. I worried that if I didn't wake up soon enough, someone might pull the plug on me.

Inevitably there were more cases. As I got older, it seemed so obvious that it made no sense to have your body go on if your mind wasn't living. My whole family was in agreement, and we just couldn't understand the other side of keeping a brain-dead person alive. My other distinct memory, though, was the nursing home. Mom, specifically, used to say adamantly, "Shoot me first."

My dilemma: Was my mother brain-dead or not? And in either case, had I not committed the ultimate sin by placing her in a nursing home?

When I first thought about caring for someone with dementia, I had imagined that most of my difficulty would be in the forgetting aspect of the disease. In fact, I thought that was all dementia was—a memory problem. I would just need to mature and get used to repeating myself, her forgetting appointments, and her not recognizing me. How naïve. If this was all Alzheimer's did to a person, caregiving wouldn't be so hard. I think I could have lived with that alone, but it is so much more. What most don't realize is that as the disease progresses, they become incapable of eating, toileting and bathing. We forget that they stop being a companion and fade into silence. We simply don't realize they lose all ability to be a part of life.

Following their memories goes their personality. Who they are disappears. Their soul to be replaced by a noninteracting, unfeeling, uncaring machine. A demanding, frail, unappreciative robot. One that saps every last bit of emotion. In short, this near-person, who is no longer your relative, is drowning and taking you down with them. Your only choice at the end is to let go.

PART 4

46

January 2018

IF YOU HAVE NEVER BEEN INSIDE A NURSING HOME, YOU REALLY will not know what to expect. If you have been inside one, you've seen them all. Emerald Gardens, not unlike its residents, was a little dated. Neatly tucked away on a tree-lined street, it might be mistaken for a Montessori school. Except schools try to prevent strangers from coming in—Emerald Gardens alarmed their doors to prevent residents from getting out.

I had joked that nursing homes were like college dorms for the elderly. You would take your meals in a common room and all sorts of activities were planned throughout the day, yet you could always retreat to your room if desired. What set them apart from all other living environments was the atmosphere. Like the pervasive smell, it was heavy and unpleasant. Nurses, physical therapists, and wound-care personnel bustled about while the patients slowly shuffled from one place to another.

It was remarkably predictable; staff members could look at their watches and tell you where a patient was at any specific time. "It's two o'clock, so George will be doing chair aerobics, and Louise is listening to the piano." A good number of residents rarely left their rooms unless prodded by staff or a relative.

Nancy MacPherson fell into that category. Most of her physical movement from one day to the next was from her bed to a chair for a few hours and then back again. If she wore a step counter, she would likely have fallen 9,994 steps short of the 10,000-step daily goal.

After signing the visitors' ledger, I dodged the wheelchair bumper car participants on the way to room 127A. Past the dining hall, where a few were playing checkers two hours after breakfast had concluded. I hope that the moaning lady of 127B was terrorizing some other hall. Only once had I been so lucky. Today turned out not to be lucky day number two. Gwendolyn R. was still in her bed facing the wall, moaning. As I had grown accustomed to, this moaning would only increase in volume once she heard Mom and me talking. Though to be more correct, it was just me talking, and Mom maybe listening.

Why did I go? It was hard to answer this, really. I tried to come at least once a week. Occasionally Carl or the girls would come, but these weren't productive visits. Children don't filter their emotions like adults. And it wasn't just what they said; they were physically repulsed. They would feign vomiting upon entering. They refused to sit down or touch anything, afraid of whatever substance might be on the back of that chair. Once Meredith had to use the bathroom. We had to leave early to go to Starbucks because of her dread of the contaminated bathrooms. As an adult, I might not have said things out loud like Meredith, but I sure felt the same way.

I used to laugh at my mom when she would talk to her plants. Yet there I was, sitting between Gwendolyn R. moaning at the wall and Mom mouthing words without a sound. I was telling stories of recent events that might as well have been directed at a plant.

Guilt? Duty? Whatever the reason, I went less often as the months went by. I began to focus on my daily routine. I was getting my life back. As intruding thoughts about my mom receded, my happiness began to return. It became harder and harder to return to Emerald Gardens. The failure to connect made the visit both meaningless and discouraging. What could possibly be going through her mind? What was she gaining from being alive?

The more I did give it thought, the more I realized I needed to visit the doctor again. What were my goals? Was I doing Mom more harm than good? Did she even need medicine anymore? The cost of her medicines really wasn't bothering me much anymore; perhaps I was resigned. More likely it was just that she was already down to nothing. Her house and money were all gone now. The state was going to pick up the tab from here. Still, why should anyone pay for medicines that were doing her no benefit? More importantly, why should she have to endure side effects for a pill that wasn't helping? Despite the high-priced pills, she had gone from independent though confused to nearly catatonic and in a nursing home.

Noticing my frustration, I thought, *I guess this means I'm not completely over the cost thing.* I had done more research, and with every new drug, I became more frustrated. I really started to notice all of the advertisements. A little research had become a dangerous thing for my sanity because I would get more frustrated with every smiling commercial.

Who had not heard that baby boomers should be tested for hepatitis C? "One in thirty have hepatitis C, but nobody knows it. And now, instead of possibly getting liver cancer, you can be treated…" They called it the forgotten disease and compared it to HIV. Why all the new commercials? Why the sudden push to be tested? Because there was now a cure. A cure that came at a price: $100,000. For something that most people who were watching the ads never knew they had. The best part, however, was who had hepatitis C. Almost all of the cases were because of doing IV drugs and sharing needles. Better yet, almost all of the people who currently had hepatitis C were currently residing in prison. Though I considered myself a fairly liberal person, I couldn't help but think where I wanted to spend my next $100,000. First off, it would take me about ten years to save that kind of money. Second, would I rather give it to someone in prison for a grisly crime they had committed who made their own bad choice to use IV drugs—or to a hardworking high school student who wanted to attend college but didn't have the money? And if, upon leaving prison, the person with the disease that was causing them no current symptoms were given a choice, a pill to cure their hepatitis C or a wallet with $100,000, which do you think they would choose? I have yet to meet the person who honestly believes they would choose the pill.

As for mental illness, same thing. I had just heard of a new medicine for bipolar disease called Vraylar. I was sure it is a good medicine, as are numerous other pills for bipolar disease. But I would bet every last dime I had that if the struggling person were given a choice between a pill that might make them feel better or the $1,200 per month cost of Vraylar, they would be far happier with the money. Imagine feeling down in the dumps, anxious enough that you felt you need to take time off work or something similar. When you go to the doctor, instead of giving you a pill, they say, "You know what might help more and would cost your insurance less money?" The doctor then just gives you $1,000 cash and says, "Come back every month for the rest of your life, and I'll give you another $1,000. Does that make you feel better?"

In other words, it was safe to say I was still pissed off about the cost of drugs. It made no sense. And I truly hated the fact that my insurance premiums were paying for all of this bullshit. These made-up costs that nobody in their right mind would ever pay. When were Americans going to revolt? When were we going to realize that we paid ten times the amount for every drug that we bought compared to the rest of the world?

47

March 2018

I HAD NEVER CONSIDERED HOW I WOULD SEE THE DOCTOR WITHout bringing the patient first. In fact, it didn't cross my mind until the perky Jennifer on the phone said, "It's just not possible."

Apparently, Dr. Metcalf was supposed to do a good-faith exam on the patient in order to bill the insurance. So, if Mrs. MacPherson was languishing in a nursing home and I went by myself, he would be defrauding Medicare by billing her insurance when she wasn't actually there.

Was there anything easy about caring for a person with dementia? I contemplated just paying cash for his time but erroneously thought that a day out of Emerald Gardens might be a nice adventure for her, even if only to the doctor's office.

Let's just say that this adventure truly was an all-day experience. There was paperwork to sign to get her out and alarms that needed to be removed from her so we didn't set off sirens like we were exiting Target with items stuffed in our shorts. I had to get a folding wheelchair to fit in my trunk. I strained my back trying to get her into the car as she was now pretty much deadweight.

While we were out, she soaked through her Depends, as I was not able to change her in a wheelchair. She seemed so miserable being moved I knew she wanted to hit me but hardly had the strength to do so. And at no time did she smile while being pushed around in the sun outside.

Dr. Metcalf seemed in a good mood but was clearly troubled when he saw Mom. "She has progressed, hasn't she? Is she able to communicate at all?"

"Actually, no, not any longer. In fact, I don't even remember the last time she recognized who I am. I would say it has been at least a year."

"I'm really sorry to hear this. I understand she is now in a nursing home, which is probably for the best, given her condition. What can I help you with today?"

Carl would have been annoyed at me if I weren't prepared. The night before I had prepared a list of questions with space to record the answers. As I pulled the notebook out of my handbag, I sensed Dr. Metcalf pull back slightly. A bit of body language that made me realize I hadn't much time. It may be that I took hours out of my day to get here, but he looked like he was ready to go in just a few minutes.

"First, is there any need for her to be on her medicines for dementia? Could she really get any worse?"

"I'm glad you brought that up, and…in a word, no. She couldn't get any worse. I would stop them. She may even do better with eating if the drugs are causing some nausea. I will write a recommendation to stop the Namzaric."

"Second, what about her blood pressure and cholesterol medicines—does she need those?

"That's a little more philosophical," sighed the doctor. "We might stop these medicines, and the following day she could have a stroke or a heart attack. If that happened, would you or another family member feel guilty? And I'll say for the record right now, it may not be cause and effect. It's possible she would have been going to have a stroke tomorrow anyway, and it would just be coincidence. What would you like to do, Allison?"

"Just look at her!" I half yelled. "Sorry, I didn't mean to come on so strong. I guess my point is, if she dies a little sooner because we stopped these medicines, then might we not be doing her a favor? In fact, that brings me to my final question: can we start her on hospice? I've talked it over with my brother, and we both know she wouldn't have wanted to live like this. We would prefer to let her go."

If we were reading a play, there would be stage directions saying, "a dramatic pause ensued." I could suddenly hear the humming of the fluorescent lights. This seemed to only bring more weight upon what he was about to say in response.

"I think you don't really understand hospice. You may be confusing it with the idea of euthanasia, which is illegal. To qualify for hospice, I would have to say that I don't believe she has six more months left to live. I would have to provide a logical reason for her to be nearing the end of life. But her last labs were excellent. Her sugars are fine, as are her kidneys and liver. True, her cholesterol and blood pressure are good because of medicines. But even if we stopped those, it wouldn't imply death would arrive within six months. In other words, she doesn't have cancer, severe heart or lung disease, or something equally devastating. She very well might live like this for years."

Why were my visits to Dr. Metcalf always so awful? I didn't know if he had ever given me good news. It was not that he was a particularly unpleasant person. In fact, he seemed caring. But each time he told me something, I thought I was going to implode. "Do you mean there's nothing we can do except watch her wither away slowly in a nursing home?"

"Allison, I guess I'm not sure what you were expecting. What did you think hospice was going to do? Their primary aim is to take away obvious suffering and help make the family comfortable, emotionally and spiritually. But nowhere in their charter is there a way to hasten the end of someone's life on earth. There have been several high-profile cases of people with brain cancer or similar who wanted to take their own lives. The Dr. Kevorkian type of idea. As you probably know, these are highly controversial."

Surprising me, he suddenly leaned forward and took my hand. "Allison, you look so sad."

"I'm beyond sad, really. I am completely emotionally spent. I've grown to hate her, I'm ashamed to say. She is like an albatross around my neck. I may feel a little ashamed telling you this, but I no longer feel bad saying anything in front of her—her mind is no longer there. This is no longer my mom. And yet I can't let go emotionally. Not completely, as she is still alive. This might be what people feel when a child is abducted. As the years go by, you pretty much know they won't come back alive. But you can't fully let go until you know for sure. It's complete torture."

Another long pause. I wasn't feeling bad; he didn't make me feel ashamed at all. In fact, he seemed to completely understand. This was certainly not his first case like this.

"What I recommend is that we put her on what's known as palliative care. I like to think of this as stronger than your typical Do Not Resuscitate order. I can't tell you how many people on DNR not only have chest compressions and rescue breaths but hospitalizations, antibiotics, and feeding tubes. I believe what you need is more like no active help. If she gets an infection, we don't treat with antibiotics. If she can't eat, we don't start tube feeding to her stomach. We let nature take its course. How does that sound to you?"

"I haven't really thought about it that way, but I see what you mean. Why call 911 when you already want to let go?"

"Precisely; I couldn't have said it better," he interjected with enthusiasm.

"Is this the course that you would recommend for Mom, or do you have another suggestion?"

Dr. Metcalf replied, "I would simply add your previous idea. Stop all medicines that might be of help such as her BP and cholesterol meds. In fact, I would have her on no medicines at all unless they are obviously giving her comfort." I nodded. "OK, I must go, but I will write a note to this effect and send it off to her nursing home. It should go into effect tomorrow." And with that, he left, gently squeezing my hand once again before he walked out the door.

"Well, Mom, it's just us again. Are you ready to go home? It's time to get back to Emerald Gardens. The good news is that you will never have to come here again."

I waved to the receptionist as I left the office. We even walked around outside for a while before attempting to get her back into the car. I liked to think she might care. That she might still enjoy the breeze, the sun.

By the time we had returned, I was exhausted and my back was killing me. Even if a visit cost $350, the next time I would just pay cash and go by myself. Which got me thinking. *Why did I bring Mom in the first place? Because they forced me to. And you know the ironic part—he never examined her!* The nurse took her vitals before he came in, but the doctor... He never even listened to her heart. He never touched her. He simply waved goodbye.

48

August 2018

A PEACEFUL DEATH. I FOUND MYSELF THINKING ABOUT THIS A lot these days. It seemed strange wishing for someone to die. But I realized that was increasingly what was happening after our day-trip doctor's visit. "Other than her mind, Nancy is in pretty good health." Somehow I had envisioned we could put her on a six-month journey to death by joining hospice.

Carl helped me understand my feelings. He was right; after we placed her in the nursing home, I considered her to no longer be living. "Her mind has died," he said, cutting through all my defensive words. That was when I realized she seemed no different to me than someone whom we have declared brain-dead. I recalled the case of Karen Ann Quinlan, when they finally allowed her to die and removed the ventilator. She didn't die. She languished in a coma for nine years. I didn't think I could survive a similar ordeal. I would have to let her die in my mind at least and stop visiting. And that is probably why nursing homes are so lonely. I was one of the few regular visitors, as Mom was a new resident. Maybe the others had had regular visitors, too—in the beginning.

I had been smoking for more almost a year before I finally told Carl. We should have no secrets. Well, none quite so large as smoking. He wasn't as surprised as I had expected. My feelings and philosophy on death had not evolved isolated inside my head. He knew I had stopped seeing old age as something to be prized. I promised him, though, that I would never smoke at home. Meredith and Sloane had only a few years ago had the sex talk. A discussion about optimal ways to die seemed premature. Carl, more understanding than I probably deserved, didn't actually agree with me. I didn't think most people would. There is just a complete mental block about death that seems to be hardwired in our minds. Not unlike the opposite end of life, the beginning. We all know that our parents had sex to create us, and they were probably still having sex when we realize this. Yet we shut these thoughts out so completely that even reading these words will get most people to cringe.

As I became familiar with the nursing home, I started to explore what our minds so wish to hide. How were these people all going to die? Not just what was written on their death certificate, but the final three-month process. I saw a patient being suctioned because of excess mucous. A wound being unwrapped, cleaned, and rebandaged. My mom getting fed. Staff holding down a confused, agitated patient. Some things even made me laugh, like seeing oxygen nasal prongs on someone's forehead. But what I observed most, what seemed ever-present for anyone who dared to listen, were the moans. A cacophony of sound and emotion that seemed to say, "Can't you just leave me alone to die in peace?"

Yet we didn't. Karen was fed through a tube for nine years before she finally died of pneumonia. And was my mom much different? If we didn't feed her, she could never eat on her own. It seems our human instinct to nurture never ends, even when life has moved on to the actively dying phase. What I was seeing and feeling, though, had pulled me away from my previously held instincts. That was when I realized it was time to call Jeremy.

It was surprisingly cool that August evening. Kids and families were still out, but festivities of the day were wrapping up early because of the wind. After countless days without rain, the river had receded notably from its springtime high-water mark. It was good kite weather. I was prepared for a very long walk.

But I wasn't prepared for his response. "Hey, sis, can I call you back? We're in the last innings of Zach's baseball game." *Ugh.* I had never liked baseball. But I couldn't very well say it was an emergency. It hadn't occurred to me that Jeremy might have something more important going on at the moment. My focus was so clearly on Mom, this upcoming conversation. I wasn't ready for a better time.

So, I walked farther than I had thought. Penance for my plans. I had already reached that point on a walk when I started to notice my discomfort. My left foot was starting to ache a little, and I could definitely use a little water. I had so worked myself up for this talk I hadn't been prepared for a long walk. But I did have cigarettes and a lighter.

I certainly understand the resentment toward those who smoke in nature. Fouling the air for a hundred feet and, minutes afterward, causing an unsuspecting jogger to become instantly irate. Outside was my only designated smoking area, though, so there really was no other choice for me. Plus, it really did calm my nerves. Though you wouldn't believe that if you had seen me jump when the phone buzzed in my pocket. I guessed my nephew's baseball game had finally ended, and it was time for me to make the sale.

"Jeremy! Hi, how ya doing? I was giving it a bit of thought, and I think for Mom's sake, the best thing we could do is stop feeding her. She'll die quickly and won't have to suffer a more miserable death many years later. Uh-huh, uh-huh. Yeah, just thought I'd let you know, goodbye."

OK, that was not what I said. It was what I was thinking, but how do you sell that idea? It was not that Jeremy didn't know what's going on. He had even come down to visit Mom once she was settled in the nursing home. Jeremy also knew me better than anyone. We really didn't keep secrets, as far as I knew. But this was more than a philosophical discussion. I wanted him to agree on a decision that would change Mom's life course.

The saying "practice what you preach" came to mind. We say that a great deal because we know it is harder to act upon an idea than to come up with it in the first place. I had always been for the right of women to choose an abortion, but had I become pregnant in my twenties, would I have been able to do it? Let's just say I was glad I hadn't been forced to make that decision.

"What's on your mind, Allison?" brought me back. "Zach's team won, by the way."

"Oh, that's great." I replied somewhat distractedly. "But I've got something to talk to you about. It's about Mom."

"Has anything happened?"

"No, actually. Nothing at all. But I've been running back and forth with an idea ever since we saw Dr. Metcalf a few months ago. Do you remember when I told you that the doctor felt she was in good health?"

"Yeah, she's a little like you, isn't she? You don't take any medicines, and neither did she at our age."

I wasn't yet ready to tell him about my smoking decision. *Ha! I guess I do have a secret from him.* One revelation at a time.

"So, aside from the obvious, sis, what is your point?"

"Have you thought not only about when she is going to die but how? Because I've been giving this a lot of thought lately. Other than talking about random stuff when I'm with her, it seems I have nothing else to consider when I'm at Emerald Gardens. Maybe I have thus become biased. That's why I want to know what you expect for her future."

"This isn't easy, you know. Working in IT doesn't exactly make me qualified. Maybe if I were a doctor, I could give you a better answer, but really, I don't have any idea."

I didn't say anything.

"I take it by your silence that's not the answer you wanted," Jeremy added.

"Well, it certainly is a typical head-in-the-sand answer. I guess I did want something a little more specific than that. Let's appeal to your gambling personality. Would you put your money on the over or under for her living more than two years?"

"Allie, you're not only an idiot, you're fucking rude. Goodnight!"

If with a cell phone one could hear a handset crashing down on its cradle, I would have heard it just then. Instead, my screen just returned to the photo of Carl and the girls that I so adored.

For at least another mile of walking, I just stared blankly ahead. Plenty of people rollerblading, cycling, or jogging probably went by, though I didn't notice any of them. I was deep in my thoughts, realizing that I had conviction without eloquence. But I needed to explain to Jeremy what I now so strongly believed: keeping our mother alive shouldn't be the goal. I knew I was biased. Caregiving brought so many negative emotions. But it hadn't made me crazy. The problem was that I wasn't explaining it well. The person I needed now was Ruth. After all, it was Ruth's idea in the first place.

Ruth, a hospice nurse, had been visiting another family at Emerald Gardens. We were all outside enjoying the warm summer morning when I heard her gently suggest to this family, "Why don't you stop feeding her?"

At that moment, even I recoiled a little bit. I heard someone echo my feelings when he angrily replied, "She needs food, obviously! You would never say to your eight-month-old, 'Sorry if you haven't figured out how to eat by now.'"

Ruth went on, undeterred. Caring simply radiated from her. She became like a hypnotherapist, providing an array of dreams and images. As I sat there holding Mom's hand, my mind seemed to slip from dream to dream. Yet here we were in the Serenity

Garden. Fresh air. Invigorating compared to the stifled, heavy air just fifty yards away. Yet Ruth's tone and imagery moved my mind all over the place. She conveyed the sadness within those alarmed doors. She spoke of the impending nature of death, the loneliness, the despair of probably every resident within. She made it easy to understand why almost all were on antidepressants. What was transformative was her explanation about what death felt like. Not the final half hour, but the months, sometimes years of decay. And I was suddenly back. Back in the war zone of Dad's ICU room. Discarded equipment, IV poles, gauze saturated with betadine. This had been the only death I knew. Yet Ruth was revealing that the woman in front of me was also dying. We were just preventing it from happening by feeding her, sending her to the ER every time she got sick. "The alternative goes like this," Ruth said to the family. "We don't feed her; we provide. Juices, straws, tapioca, spoons. Her body needs less now. Have you noticed how much of a struggle it is to feed her? How often she refuses even water? After a few days, she will start sleeping more. Every day interacting less. You will not see her struggling. She will no longer be taking any food. And then one day she will gently pass."

I looked up at Mom at that point and asked, "Isn't that the type of death everyone would want?" If this were a movie, I would see some kind of sign. Her head would fall forward in a nod. Maybe there was the hint of a smile. Maybe it was because of the chirping birds.

The answer was clear to me. And yes, there was a selfish component. I acknowledged that I would no longer need to feel guilty about not coming to Emerald Gardens, no longer need to worry about more expenses, no longer feel unable to move on emotionally.

But those facts didn't change that goal number one was a peaceful death. I knew that if I could grant my daughters serenity, it would be my preferred option on my deathbed. I was convinced my mom would similarly want that for me.

My phone began buzzing. It was Jeremy. *Should I answer?* He was rightfully pissed.

"Hi, Jeremy," I tentatively said.

"What the hell, Allie! Why do you have to be so different? I know I shouldn't have hung up on you, but..."

"I wasn't sure if I wanted to answer the phone" was all I could say.

But then we got to talking. I tried my best to channel Ruth. It helped. Not that he agreed with me—far from it. But he said he would come and visit. He needed to see Mom to help him understand what was going through my head. Whatever the reason, he was coming out, which was great. Though I later thought, *Maybe his goal for coming is to change* my *mind.*

One thing that my brother could always get me to do was laugh, and tonight was no exception, even after our somber conversation. He began, "I know you think I never listen to you, but I did read that *Inferno* book you recommended, by Dan Brown."

"And?"

"Well, I totally agree he made a great case. Too many humans, only way to save the planet would be less people. But when you talk like Aldous Huxley's society and say people who get too old have no further purpose, that's a very tough sell.

"Allie, let me burst your bubble right now and say that will never happen. Humans are never going to accept your idea of planned deaths at age seventy or any other number you choose. Even if you said one hundred, the people at age ninety-nine would swing their canes at your head, saying, 'I've got plenty of life left in me, missy.'"

"OK, that's pretty funny. I can just imagine that person."

"But the best part about the book is that Dan Brown's idea was so much better than yours. In fact, I'd say it was pure genius. Having a virus making 33 percent of the world sterile is the best thing that could happen to the human race. It's fair, it doesn't kill anyone, and it arguably saves a lot of horrible deaths from war, global warming, vanishing resources, and the like. The more I thought about it, the more I felt I would be willing to unleash that virus."

"Are you trying to tell me in your roundabout way that you think I'm not as crazy as you thought?"

"I wouldn't go that far."

"Jer, I'm so glad that you want to see Mom again. I know she probably won't recognize you either. But I have to think that it means something when we visit, at least to us."

49

August 2018
Nancy

Hot. Too hot. Burn. Stop! Gooey. So salty.

"Nancy, just a few bites more of your oatmeal."

Who is this? Not hungry. Hot. No more. No more. Why? "Thhhrrrr."
Mean. Leave alone. Shoo. Arms stuck. Go. Can't move. "Rrr. Rrrrr."

"OK, dear, have you had enough? You're starting to really wriggle. Oh, I hate tying you down, but it's the only way to stop you from knocking the spoon out of my hand. I'll let you loose now, but stop spitting at me. And if I let you go now, be good and don't hit me."

"Turn on her music!" yelled a voice from the hallway. "That way she won't claw at you."

"Not a bad idea. OK... You like your music, don't you? I can see the smile in your eyes. Well, I like John Denver too. Let me clean you up, and then I'll let you go."

"Is that better? Thanks for not clawing me today, I really appreciate it. It's getting harder and harder to explain these bruises to my friends. One day soon they're going to call the police on my husband. True, he can be a stubborn goat at times, but he'd never hit me. I hope your husband never hit you. I hope you had a good life."

I'm thirsty. Why go? I'm thirsty... Oh, she's back. No... not my chest. Why chest? I'm thirsty. Now my face. Yuck, washcloth smells. So thirsty. Who are you? "Rrr." *Please get that off my face. Can't move.*

DON'T. That washcloth. I can't move. Just go. "Rrrr." *Oh, she's gone. Please, water.*

My music. Ahh. Love this. Nice voice. Glen Campbell? Guitar. That voice. John Denver? I'm free. My arms. So nice. Not a witch.

"Heelllp! Heelllp! Heelllp!"

Who's screaming? Can they stop screaming? "Rrrrrrr. Rrrrrr."

"Jessica! Can you go in that room from hell and shut those women up? Take out Mrs. Renfro. Once she starts screaming, she won't stop."

Finally quiet. Never stops. I'm exhausted. Leave me alone.

"You can go ahead and try to wake her if you like."

"Mom, Mom." Someone touched her gently on the shoulder. "Guess who has come to visit you. Your favorite son. You remember, the one who made you start to color your hair when he dropped out of college."

"Scoot over, sis. I feel like we are trying to wake someone up who has been sleepwalking. I say we shake her—I don't think her hearing is too good, anyway."

More people. No! I am so tired. I don't want anything. My eyes don't want to. Stop shaking me. I'm old. Who are they? What a nice voice. And warm hands. I'm so thirsty. Maybe water.

"What do you think is going on in there? When's the last time she talked to you?"

"Jer, I don't know. Months and months, maybe a year. I can't remember when I felt she knew who I was."

Back hurts. I need to be flat. Sleep. Back hurts. Let go! Just go. Warm hands. Gentle.

"It feels good to be connected. Jer, I'm glad you came. This is our family now. The circle seems so close. I'd like to believe these times mean something to her. When I visit; now that you are here."

Music would be nice. They're leaving. I'm tired. Maybe I can sleep. I feel good. I feel good.

50

October 2018

"'I AM DYING, MAXIMUS. WHEN A MAN SEES HIS END, HE WANTS to know there was some purpose to his life. How will the world speak my name in years to come?' Do you know where that quote comes from?" Jeremy asked.

We were flanking Mom, each holding a hand. She would squeeze at times, making me think she was paying attention. It seemed she was too tired to keep her head up.

When Jeremy asked this question, he was looking sadly at Mom, though I knew it was meant for me. I didn't care where it was from; I knew the point he was making: Nancy MacPherson wouldn't want to be remembered like this. As Mom sat there, seemingly oblivious to our presence, I knew he knew this was not the person she would want remembered for years to come.

"By the name, it sounds Greek, but that's all I can guess."

"Not bad, Allison. It comes from one of my favorite movies, *Gladiator*. Mom was a warrior. She inspired so many and gave hope to so many random people. True, she wasn't an actual fighter, but she had more heart than anyone else I've known. I can see other people questioning our decision. They will talk about the moral slippery slope. Kind of reminds me of the dictum about pornography, 'I don't know how to define it, but I know it when I see it.' Maybe it's not so easy to define when someone is no longer creating memories and actively living, but this case is really quite clear."

"It's funny—even though I feel the same as you, it hurts a little to hear it out loud. It's also funny how your mind can come up with some odd, random, yet perfectly understandable analogies. How do you end up with death and pornography in the same sentence?"

"A talent of mine, I suppose. What will you remember most about Mom?" Jeremy asked.

"That's becoming a difficult answer. What I so didn't want to have happen has happened. This version of Mom is what has become my reality. The one where she can't talk, can't help herself. The version that never laughs or shares a story. I don't want it to replace the regal memories. In truth, I always wanted to be a bit like her. I still wish I were as altruistic. And you?"

"What drove her? That's what I would like to know. I wish I could bottle up that passion, drink most of it for myself and then give sips to everyone I know. I also have so many funny memories. She loved to make you laugh and didn't mind being teased. But what's great about having had her for a mom is we get to remember the early days when she would comfort us like only a mom can. I guess I look upon it as a privilege that only we will remember what it was like being read to every night or how she made us cinnamon toast cut in three when we were sad.

"I think I'm ready to say goodbye. I never pictured death like this, Allison. And for the record, let me just say, I would want you do the same for me."

"We love you, Mom."

When we placed her hands back neatly on her lap, she seemed at peace. Something I thought I would feel comfortable remembering.

There were two surprises after that. The first was how long she lasted without food or water. I tried to fast once for twenty-four hours. Coincidentally it was to help raise money for a program that Mom had started. The goal was to get people to pledge money for her cause. Instead of it being a jog-a-thon or similar, this was eat and drink nothing for twenty-four hours to show solidarity for prisoners of war. I was all for the cause, but in retrospect, I realized I would rather have just donated the money. My mind was no longer working by the end. I had a terrible headache and contemplated eating my own arm. I couldn't even recall what I ate the following morning. It could have been three-day-old leftovers, and I would have been happy. Plus, I was so thirsty.

So, I didn't foresee our frail mom lasting more than a couple of days. But it was eight days later, in fact, when I finally received the call. Which leads me to the other surprising thing. She didn't seem to suffer at all. She just lay there quietly most of the time. It was hard to imagine she could have slept more than before, but she probably slept eighteen hours or more per day those last few days.

In other words, I got my wish. After all the thought about how someone might die, she basically chose the best way out—peacefully, in her sleep. She never seemed to struggle at all. Which for me meant the world. I couldn't thank the hospice nurse enough for giving me the idea in the first place. And, like Phyllis had done for me earlier, to allow this choice to seem both valid and the right thing to do.

51

October 2018

Where was life supposed to go from here? I had invested so much time the last several years caring for and thinking about my mom. During that time, Jeremy and I also sold her house and divided her many possessions. The funeral was still to be planned. My family already thought I was strange, but I was looking forward to this. I wanted to be like a courtroom lawyer. I wanted to appeal to the jury, all those present, and let them know her character. I wanted to provide them with a memory of my mom that was different than those last few years. It was a case that I needed to win. And the person I most needed to convince was myself. I wanted my lasting memory to be the vibrant, firebrand social-justice worker that defined her.

I certainly can't say that it snuck up on me. The funeral was scheduled for November 4, 2018. Almost three weeks after she died, and a full month since we made the decision to stop providing nutrition.

I can't tell you how many people, upon hearing the news, said, "Oh no, was it sudden?" I found this curious because I presumed that implied that if it were expected, then it shouldn't hurt so much. My hurt had been going on for months, years, and I was convinced this pain was just as devastating as if she had died in a plane crash. Dying a long, slow death is just different, not less painful. But there was a difference. For me, Mom had died many months prior to that cool fall day. Thus, when the call came, relief outshone grief as my dominant emotion.

During those weeks, I wrote and rewrote my eulogy. I couldn't find the right tone. And I certainly didn't want to make it long. What saved me in the end was that the day of the funeral arrived. Deadlines are a wonderful thing when you think about it. The time comes, and you must come to terms with this is the best work you are able to create. We may think we could do better with more time, but if we are honest, we know otherwise.

It's an odd privilege at weddings and funerals to be seated in the front. Aside from the engaged couple or the deceased, you are the next most important in the room.

I was so nervous. It felt as if I were about to give the most important speech of my life. I guess it was, if you compared it to my debate about Manifest Destiny in high school. I was so focused, I completely tuned out the minister, who was intertwining a speech about love and service to the community with the work of my mom throughout her life. So, it took me a bit by surprise when I realized he was stepping away from the podium after inviting me to come up and say a few words.

Looking back toward the entrance, I stood carefully. The Unitarian church was full. How many lives had she touched in her seventy-seven years? It seemed they had all come to say their goodbyes. Had it not been raining cats and dogs, I knew Mom would have liked this service to be held outside. But for me, this unassuming church, the only one she ever professed to enjoy, seemed the better venue. Like her, this church didn't come with a lot of outward frills: it had no beautiful glass, stately domed ceilings, or pipe organ. Its power lay in the fact that it made clear everyone was welcome. Straight, gay, Black, white, lawyer, homeless, believer or nonbeliever—all were welcome. That was why my mom loved this place. She wanted a world like that.

While I approached the podium, notes in hand, I remembered that I had thought about researching eulogies. I hadn't, though. I feared I might be swayed to plagiarize others to some extent, and I wanted mine to be unique, originality to trump any of my misguided ideas of what to say. I wanted this to be about my mom and her alone.

Alongside the podium there was a picture of her. She would have liked the image but disliked that she was alone. She wasn't one to crave the limelight. Well, like it or not, this was a time to celebrate her shine. And it fell on my shoulders to deliver her life's summary.

"Friends! Each and every last one of you sitting here today. And all those who aren't here, even ones who've never had the pleasure of meeting my mom—they are also friends. She truly was liked by all because she believed in everyone's goodness. Even about a convicted murderer on death row, she would have found some positive attributes. And as Mom would have said, 'Why not focus on the positives?'

"My first memories were stories. Without a doubt, she was a storyteller. She would read to Jeremy and me at bedtime, telling all sorts of tales. Like an actress, she would voice the different characters so they came alive. Stories I remember vividly include *Gulliver's Travels* and *Old Yeller*. I'm sure I had cried many times before she read me *Old Yeller*, but not like that. She brought us into those worlds so profoundly, it felt as if we actually knew everyone in the story.

"She taught us charades, Pictionary, and all sorts of games. I am so glad we grew up before the internet was constantly asking for our attention, because she gave us something so much more magical. Imagination. She taught me how to read, not just for concepts. When I read, a flood of colors, smells, and emotions fills my brain. It is so vivid that if they turn the book into a film, I find nothing but disappointment.

"So, you are probably wondering, what did she do wrong? Well, I'll tell you. Not everything, mind you, as we don't have the time." The audience chuckled.

"She forgot my dentist appointment in the third grade. I had remembered, which was why I hadn't done my homework. I knew I was going to be taken out of class. I think that was the first time I got an F. Though, sadly, not the last." More chuckles.

"She once helped me on an art project because I am woefully bad at art, and she got a C!" Jeremy laughed heartily through his tears. "What's the point of asking for help if the best grade you are going to get is a C anyway?

"She once completely forgot her own wedding anniversary. Conspiratorially, she made me ride my bike to the store to get a card and whatever present I could think of. The best part about that deal was she gave me twenty bucks and told me I could keep the change. That was her second mistake on the same day. Let's just say, Dad didn't get much of a present for that anniversary.

"And, certainly at the top of the list, she forgot to play favorites. I was supposed to be her favorite child. I was first, after all. And somehow she managed to make Jeremy feel that he was equally loved." I saw a tear roll down my brother's face.

"Speaking of loved, she cherished our dad. I'm not sure what kind of life he would have led without her, but I can't imagine he would have had the same success. She completely believed in him. So completely, he achieved more than he would have otherwise. The same happened to us. I used to wonder why someone who was clearly the best, like Roger Federer, the tennis player, needed a coach? He is certainly better than his coach. And yet, having someone in your corner can really make a difference. Mom was the best coach we all could have had. She made us better than we ever would have been without her. You might ask how. I'll tell you. She never spanked or hit us. And she did more than just encourage, because we weren't exactly always perfect. Her discipline style? Guilt. She could have been Roman Catholic. If you failed, you failed *her*. Your actions made her feel sad, and that could make you feel downright horrible. It was worse than any punishment. I lied once. When she caught me, you would have thought I had stolen shoes from a homeless person. She hardly spoke or looked at me for weeks. It was true agony. But it worked... I became a better liar." The crowd laughed. "Just kidding!

"Probably the main reason why there are so many of you here is because of how she spent her free time. She did work to pay bills. But once she retired, she spent even more time doing what she loved—helping those less fortunate. She envisioned a more peaceful world. And even if it couldn't happen in her lifetime, there was no reason not to try right now. 'Every little bit of kindness helps' was her motto. If there were a character in literature who personified Mom in a nutshell, it would be the priest from *Les Miserables*. The one who took in the prisoner. Provided him with clothes, food, and shelter. And then, after the prisoner stole his golden candlesticks, gave them to him as a gift so he could better his life. In summary, I would like to say this. If you are here not only to seek comfort for the loss of Nancy MacPherson but also to honor her, I would like you to do this. Honor her by, at least once in your life, being that character. Help someone downtrodden, even better if it's a complete stranger. Altruistically give with no desire for accolades or reward. And see how that person, how your little corner of the world, begins to blossom. And when you experience the joy of selfless giving, you will have ascended. You will have felt as good as you could possibly feel. Is there a more noble thing to do in life than that?" I saw some nods.

"Thank you. Thank you all for listening. Thank you all for coming. And please, honor my mother with your deeds.

"Oh, and one last thing. I asked them to play a song that my mom grew to love. She gave me a love for music, and she not only liked this song, she felt it had something to say that was important. I'll let you judge for yourself."

I hit play on a Green Day song I'd introduced her to. The actual title of the song is "Good Riddance," but everyone called it by one of its lyrics, "Time of Your Life." Kind of perfect.

52

August 2019

W‌HEN I WAS ABOUT SEVENTEEN, MY MOM ASKED ME TO JOIN her for a hike. This was the age where it seemed everyone had the T-shirt that said Go Climb a Rock. Maybe that was what inspired her; I'll never know. Several of her friends had organized the trip, but she didn't want to go alone. Which was a sly way of saying she didn't want to be the only novice in the group.

Let's start by saying this was no ordinary hike. In fact, it was such a long way, it was expected that you would spend the night at the top before coming back down the following day. I had never gone camping before, so I was a little dubious. I also felt that ten miles each way sounded challenging. She casually added that the climb was almost five thousand feet, and we were to carry backpacks. With Mom, life was always an adventure, and she was so enthusiastic, I couldn't help but agree to go.

Weeks of training became comical. Mom would even make dinner in her hiking boots to help break them in. Neighbors, I'm sure, had a good laugh at her barreling along the sidewalks with my school backpack filled to capacity with books. She even sported a floppy hat and poles, looking like a cross between a Sherpa and Gilligan. By the time the final week came around, she had worked up to walking as much as two hours at a time. Her confidence brimming, she felt completely prepared.

The night before the trek, we had our dehydrated food, tent, water bottles, camping stove, flashlights, and every imaginable thing we might need laid out all over the floor. Up until this point, I really hadn't participated that much in the planning. I had agreed to go, but I didn't actually train. I had been on the soccer team, after all. But I never really thought about carrying this kind of weight. Looking at all this gear spread out before us, it was obvious these would be significantly heavier than my school backpack. Certainly because we really had no clue what we were doing, it was after 9:00 p.m. when we finished dividing everything into our rental backpacks. They must have weighed forty pounds each!

I must have been showing my fear, because Mom started to encourage me. We started parading through the house with our packs on, her jumping around as if she were on the moon. Dad and Jeremy joined in with the cheer, and the pack did seem to feel a little less heavy. Mom made it seem effortless. Maybe I should have done some training after all.

The next morning, we left long before dawn to get to the trailhead and join the group. There was a tension before the group left. For the more experienced, maybe just excitement. But no matter who you are, this kind of hike takes effort. Sprained ankles, pulled muscles, and blisters could derail your hopes of making it to the top. And what was suddenly derailing my mother was her backpack. We were both sporting these monstrous frames, heading toward the rest of the group, when she asked if my backpack hurt. I wasn't sure what she meant, but she was very concerned about her hips. "It's really hurting; I don't know if I can make it."

So, we tried the obvious—we switched packs. She was suddenly in heaven. "Oh, that's much better, but how are you?" I might have lied even if it had hurt, but the good news was that it felt just as good as my backpack. She chalked it up to being taller than me. But let's face it, at seventeen, I was built like a boy. Either way, we were ready to start our adventure.

The group was really a lot of fun, and it was a stunningly beautiful hike. So, it took me by complete surprise when Mom suddenly announced at lunchtime that she was turning back. In my entire life I could count on one hand the number of times I saw my mom cry. This was one of those times. She felt so defeated.

Mom stood in front of the group and began talking. "I asked Russell, who has done this hike a few times, if we had completed the worst of it so far. When he told me we were just halfway, I realized that I'm more likely to injure myself than make it. But don't worry about me. While you are freezing and eating your warmed-up rehydrated lasagna, I will be sleeping like a queen in the camper van, sipping a glass of wine."

After lunch and before we left the lake, Mom said to me, "Well, I might as well give you all the good stuff I've got. I won't be eating this crap once I get down there." She gave away every last piece of food and all but one water bottle, partly to get rid of her ballast but also partly to let it be known she was going to have a nice meal that night.

The view from the top was amazing. After the sun set, I saw something I had never seen before, the Milky Way. The stars shone so brightly without a moon on the warm summer night. I was having the time of my life—they were really a great group of people. With them I was experiencing a memory I would never forget. And yet it was incomplete without Mom there. This was her dream, not mine. And somehow I got the chance to be there and not her.

What made this story especially tragic was learning the next day what had happened to my mom after she got back down. The first trouble was that when she got to the Volkswagen van, the refrigerator was completely empty. After an eight-hour roundtrip hike, you kind of hope for more than warm fountain water. Then, as she told it, the real tragedy crept into her mind like a slow-motion accident. The smile that had started to form as she began to go through the backpack to get her wallet faded quickly, because it was then she realized that not only had she given away all of her food, she also had never retrieved her wallet from her original backpack. The one I was carrying, several thousand feet up from where she stood. She was hungry, thirsty, more tired than she had ever been in her life, and...penniless.

I was never sure how homeless she had actually appeared on that day outside the ranger station. But she must have looked pitiful as she began to beg for money. She began to tell her tale of woe to anyone who was willing to listen until she finally managed to get ten dollars from a hiker. She bought a salami, some cheese, and water. Ten dollars clearly did not provide the nice meal or lodging that she had envisioned. And it had to last the entire next day because we weren't going to be back until late in the afternoon.

The only good news from my perspective was that I didn't know any of this was happening. I wouldn't have enjoyed myself knowing my mom was so miserable.

When Mom was alive, I had never thought of disobeying her wish about her remains. She had told me that she wanted her ashes buried beneath a newly planted tree so she could live in it forever. This seemed like such a nice sentiment that I never gave it another thought.

But after she died, I came up with a better idea. I wanted her to complete the journey that she so wanted to have finished. I needed to take her to the top of that mountain. That was how I found myself again with a heavy pack at the trailhead for the second time in my life. This time Mom was going to make it to the top, even if it killed me. Hiking ten miles is definitely different when you are seventeen than it is in your midforties. But it wasn't actually as bad as I remembered. What I lacked in youth, I guess I made up for in ambition. I couldn't think of a better tribute to pay her. Part of me wanted company, but I wasn't unhappy that I ended up alone with my thoughts.

I went over my life with her from start to finish. They always say that we get to the end of a life and we recount only the good things and not the bad, our nostalgia having no place for the times when that person made you miserable. I guess that was what I did in the eulogy. Listening to what I said, you would think she had never had dementia. I suppose that was how I wanted others to remember her. That was how I want to remember her.

The top of the mountain was as beautiful a view as I had remembered. I felt accomplished making it that far, though I was somewhat humbled trying to set up the tent on my own. I finally had to procure a large rock to anchor the pole on one end while I used all my strength to bend that stupid pole into the small ring on the other side. After repeating this process a few more times, I was spent.

I was not sure if it was illegal to dump ashes off a mountaintop. I couldn't imagine anyone up there would take the time to arrest me. But for some reason I wanted to wait until morning anyway. It was time to quietly celebrate our achievement. And it sounds corny, but to honor her, I had brought up a salami, some cheese, and a small bottle of red wine.

How I could be so tired and sleep so poorly remains a bit of a mystery. Perhaps I should have brought more wine. It seemed every hour I would clamber out of my tent to marvel at the stars above., preferring all along that I was snug and resting in my bag. I must have finally fallen asleep because I did startle with the alarm buzzing on my wrist. And despite being remarkably tired, I knew it was time. It was cold and quiet in the early light of dawn. I was ready. Mom's ashes sat across from me. This would be her final journey. It was true, she wanted to be placed at the bottom of a tree. The way I reasoned it, the wind would carry her to hundreds of trees.

There weren't many tents up this time of year, still, I quietly eased my way out toward the edge. As expected, I was the only one out this early, and so with little guilt, and perhaps to put off the inevitable, I sat down to smoke. There was no one near to tell me to stop. Yet if there were, I think I wouldn't have cared. It would not be the first time nor the last that I would tell someone my story. And I think by the end I could get them to understand why someone would choose the dangers of smoking over the dangers of living too long.

Indescribable. It's hard to convey all that I was seeing and feeling while sitting upon what seemed like the edge of the world. That moment will live with me forever. The dawn light just perfect. The sound of the wind through the trees. The magnificence of being thousands of feet above the ground. The sense that I was controlling my own destiny. All together created a mood that signaled the end of a journey for me. It was definitely the right time.

Mom waited patiently at my side for me to tap out my cigarette. Then more patience as my chewed nails made it somewhat difficult to get the scotch tape off the top. Once completed, I hesitated. Truth be told, I stood up and completed a full pirouette to ensure no one was actually watching me perform what I was about to do. And then with one quick motion I lifted the urn and poured. The wind suddenly picking up carried her far, dispersing, restarting life below. I stood forever, watching the trail of ash drifting in the poor light. With one last blink, I lost sight of her. She was gone. And now my job was officially over. It was time to rest and await the new world, my new world. I was now the guru at the top of the mountain. I wondered how many would make the climb to learn what I knew. I would just have to wait. So, I sat, feet dangling over the sheer drop. Yes, I was terribly afraid of heights, but I was no longer afraid to die. I was not afraid to achieve all that I wanted with the limited time I had. I was afraid not to live.

Afterword

HAVE YOU EVER THOUGHT ABOUT HOW YOU WANT TO DIE? VERY few people do. And before modern medicine, it didn't matter; people would often succumb to the first severe illness that they contracted. The twentieth century, however, ushered in something new for mankind—the ability to postpone death by relying on antibiotics, surgery, dialysis, chemotherapy, and other modern medical treatments that empower the individual to make a choice: fight and postpone death or die. All too often, people choose to fight without seriously considering the alternative.

Social norms tend to push our loved ones to continue painful, exhausting, nauseating treatments that deeply erode the quality at the end of their lives. While some additional time may be gained, how should it be balanced against the quality of life? After all, eventually everyone dies.

I suggest that a new philosophy must be developed. Under what circumstances should a person say that they are prepared to die when modern medicine might prolong the span of their life? How should quality of life be factored into this existential decision?

In this novel, I explore this question through the eyes of the caregiver. As death is inevitable, the decision often becomes "When should I stop fighting?" Caring for her mother with dementia, Allison must decide for everyone when her mother's life is no longer worth living.

Hopefully this book provokes us to consider fundamental questions about quality of life and death, both for ourselves and for our loved ones. Under what circumstances should the decision be made to stop fighting and to die? And by extension, would making the decision to die force us to pursue more purposefully our ultimate goal—to live a full and meaningful life?

Acknowledgments

I AM INDEBTED TO SO MANY WHO HELPED MAKE THIS BOOK possible. Most of all is my college roommate, Ben Steinberg. I gave him my very first draft after fifty pages of writing and asked him if I should go on. It was his enthusiasm that encouraged me to complete the project.

I would also like to specifically thank Laura Garwood, who became my first editor. She not only improved the work tremendously, she encouraged me to not give up on this dream. And she led me to Vinnie Kinsella and Circuit Breaker Books. It would be safe to say that one of the best days of my life was when Mr. Kinsella informed me that he felt the work was good enough to publish. His team, especially Kristin Thiel, has been nothing short of amazing in creating a much more relateable story.

Share Your Opinion

Did you enjoy *Allison's Gambit*? Then please consider leaving a review on Goodreads, your personal blog, or wherever readers can be found. At Circuit Breaker Books, we value your opinion and appreciate when you share our books with others.

Go to circuitbreakerbooks.com for news and giveaways.

C. A. Price is a family practice physician in California. The philosophy of *Allison's Gambit* was inspired by patients of his who have been caregivers to those with dementia and his continued observation that these family members often end up with tremendous guilt. His work with hospice has taught him that those who change their views about dying seem to live so much better. This is his first novel.